The swee

Albert Wood

Contents

Chapter 1 – On the home front

Paul often looked back in wonder at the peculiar events in his life that had transformed him from being a self-confessed geek, who worked selling insurance, to becoming a master of deception and intrigue, who was familiar with covert operations and knew violence and crime as daily acquaintances. The path hadn't been an easy one. Even now, his blood ran cold at the memory of some of his experiences.

It all began in such a small way, after he'd been working for some years as an insurance broker. In the course of his work, he began to feel the occasional discomfort. It wasn't a pain exactly; he might have called it a slight itch, but it wasn't really that either. One thing was for sure, it was happening more frequently, and it was reaching the stage when he could almost predict its onset. Its first occurrence had been while Paul was working at his desk with a potential client online. In the nature of his business, there were many potential clients. Most of them came to nothing. In this case, the contact had been looking particularly promising, though he couldn't remember who it was. He did recall that his sales package had been nearing completion, and the enquirer was still sounding keen. The moment came to 'hook' the client, so he'd clicked 'send.' It happened then as his sales suggestions sped along their electronic path to the client. The sensation was like a slight shadow passing over his consciousness, reminiscent of lying in the sun on a bright summer's day, when there's just that marginal dimming of the light as a wisp of high mist drifts across the face of the sun; barely perceptible, but there all the same. This impression of a shadow crossing his consciousness was just as faint and transitory.

He thought little of it at the time. Indeed, he barely noticed it, and after another cup of coffee he'd almost forgotten it. He would have forgotten it entirely if it hadn't happened again. That had been about a week later. The circumstances weren't quite the same. On this occasion, he'd been speaking on the phone, discussing the kind of policy that would best suit the needs of another potential client. Paul had gently probed the customer's circumstances and concerns. Once he'd been satisfied that he had a clear understanding of what was needed, he'd agreed to send some outline proposals. As he put down the phone that suggestion of a shadow passed over him again.

Now if Paul had been doing something unethical, that might have been an explanation. Men, or women come to that, in his business were almost a byword for sharp practice and shady dealing. Not so in his case, he took pride in the fact that his business was squeaky clean. He not only followed all the rules and guidelines to the letter, he even followed their spirit. He was assiduous in looking after the interests of his clients and was sure that his business success was the result. He produced satisfied customers, who spread favourable reports that generated inquiries from their friends. His business had thrived. Paul's self-confidence was well-placed, and his reputation for integrity and fair-dealing was the envy of many others in his field of work. He made good money from his commission, but one would have to search long and hard to find a client who would begrudge him his cut.

When it came to his life in general, the situation was different. Here, he was his own chief detractor. Though he took great satisfaction from his business achievements, he was far less confident about his success in domestic life. The fact was that his wife was an enigma to him. As it turned out, that enigma would grow into a most disconcerting mystery and reveal a skill set that, on its own, would give grave cause for concern. At the time however, he had no idea about all that and no more idea what Chris thought about the long hours he spent in his 'office.' She didn't complain, so his doubts weren't based on any evidence that he could put a finger on. Despite that, for a long time there'd been, at least to his mind, an air of tension. One contributory cause might have been that their working arrangements had created a physical space between them.

At first, they had both tried to work in their living room. Chris had used a desk on one side of the room, while Paul was on the other side, at a workstation, facing her. Naturally, they'd seen more of each other then. Nevertheless, the arrangement was doomed from the outset. The main issue was that Chris worked as an online tutor, so she was speaking for much of the time. Consequently, Paul had to leave the room when he needed to deal with a phone call, and when he had to chat online there would be both of them speaking at the same time in the same room. The sound interference was difficult, even though they both wore headsets. It was obvious that they required a different system, so Paul moved into the kitchen. That was scarcely better for Paul, because the kitchen was unpleasant as a working environment. Although it was fine when he fancied coffee or soup, for the most part the echoes made it like working in a bathroom. In addition, the background of a kitchen for video calls created a poor impression, and furthermore, the space available was limited. As his business grew, Paul didn't have the space for all the equipment he wanted. They agreed to have an office built in the garden. With hindsight, perhaps they should have built something they could both use, but it had never occurred to them that they could have twin offices in the same building. At least, it had never occurred to Paul, and he assumed that it had never occurred to Chris either.

Another thing that had never occurred to Paul, was to wonder exactly what Chris was doing in her work. He knew very little about it. They never spoke about it and he never asked. In retrospect, perhaps that had been a mistake. Then again, perhaps too many questions would have made things worse.

Anyway, although the addition of the office might have seemed like a perfectly good and reasonable arrangement, it hadn't helped their relationship. Once their work spaces moved further apart physically, it soon felt as though Paul and Chris were moving further apart in their married life. When they had both been in the house, chats over coffee during

Chris's work breaks, which hadn't been very frequent in the first place, were now a distant memory. It was quite true that Paul could have gone indoors to take a coffee break, but in practice, though he often took coffee, he seldom took a break to drink it. He preferred to work with the coffee at hand. Even if he had taken downtime, it was unlikely that the time away from his work would have matched the intervals between Chris's students, so what was the point? In Paul's mind, the situation had been inevitable. One might have said that they had come to an unspoken agreement that their time together was bound to be limited. That wouldn't have been the truth of it; in practice, they had settled for the arrangement with neither agreement nor protest.

Paul regretted having less warmth in their relationship. He lived with it by considering that his work, with its associated large income, was keeping them in the style to which they had become accustomed. By which he meant that it paid the lion's share of the mortgage, the fees for a local firm to maintain the garden, and the cost of a home help. These days they seldom went out together, and most of their meals were convenience foods, which they sometimes ate together. Their relationship didn't live up to the cosy togetherness that Paul had envisaged when they were married. He wouldn't have said that they were unhappy, it was just that he vaguely sensed a kind of static charge surrounding Chris, as though she was permanently on edge. Perhaps in reality that was the dimly-felt guilt of his own responsibility for the way their marriage was turning out.

Of more immediate concern was that Paul could now feel himself growing apart from his very lucrative business. The shadows that had been passing over his mind were growing in both frequency and intensity. They were also increasing in length. Whereas at first, they'd been like a brief fading of the light, now the shadows were deepening and sometimes even merging together. He was beginning to think and fear that there was a time ahead when his whole life would enter one long, dark tunnel of despondency. What was wrong with him?

His business was to sell peace of mind to clients, who seemed genuinely happy with his work for them. Perhaps this was a zero-sum game. Maybe there was a fixed amount of peace at his disposal. As he gave some of it to create peace of mind in his customers, perhaps he was losing the same amount of peace from his own mind. But this was his life's work! He had invested time, education, and money to build a thriving business, all based on his own expertise and on his enthusiasm to do his very best for his clients. How could that possibly give cause for the disquiet that was enveloping him?

Of course, if he'd had the slightest inkling of where all this might lead, he would have been filled with a good deal more than disquiet. Terrifying alarm and dread would have been much closer to the mark, rather than just a hazy sense of unease. As it was, he continued in ignorance of what the future held and concluded that his problem was a slight case of depression. Perhaps he had been working too hard. After all, his professional journals often promoted the importance of 'work-life balance,' so maybe he did need to live a little more. Once his thoughts moved along those lines, he determined that he should do something to rescue his marriage before it was too late. A good beginning would be to stop taking sandwiches to his 'office' for lunch. Yes, he would spend more time with Chris, and the times of darkness would surely pass.

Chris was fluent in a whole batch of the world's languages, and her students were scattered across the world or, more to the point, they were spread across the world's time zones. Her mornings began early as she spoke with those who lived to the east, and her evenings ended late as she contacted those in the Americas. Although Paul and Chris did sleep together, it would be more accurate to say that they collapsed in bed together. Even though her days were long and tiring, Chris often had time between lessons, which she filled with exercising and sketching. She had always enjoyed art, but it had never been part of her academic training. Now, as a leisure activity, she was keen to hone her technical ability. Her sketches were all based on famous works of art, which Paul didn't remotely understand. Although he could appreciate the skill of the original artist, as well as the craft of his wife in making her copies, he had no real interest in the subject. Despite his indifference to art, over the years Paul had been introduced to a great variety of famous artists. Whenever Chris completed a sketch, her latest representation of a masterpiece would adorn the 'art space' on their bedroom wall. Paul had no objection to the practice, though despite the wide range of works that he'd been presented with, he never perceived any meaning in the images she produced. They didn't 'speak' to him, but simply remained pleasant to look at.

The latest piece of work in the art space depicted an ancient banquet, and that night Paul asked Chris about it. She explained that it was a copy of a much larger painting in the Louvre Museum of Paris. That information flowed over Paul like a passing summer breeze. He hadn't asked the question out of interest in knowing more about the painting. He'd simply noticed that the picture involved food and a meal. The point of his enquiry had been to begin a conversation about food, which would lead towards a suggestion that they went out for lunch together the next day. When he finally made that proposal, Chris's surprise bordered on shock, tinged with concern.

"What brought that on? Has something happened? Is it good news or bad news?"

"Nothing has happened. I just thought that we spend so much time working that we are usually worn out by the end of the day. It might be nice to spend more time together when we're awake."

"That would be lovely. As it happens, tomorrow would be good for that because I do have a slack period right across the middle of the day."

Domestic chores had passed out of their lives long ago when they began to pay for help in the home and garden. They had only ever had two home-helps. In the early days there had been Chloe, whose degree in Media Studies had not resulted in a related career path. After a year or two there had been a change. Paul had no complaint about Chloe's work, and the girl herself had been keen to continue. The fact remained that Chris had been insistent on someone new. That was something else that Paul had accepted without question so, since then, Jacquie had been employed.

Everything about Jacquie proclaimed efficiency. She was a year or two older than Chris and Paul. Were it not for the blue apron she habitually wore, she would have been easily mistaken for a librarian of the old school, the ones with their hair severely pinned back, who ruled with a rod of iron, and glared over half-moon glasses to command the silence of anyone who dared to whisper. One might have expected such a person to appear with clockwork regularity each week. In fact, Jacquie arrived at a wide variety of times, though always on the same day. Chris was more than happy with the arrangement, and that was all that mattered to Paul.

In former times, one might have paid a home-help weekly, with cash, which was in pre-history for Paul. Both Jacquie and the firm, Lawn Lovers, that maintained the garden, were paid by standing order. Lawn Lovers was a local firm, represented by an assortment of men and women workers. At one extreme were young girls, who looked as though they must have been playing truant from school, while at the other end of the scale was an elderly man, who would have looked more at home with a Zimmer frame than a lawn mower. Their common feature was that they would arrive at a random time, in a pick-up van with a lawn mower on board. Paul would often see them at work from his office. The effect of their domestic employees was that everything around Paul and Chris was immaculately kept, with virtually no effort on their part. So, with their new-found time for each other, they began to enjoy their home and each other. A fresh period of marital bliss washed over them. They were less tired at the end of each day, and in bed they did more than just sleep together.

Although Paul and Chris were both in their mid-30s, they had no children. The idea of a family had never been particularly attractive to either of them, in contrast to their friends from university, who virtually all had lives punctuated with school runs, football, ballet and children's parties. Paul occasionally thought that they might be missing something, but it only took a little more thought to confirm that whatever it was, they didn't want it or need it. Perhaps it was something to do with the kind of childhood they had in common; one of the very few things they did have in common.

Paul had never known his parents, because they had both been killed in a car accident when he was only a few months old. It had happened while they had all been staying for a few days on his grandparents' farm in Sussex. His parents had taken the opportunity of grandparent baby sitters to enjoy a rare evening out together. There was a traffic collision, and they never came home. Paul had been their only child and he simply continued to live on the farm, where he was brought up by his mother's parents. His other grandparents had been alive at the time, though both were in poor health, living in the North of England. During his early years he'd seen them occasionally, but he barely remembered them now. Before many years had passed, they died, leaving his grandparents on the farm to be his only known relatives.

Chris's experience wasn't the same, though it was certainly similar. She had been the only daughter of a single parent mother. The sole piece of information Paul had been able to extract about her father was that there was no information to be extracted. Even her birth certificate said, 'Father unknown.' As if her circumstances were not difficult enough, Chris's mother had become ill, and she died when Chris was only five, leaving her to be brought up, with some reluctance, by her only living relative, a middle-aged aunt. The aunt was unmarried and was a diplomat so, over the years, her postings had dotted the globe. Chris had been moved from one boarding school to another as she followed her aunt's career from country to country. The girl's education didn't appear to suffer from all the moves. She was highly intelligent, and one result of all her aunt's postings was that she had picked up a great variety of languages by the time she went to study International Politics back in England.

Paul's life and happiness revived out of all recognition as he and Chris recovered their relationship. He felt himself regaining the lightness of spirit that he had known in the early years of their marriage. He had just begun to think that life was very good, when it began to happen again. The fleeting moments of darkness washed over him once more. As previously, they were barely perceptible at first. Again, they focussed around his business dealings and became increasingly noticeable as the weeks passed. What could be wrong with him? He had everything – a thriving business, happy customers, a contented, loving wife, and a beautiful home. What more could he possibly want?

He said nothing about what was happening to him. In truth, he didn't know what there was to say. When he tried to formulate words to describe his disquiet, they just sounded ridiculous. How could a grown man seriously complain about vague feelings of shadows passing over his life? It didn't only sound ridiculous, it was ridiculous. So, he bottled it up and kept quiet.

Chapter 2 – The Scream

Out of the blue, two things happened that changed Paul's life for ever. On the face of it, neither of them appeared to be life changing. To any dispassionate observer they would have been as no more than the flapping of a butterfly's wings in the face of a vigorous breeze; mere nothings, such as one would normally pass without a second glance. Nevertheless, they took hold of Paul and his life, and they shook him to the core. The first was Chris's latest sketch. The second was an advert that popped up briefly on Paul's computer. Both were trivial in themselves. However, their order was important, because it was the dramatic effect of the sketch on Paul that prepared him to take notice of the advert that came later.

Chris's latest sketch wasn't a copy of a pretty picture. It showed a misshapen image of a man on a distorted representation of a seafront, where he seemed to be screaming in agony. It was that image that burned itself into Paul's mind. He'd never seen the first hint of meaning in any piece of artwork before, but this picture had a powerful significance that hit him like a mental sledgehammer. His whole life view was shattered in an instant, before it re-formed with terrible clarity. Paul was physically trembling as a cold hand seemed to take hold of his heart with a vice-like grip. Its chilly fingers were trying to squeeze the life out of him as the truth was revealed: he was the man on the promenade!

Paul began to calm himself. His reaction was surely exaggerated beyond reason. He *wasn't* screaming in agony, he merely experienced periods of darkness. Sadly, however much he tried to reassure himself, it didn't prevent him from identifying with the agonised cry, *and* he knew the source of his distress. With sudden sharpness of vision, he recognised in the picture the origin of the pain within himself: he was seeing and feeling his world to come. Although he wasn't yet in the state of utter despair portrayed in the sketch, he saw that he would be. This was his destiny. He didn't believe in fortune telling, or horoscopes, or any such mumbo jumbo. The future hadn't happened. He was perfectly persuaded that no-one could possibly know what it held on the basis of crystal balls or the movements of the planets. All of that was mere superstition. So how was it that he could see the future of his lifepath with such vivid certainty? Until now, the future had always been clouded in comfortable uncertainty. Recently, those clouds had been bright with promise, but here, in the blink of an eye, the mist had cleared from his mind to reveal his own sure path to screaming terror. Was this the beginning of progressive insanity? How long did he have? Could the path be changed? Was this some kind of divine warning?

He decided to ask Chris about the picture, but he would have to be careful. His dreadful agitation should be kept in check, otherwise she would suspect a nervous breakdown. He could give no hint of the doom-laden future he had foreseen. No, he must sound casual. His opportunity came when they visited a local café for lunch. There were several restaurants within a short walk from home, and Chris was insistent on varying their destination. She claimed that it would save them from settling into a dull routine. Once again, Paul accepted her strategy without question.

On this occasion, they had been chatting about the theatre – their main shared experience. Paul had been at an all-boys school where, as he would freely admit, he had been a geek. He'd never been in poor physical shape; his outdoor life on a farm had seen to that. Having said that, although sport was a much-vaunted feature of the school, he wasn't keen on any of the organised games on offer, and he took care to keep clear of all the school sports teams. He only played games when they were compulsory. On reflection, he knew he'd been a bit of a loner. It was during his GCSE year that his maths teacher suggested that he might like to help with the stage lighting for a school production. He did help and he enjoyed it. By the time he was studying 'A' levels, he was more-or-less in charge of the lighting for all the school's productions. Once his teachers had satisfied themselves about his technical competence, their confidence in him grew rapidly. Within the world of stage lighting, his authority was soon unchallenged. In the course of that technical role, he sat through endless rehearsals and performances and began to enjoy the on-stage drama as well as his work behind the scenes. He became virtually word perfect in every production and picked up words and phrases that lived on in his everyday thought.

At university, he'd been a geek studying maths. With his previous experience, he did join the drama society, where he again took command of the lighting. This was where Chris had come on to the scene in every sense. It was during his second year when Chris, also in her second year, brought paradise to the stage as the star of a show. He framed her in the spotlight and held her bright image indelibly in his mind. The fluidity of her every movement enthralled him as she flowed sensuously across the stage of his life. The cadences of her speech were as music from heaven, and her every utterance was a velvet caress. He worshipped her from afar - always from afar. He was awkward in the presence of all girls, and when this girl was near, he became virtually incapable of both speech and coherent action. He'd never had a girlfriend, and he was clueless on how to begin a relationship. His lack of experience made no practical difference, because Chris was way beyond his reach. She was the uncrowned queen of the female students, and he guessed that most of the male students were already in love with her. He resigned himself to frustrated love at a distance.

After one particular rehearsal, he had already begun to feel the flush in his cheeks as he saw Chris walking towards him. By the time she spoke to him, he was bright red to the gills. His heart was thumping like a steam hammer, even before she suggested that they might have coffee together. At that, his brain threatened to take leave of his body while he struggled desperately to reply through the sandy dryness in his throat. His mind was at the gates of an unexpected and wondrous new world, yet the paralysis of his tongue threatened to keep that gate firmly closed. Despite his debilitating embarrassment, Chris had persisted, and that was the beginning of their relationship. Their lone childhoods and their shared love of theatre were all they had in common, but that was more than enough for Paul. The other students looked on with awe and wonder. How could this have happened? What earth-shattering event had reversed the natural order of things? It was beyond comprehension that such a vision of beauty should fix her attention on this gangling geek. Surely that couldn't last, there was nothing about him to inspire devotion. To everyone's surprise, it did last. Despite the best efforts of the other male students, there was no distracting her attentions from Paul.

Had he been more a man of the world, Paul himself might have wondered how or why this amazing turn of events had occurred. As it was, he didn't look for any explanations, he simply basked in the glow of her presence and grew in confidence as their relationship continued. The princess had kissed the frog, and he was transforming daily.

His thoughts returned to the present reality, and Paul changed the subject.

"Your latest picture is quite remarkable," he ventured, "I've never seen anything like it."

"Oh, it's pretty famous, partly because of the controversy connected with it."

"So far, so good," Paul thought, as he wondered whether the controversy might do something to explain his own reaction.

"What kind of controversy?" he enquired.

"It's a bit of a hodgepodge really. The picture seems to exert a strange compulsion over some people. Different versions of it have been stolen over the years, and on at least one occasion there was no good explanation of why the thieves had done it. That on its own was weird."

This was now sounding a good deal more ominous. The picture might have exerted a peculiar influence on others, but Paul could hardly believe that he was himself in the grip of a mysterious painting, especially since he hadn't even seen the original. He hardly dared to ask any more, yet he did, "You say, 'that on its own was weird.' Do you mean there was more?"

"Oh yes, there's plenty more. For example, the whole question of whether the artist was insane."

Paul felt himself turn pale and he hoped that Chris wouldn't notice. This was exactly what he secretly feared. Now he was screaming inside, "No!! Please!! I can't be going mad! What will become of me?"

Chris appeared not to have noticed, and she carried on, "The painter himself lived in mortal fear that he might be mad, especially because there was insanity in his family. That clearly preyed on his mind to the extent that on one of his paintings he even wrote that only a madman could have painted it."

Paul was now in a cold sweat, and he began to feel a little sick. He attempted to appear casual and unconcerned as he undid the top button of his shirt. He tried to look deep in thought as he lowered his head. All this was in a desperate attempt to look normal while he was trying not to faint. He wasn't sure how much time had passed, but he hoped that the hiatus had not been too long before he was sufficiently recovered to say the only thing he could think of, "Fancy that."

His head was still in a whirl, so he tried to mask his confusion by applying himself to his sandwiches. In the face of what he had heard, he was no longer hungry. In his present state, food was the last thing he needed. Nevertheless, he completed the meal with a silence that he hoped was explained by eating. As he ate, he was working to calm himself with thoughts of objective reality, "It's only a painting. You're over-reacting. Of course, you're not mad, you were just caught by surprise."

The problem was he didn't actually believe any of his own reassurances, and his heart was filled with fear and dreadful understanding. He would have to find a quiet space, where he could try to organise his thoughts. One thing was for sure, he certainly couldn't tell anyone of the horror he had seen so clearly.

Paul spent the afternoon in his office, in front of his computer. He was in no state to deal with clients as he concentrated on attempting to make some sense of what he had seen. If anyone heard the unvarnished truth, that would undoubtably mark him out as an object for ridicule, but it bubbled up inside him and pressed for release, and that would never do. The best he could think of was to adjust what he knew in a way that would keep it true to reality, whilst making it more socially acceptable. By 'socially acceptable' he meant acceptable to Chris. He began to work out what he could truthfully say, without being accused of insanity. On the one hand he wouldn't be able to conceal his turbulent state for long. On the other hand, his vision of doom, and inevitable helplessness in the face of disaster, couldn't be allowed out for public scrutiny. As he worked out how to disguise the full truth, he gradually came up with a cover story that would express some of what he knew, without revealing too much.

His business dealings had been what started all this, so they should be incorporated as part of his cover story. He couldn't say that he was terrified. Maybe it would be okay to say that he was dissatisfied. That much was certainly true. Although his business work was absolutely fine by any moral standard, he could say that it was leaving him unfulfilled. That was it! He could say that he was helping people to prepare for bad things that might happen, but that work was leaving him with some discontent because he would rather be trying to prevent bad things from happening in the first place. That was all a vast understatement of what he now knew, yet it was close enough to the truth to pass muster, and it certainly wasn't a lie.

It was as he came to that conclusion that an advert popped up on his screen. Though the thought was absurd, it was as though someone, somewhere, had known what he was thinking – 'Tired of the rat race? Join us and make a difference.' The gist of the advert was an offer from 'Michael & Co.' to provide life-affirming choices to suitable candidates who were tired of conventional business careers. No paperwork, no application forms, no obligation, just stop by one of their offices for a chat. A list of office addresses was provided, and one of them was local. The information was intriguing, especially because he had never heard of Michael & Co., yet there was an address in his own High Street. A few minutes later he discovered that he wasn't the only one who had never heard of the company; even Google turned up a total blank. That was a first in his experience. He was fascinated and oddly attracted. It would do no harm to walk by one day to see what this office looked like.

Meanwhile, how could he talk about his state of mind with Chris? Now that he had a cover story, he would feel much better if he spoke sooner rather than later. He would have to be careful over what he said, but saying something would help to give him the peace of mind that he usually offered to his clients.

The next day was warm and sunny; spring at its best in England. Paul and Chris sat out of doors over lunch. When they visited restaurants that spilled out on to the pavement, Chris generally chose to sit inside, even in the warmest of weathers. Once they were inside, she always picked the seat facing the door. However, on this occasion she was happy to sit on a patio at the back of the café, which could almost have been out in the countryside. They were far enough from the road for the traffic noise to be little more than a hum, while the potted trees and shrubs completed the illusion of a rural environment.

"Chris," he began. She looked at him enquiringly as he continued, "Do you ever wonder about the value of what we do? I mean what is it really worth?"

She thought briefly before answering him, "I take it you're talking about work, and no, it's not something that troubles me at all. I teach people, and that helps them, but the bottom line is that I work and earn money. I do enjoy the work, and thinking about it, I would have to say that education is worthwhile in itself. It's certainly interesting to meet people from so many different backgrounds. Don't you find that as well? Surely your clients are a good mix too, aren't they?"

"They are. The trouble is that, in essence, all I'm doing is helping them to find the best insurance policies, which will pay out if some kind of disaster strikes."

"Well, that's good, isn't it? Isn't that a useful and worthwhile thing you're doing?"

This conversation wasn't going in quite the direction Paul had hoped for, but perhaps he could set it back on its track. "It has its good points, it's just that I wonder sometimes whether I'm just making money out of people's fears. Also, times have moved on. It's not like the old days when people had one career that took them from university to retirement. There's almost an expectation of having more than one profession, and I occasionally find myself trying to imagine an option that would be a more positive one."

Chris just looked incredulous. "You can't be serious! You've spent forever training and working at what you do. You're good at it and it gives us a good income. Why on earth would you even think of starting again on something else? When you already own a goldmine, you don't look round for an alternative source of cash. You might as well think about digging for pirate treasure at the end of the garden."

It was true, Paul had committed an enormous amount of time and effort to his career. Following his maths degree, he'd joined a large firm of insurance brokers, where he had worked and studied to gain more qualifications, and he'd become very skilful at what he did. All the awkwardness of his youth had been overcome, and his social skills had been transformed, largely by Chris. He'd learnt to make connections and to develop the best of relationships with customers from all kinds of backgrounds. After several years with the firm, he had ventured out on his own and painstakingly built up a very successful business, with a strong client base.

That had not been Chris's path. Even when they met in the second year at university, she told him that she'd already come to the notice of an international firm that wanted to use the combination of her academic work and her language skills for online teaching. A career path had been laid out for her, and she had more than willingly followed it.

Paul cast around desperately for something he could say. There seemed to be no way of adding anything that would further his cause, so he retreated with dignity by saying, "It was just a passing thought. It's just that work sometimes seems to be in a bit of a rut, and it makes me wonder."

"Wondering is fine, but don't be tempted to do anything silly. There are plenty of ways of doing some good in the world without throwing up a whole career, especially when you have responsibilities."

That caught him off guard, and Paul leapt in to reply with far too little thought, "Do we really have responsibilities? We have no debts, and we pay a couple of people to do some work for us. We're hardly responsible for them, and they don't depend on us in any meaningful way."

"Of course you have responsibilities *and* debts! Are you seriously suggesting that you're ready to wreck our lives in the pursuit of some fairyland career, with no prospects beyond a warm fuzzy feeling that might last for all of the first two days. How could you even dream of such a thing?"

She was right, of course, he did have responsibilities and a large debt. His grandparents had been tenant farmers, and they were never rich. Although he had been their sole heir, he hadn't inherited a fortune. It was true that his parents had left a trust fund that paid for his education, and after that, he had still been left with enough to provide a substantial deposit on their house. That had been an expensive purchase, principally because it was in a smart part of London. Their mortgage was sizeable. With Chris in the right, this was an argument he needed to defuse, so he resorted to a calming lie, "I'm sure you're right, my dear, it's just a crazy thought."

"Yes, you're right about that at least. It is crazy thinking."

The sun went behind a cloud, and Paul felt himself withdrawing into renewed darkness of mind and thought. How had he come to this? He remembered his life on the farm. Though the weather must have been terrible through a large part of every year, his memories were all of sunny days, out of doors, surrounded by animals. There were cattle and sheep that would come at his call. He recalled the warm, soft coats of the cows and the rough lick of their tongues. There was the wagging of tails as excited dogs rushed to greet him. His favourites had been the golden Labradors. For many years that had been Lucky, who had been the tenth in a litter. She had shown such poor weight gain that her survival was little short of miraculous. During Paul's early teens, Lucky had been replaced with Charles. Neither dog had the training of his grandfather's sheep dogs. Their understanding of 'sit' and 'stay' were both rudimentary at best, and the concept of 'heel' never brought the faintest sign of response. Secretly, Paul thought the dogs understood perfectly well, but chose to fain ignorance. It mattered not, he loved their friendly exuberance and the flapping of their ears as they raced across the meadow ahead of him. He overlooked the times when they emerged from the pond and insisted on standing right beside him to vigorously shake themselves dry. What with ducks, chickens, and cats, he'd lived with animals at every turn. How different were the sunny days of boyhood, from the gathering clouds of his life now! Those days couldn't have been as carefree as he remembered, of course, and his grandparents' lives had certainly been filled with long, hard days. They must have worked themselves to death on that farm because they both died after only a few years of their retirement, during the first few years of Paul's marriage. Chris was right, it was crazy thinking to look for anything more than the life he had now. Unfortunately, although he tried to convince himself of that, he never quite succeeded.

Chapter 3 – Michael & Co.

Although Paul spent long hours in his office, his young life on the farm had given him a continuing love of the outdoors. He made a deliberate practice of taking a walk as part of his daily routine. His area of London was well endowed with parks and gardens, where the birds, and in some cases the animals, reminded him pleasantly of his childhood. The walks kept him respectably fit and, despite his largely sedentary work, kept his weight in check. Though Chris would walk for exercise on occasions, she preferred more vigorous activity. She went to swim at their local Leisure Centre each week. There was no set time for that. Nevertheless, she went without fail. However, her main exercise was in their home gym upstairs. Installing that had been their first project when they had bought the house, and Chris made good use of it. Paul would often hear her exercising as he worked in his office, and the result was that she was impressively fit. He knew that her trim physique drew admiring glances from many, and he was chief among them.

Within a day or two of reading the pop-up advert, Paul took a walk in the direction of Michael & Co. It was no wonder he had never noticed the office before; one could easily walk straight past without a second glance. He found the address in a quiet part of the High Street, where he discovered its plain wooden door with a yellow-tinted fanlight above it. The door itself was painted dark maroon, though its number, 77, gleamed in shining brass at eye height. Below the number was a less shiny, circular bell-push, and where one might have expected a letterbox there was instead a small black plaque, engraved with yellow print – 'Michael & Co. Please ring and enter.'

He had no intention of doing anything more than taking a look, so Paul turned on his heel and headed for home. He used the long way home through the park, where he sat on a bench to think. In front of him, the lawn and its borders were filled with the green shoots of spring. The swelling buds were beginning to show colour, giving the promise of a glorious display in the days ahead. As he sat in thought, he was aware of a man coming to sit on the same bench, who began to speak to him, "Isn't it a miracle, how after all the gloom of winter, the flowers burst into new life?"

Paul snapped out of his reverie, "Yes, it's an amazing part of the cycle of life."

The stranger had more to add, "That's exactly it. Life goes in cycles like that. It's easy in the dark days of winter to become despondent. The trick is to look forward to the spring ahead."

Paul didn't know where this conversation was going. It was beginning to seem heavy for a casual chat with a stranger on a park bench. He attempted to shut it down with, "I'm sure you're right."

The stranger was not so easily put off. He continued with more of his philosophy, "Isn't it a shame how often we see people making ill-advised decisions about their future, just because they are caught up in the gloom of a few dark days. All they really need to do is to remember the good days of the past and the cycle that will bring more good days ahead."

This interaction was breaking the bounds of social etiquette. It wasn't acceptable to inflict home-spun views on perfect strangers. It might have been better if Paul hadn't engaged further; he could have simply excused himself and left. As it was, he didn't leave. Instead, on the spur of the moment, he answered, "What do you mean?"

"Only that people can have times of despondency when they easily make rash decisions." The stranger's voice seemed to take on an edge of menace as he added, "That can put themselves in serious danger and expose their friends and family to some dreadful perils. It would be much safer for all concerned if they realised that the depression would pass, just as winter always turns to spring." Then, in a much more breezy tone, "Still, you're obviously a man of intelligence, so I don't know why I'm telling you all this. You'll work it out for yourself."

With that, the stranger rose and walked off, leaving Paul to wonder what had just happened. The stranger had spoken as though he knew Paul's thoughts and had been giving him unsolicited advice. No, it sounded like more than advice. Were there thinly-veiled threats?

Paul couldn't deny that the stranger's words had produced disquiet. However, his uneasiness was more than balanced by curiosity, and his thoughts were not distracted from their focus on that intriguing door. There had been shop fronts on both sides of the door, so he concluded that there must be a staircase behind the door, leading up to an office on the first floor. Although the pop-up advert had claimed premises in a wide variety of locations across the length and breadth of England, number 77 certainly didn't look like the entrance to a large and successful enterprise. It seemed unlikely that Michael & Co. could live up to its advertised claims; it hardly looked like the kind of place where an already successful executive would be enabled to change careers and 'make a difference.' Nevertheless, that door attracted Paul as surely as cheese draws a mouse to a trap. Sheer curiosity would be enough to propel Paul through to whatever lay behind that gleaming brass number.

For the present, he would say nothing about it to Chris. After all, if there was no practical outcome to his visit, and that was the overwhelming probability, then it would be the height of folly to create an unnecessary rift between them. If, by any chance, Michael & Co. did live up to their promises, there was still no guarantee that they would be what Paul wanted, or even that he would be what they were looking for. Judging by the unimpressive venue, he was likely to be over-qualified for whatever might be on offer. None of that changed the fact that Paul was back at the maroon door on the very next day.

At the last minute, he was hesitant. It wasn't fear of who, or what, he might find on the other side of the door. No, there was just the faint possibility that he was about to have a life-changing experience, and he wondered whether he was ready for that. He took a deep breath - only one way to find out. He rang the bell and pushed the door. As he had expected, it opened on to a flight of stairs, which were dimly lit, despite the fanlight over the door. He climbed the narrow stairs noiselessly on the soft grey stair carpet to arrive at a small landing, where there was a blank wall ahead and a door with a frosted glass panel on either side of him. The one on the right was marked 'Reception.' He turned the handle and pushed it open. Inside, he was confronted with a polished wooden counter, which created the atmosphere of a hotel check-in. On the counter was a mechanical bell labelled 'Ring for attention,' so he pinged the bell.

To his right, was a waiting area where two armchairs were placed by a large sash window, which gave a view of the street below. It all looked clean and efficient. That impression was reinforced by the young woman who emerged from a back room and came to the counter. The name badge on her crisp, white blouse informed him that it was Annette who was treating him to a bright smile.

"Good afternoon, how can I help you?"

After all the mystery, this seemed so normal - a little antiquated, but still normal.

"I read your advertisement, and it said that I could just arrive here to enquire."

"That's great! I'll find someone you can chat with. Could I take your name please, sir?"

He hadn't thought this through. Now his name was going to appear on someone's records. Should he make up a name? No, that was being paranoid.

"It's Paul Keating," he answered truthfully.

"Thank you, Mr Keating. Please take a seat and I'll find someone to help you."

She disappeared into the back room, where Paul could hear her in soft conversation. It can't have been more than a minute before she returned and announced, "Mr McDonald would love to see you in his office on the other side of the landing, Mr Keating. He's expecting you, so you can open the door and go straight in."

Paul thanked her as he stood and followed her instructions to the office, where a stocky, middle-aged man rose from an armchair by an unlit fireplace. He laid aside the book he had been reading and extended a hand, "Welcome to Michael & Co, Mr Keating, I'm Malcolm." After shaking hands, Malcolm indicated a second armchair on the other side of the fireplace. They made themselves comfortable, and Malcolm waved his hand towards the refreshments on the coffee table beside Paul's chair.

"Please, help yourself to rations Mr Keating - may I call you Paul?"

"Yes, please do, Malcolm."

Once Paul had a warm mug in his hands, Malcolm began, "It's a pleasure to see you, Paul. I gather that you saw our advertisement. Perhaps you could tell me what made you follow it up."

Malcolm's every movement and gesture was sharp and precise. His speech was crisp and reminiscent of a military briefing. The possibility of a military background was made more likely by his tie, which Paul thought might well be related to one of the armed forces. There was no hint of stuffiness about him, rather, as the light from the window behind him glinted on the bald dome of Malcolm's head, his eyes twinkled with friendly sincerity. Paul felt an almost irresistible urge to respond with equal truth and honesty. It required a conscious effort to hold back the pressure of the words that were trying to gush out. He succeeded and kept to his cover story, "I'm an independent insurance broker, and my business is thriving, but I was attracted by the idea of contributing something more positive to life."

Malcolm looked him in the eyes. If he hadn't known better, Paul would have imagined that his mind was being probed by the mild-looking man opposite. "That sounds very good, but let me be honest with you. In our experience, although many people have the kind of thoughts you describe, very few of them find their way to our humble and rather narrow staircase. When they do, I usually find that they have a rather stronger motivation than the one you have described. Those who want to contribute to society can easily find more obvious ways of doing that: they join their residents' association, or become school governors, and so on. In contrast, those who end up coming to us are usually urged on by something more compelling; something more pressing than just wanting to do good."

As he spoke, Paul was beginning to feel that here was a man who might truly understand. In his presence, Paul could believe that the truth could be spoken without it sounding like insanity. It was even possible that this man would hear about Paul's reality with sympathy. That remained to be seen, because before he could form any words of his own, Malcolm was continuing, "You'll have seen that our advert referred to 'suitable candidates.' We've found that those are few and far between. Our judgement of suitability is largely a matter of assessing their motivation for coming to us, and you may find it hard to believe, but we have often found the best motives to be ones that are viewed with ridicule by others. I like to think that we are far more discerning, and I can assure you that anything you say will be heard without criticism, so please, Paul, can you tell me more about why you are here?"

Malcolm settled his hands together in his lap and sat back as he allowed silence to descend.

"You're right that there is more," Paul replied, "It's very hard to put it into words, but I'll do my best. I've been experiencing something that almost amounts to mental pains. They're always in connection with my business. I don't mean headaches, or anything like that. In fact, 'pain' is too strong a word. It's more like shadows passing through my mind. I know how that sounds, which is why I haven't given anyone else the opportunity to tell me it's ridiculous. I can't help thinking that for myself, so I don't need to hear it from others."

Malcolm was nodding encouragement and Paul continued, "I'm already worried that my mind is becoming unhinged, so I haven't wanted to talk about this to anyone and especially not to my wife. She doesn't know I'm here. When

I tried to broach the thought of changing my work to something that would be more useful to society, she was pretty hostile to the whole idea, so if I mentioned mental issues connected with business dealings, she would be wanting to have me sectioned."

Somehow, in this room, with this man, though there was the harsh reality of traffic rumbling outside in the real world, all Paul's outlandish anxieties and fears sounded normal. All the same, conducive as the surroundings might be, he had no intention of revealing the true depth of his fear. He did mention the picture, but even with that he kept to the simple thought that it showed a world in need of help. If he spoke about the true extent of the hellish menace and the evil that he'd seen so clearly, that would surely have any sane person suggesting psychiatric help.

As Paul ran out of verbal steam, Malcolm sat forward in his chair, "What you are describing may well be exactly what we are looking for here at Michael & Co. Be assured that others have known very similar effects, and that leads me to think that you may be experiencing precisely the reality that we are interested in. If that does turn out to be the case, we could certainly offer you employment. Now, I quite understand that this could cause difficulty with your wife. You need have no concern over that. Effectively, you could describe us, with complete truth, as being an ethical international company that is interested in becoming one of your clients. You could maintain other parts of your business and work for us part-time - which would suit us well. In short you would give us whatever time you wished, and we would pay for that time. Your income wouldn't suffer – we have good sponsors and deep pockets. I can say that working for us wouldn't be like anything you have done before, and I can promise that you would have the adventure of a lifetime."

Although this was all very encouraging, it only left Paul thoroughly mystified. What on earth did Michael & Co. actually do? How could it possibly be the adventure of a lifetime? "What exactly would I be doing?" he asked.

"Unfortunately, I can't tell you that now. I do understand that we are a bit of a mystery. Although at the moment I'm not in a position to explain more, if you decide to explore the possibilities further, I will then be able to give you more detail. Sadly, in the immediate future, we have certain procedures that I have to follow, so what I suggest is this: I will need about seven days to deal with our protocol. If you would like to pursue matters further, perhaps you could come to see me again next week."

Paul was attracted by the prospect. He was intrigued and exhilarated by the mystery, but he tried to remain restrained in his agreement. As he stood to leave, Malcolm added, "One more thing – do you have any allergies?"

That question had Paul even more puzzled. What did allergies have to do with anything?

"Not that I'm aware of. Why? Is that important?"

"Yes, it might have been. However, since you don't have any, it isn't, so I look forward to seeing you next week."

During the walk home, Paul was running through in his mind how much he should tell Chris. He obviously had to say something, because it wouldn't do to have a sudden change in his routine without some forewarning of the possibility. He couldn't foresee any great difficulty. Malcolm had given him a good steer on how to present things on the domestic front.

When he arrived home, Chris was just finishing with one of her students. She looked up as he came into the room, "Oh! You've been out. I didn't hear you go."

That wasn't surprising. Paul had taken care to leave very quietly from his office, without coming through the house. He'd left the premises using the gate in the garden, which he had closed behind him with only the faintest of clicks. "I didn't want to disturb you," he answered, "I've been down to the High Street. It's a bit strange really, because after all these years of clients who have been based at a distance, I have a potential client who's only a few minutes' walk away. It may come to nothing, but I might actually have a customer that I go to see face to face. I'm due to visit them again next week, so we'll see how it pans out."

"Well, that would be a change. Who are they?"

"It's a company I'd never heard of. Even so, they have offices all over the place, so they could possibly produce quite a lot of work. We'll just have to see what develops."

"Let's hope it works out well. That could be just the kind of change that will help you to snap out of any odd ideas you might be having. Anyway, I must get on, there's another pupil waiting online, so I'll chat later." They never did return to the subject, much to Paul's relief. He'd already said as much as he could. In fact, with the remaining mystery of Michael & Co., he had said all that he knew.

Chapter 4 – The Infection

A week had flashed by. Paul had tried to research Michael & Co. in idle moments. For a supposedly international concern, they had amazingly little online presence. No, it would be more accurate to say that they had precisely zero online presence. How had that advert popped up out of nowhere? Where was the customer chat, or the user reviews? How could a company do anything at all without appearing online in some form? Did it consist of just two people in a small office in the High Street? Even if it was no more than that, who paid them? Anyway, the advert had given addresses for many offices. To find no trace of them on the internet was incredible. The more he thought about it, the more peculiar the whole business seemed to be. Could there be a scam of some kind going on? He should obviously be alert to the possibility, though if that was the case, surely his search would have come up with warnings from those who had been caught, yet there was nothing.

By the appointed time, Paul had decided to proceed - with very great caution. On the one hand he remembered Malcolm's apparent sincerity, on the other hand, he was also fully aware that the key skill of the successful conman was to create precisely that impression. Paul would make no financial commitments, nor would he rush to reveal any more personal information about himself. On reflection, he realised that he had told Malcolm next to nothing about himself: only his name and that he was married. So, no harm had been done thus far.

He rang the doorbell and entered as before. At reception, Annette was clearly expecting him and asked him to go straight in to see Mr McDonald. Malcolm was effusive with his welcome, and the two men were soon seated with coffee, just as they had been a week earlier.

Malcolm began, "I thought you would be back, Paul, and I'm delighted to see you. I do know that we've been a little secretive, but today I hope that we can clear up some of your inevitable questions. I have been able to complete our procedures for new contacts, such as yourself, and I now have authority to tell you more."

This gave Paul the opportunity he needed, and there was no point in holding back. If this company was pulling some kind of con trick, he needed to address the issue straight away, "My first question is about why I've been able to find out nothing about your company. How can a company with so many offices, or one conducting any kind of business, fail to be found by any search engines?"

"The answer to that is both simple and complicated. The simple answer is that we don't wish to be found in that way. The complicated answer is that we have a department of skilled technicians, whose work is dedicated solely to preserving that state of affairs. With your background, you will realise that their task is extremely difficult, but they are very skilled. We pay them extremely well and, as I said, maintaining our anonymity is their sole purpose."

"I won't pretend to understand how you could do that," Paul commented, "though I'll let it pass in favour of another question. You speak as someone knowing much more than just my name, even though that's the only thing I told you. How did that happen?"

"Hmm," Malcolm smiled thinly, "yes, we have a human resources department that is also very good. You will have seen that we don't use application forms and all that bumph, which avoids the embarrassment of people telling us things that aren't quite true and the creation of an information trail that we would like to avoid. You must know that pretty much everything about you is held as electronic information somewhere, so I leave you to draw your own conclusions. You may rest assured that we will not pass on any information about you. We wouldn't dream of doing such a thing, and it would compromise our non-existence if we did. I might add, that your work for us would be another thing that wouldn't exist, but we'll come back to that."

Paul was stunned at the enormity of what he had just been told. Surely, that wasn't possible! He quickly regathered his wits, “Exactly what work would that be? What does your company do?”

“That's the main question I expected you to ask, and I'll try to explain. Before that, I would be grateful if you could be a little more open with me. On your first visit, you explained to me about sensations of shadows or darkness, and that was most helpful. Indeed, it was what most commended you to us. At that time, I had the distinct feeling that there was more that you were not telling us. As you spoke, you were being very careful in your choice of words when you told me about that picture. I don't mean to criticise you for that, because whatever you were not saying was clearly a source of great disturbance and anxiety for you. Having said that, if you could try to explain, it would be most helpful, I believe as much to you as to us. Although you only have my word for it, what you tell me will be confidential.”

Again, Paul felt words and feelings welling up and pressing for release. It would indeed be a relief to let the dam break and speak to someone who might conceivably listen with understanding. For the first time, he didn't hold back, “You're quite right, I saw something incredibly dark and sinister in that picture. Even as I've thought about it since, I've struggled to believe that anything so awful could possibly be true. I haven't dared mention it to anyone, mainly because I can't avoid the conviction that I've seen such a dreadful vision of reality, that any sane person would surely dismiss it as impossible, before carrying on to call my own sanity into question.”

“I'm not going to call your sanity into question, though I would like to know what you saw. It could be of vital importance to both of us. So please try to explain.”

“Okay, I'll do my best. The picture was of a distorted man screaming in agony. That much was there for anyone to see. The thing is, I saw why he was screaming.” Paul was beginning to relive the terror of the man on the promenade. He swallowed and continued, “He was screaming, because he knew that his whole world was infected with something truly horrible, it was all around him, everywhere he looked there was infection, and there was nothing he could do about it. He was screaming in fright and in dreadful frustration."

Paul paused, but Malcolm wasn't ready for him to stop there, "There's still more isn't there?"

"Yes," said Paul quietly, "I realised that I wasn't just seeing a philosophical view of the world in general, nor the artist's impression of his own environment, I was seeing the reality of my own world."

Malcolm didn't reply immediately, and Paul was given time to recover himself. Then Malcolm spoke, "I'm very sorry to say that what you have seen is real; it is the true state of affairs. There is some sort of plague active in the world. You've caught a glimpse of it, and that places you amongst a very small group of people. You used the word 'infection,' which happens to be what we call it. The vast majority of people don't know that it even exists, and worse still, if you try to tell them, it's nigh on impossible to convince them. The fact is that there is a problem, and it represents a great threat to the whole of humanity. That's the reason why Michael & Co. exists; our work is to resist and fight back against the infection as best we can. We are in desperate need of people like you to help in that struggle, and there's no doubt that we can offer you employment. Your work would be to assist us in doing something about what you have seen."

Paul didn't know whether to be relieved, or even more disturbed. It was a relief to be understood and believed, set against that, it was highly disturbing to find another apparently sane person who thought that what he had seen was the truth.

"I can tell you a little more about what you've experienced," Malcolm explained, "I'll be honest, we don't know exactly what we're up against. We do know that it's not a virus or a bacterium. From a scientific point of view, we can't even test for it. How it's transmitted or passed on is a mystery, but when it's active it causes harm. The damage isn't often physical for humans and animals, rather it affects their whole mindset and thought processes very much for the worse. In addition to that, it can affect inanimate objects. In that case, it can cause all kinds of physical disruption and destruction. The good news is that we do have ways of tackling it. The bad news is that we are hampered by the fact that most people refuse to believe that there's a problem, and we are further hampered by the fact that we have no scientific test to discover where the infection is active."

"Then how can you fight something that you can't detect?"

"That's where people like you come in. It was discovered some time ago that men and women with your kind of sensitivity can be trained to sense the infection. We refer to them as 'Spotters,' because they are rather like some of the guidance systems employed by the armed forces. In those systems, a laser beam can be used to 'paint' a target, so that weapon systems can lock on to it. Our Spotters perform the same kind of function. If they can locate infection, or sources of infection, we stand some chance of working out ways to neutralise the effects, or maybe to remove the infection altogether. You'll realise that without our Spotters we can do nothing."

"That sounds great, but would that work make my dark shadows go away?"

"Yes, I believe it would. That's probably not for the reason you think. What you have been suffering from is rare; not unique, just very uncommon. Others like you have found that the shadows are caused by their unusually sensitive mind urging them to do something more with their life and demanding more than just doing a little good here and there. Our experience suggests that if you do agree to work for us, that need will be satisfied, and the shadows will rapidly pass."

"How sure can you be about that?"

"I can't say it's one hundred percent certain. All I can say is that it's worked in one hundred percent of the cases I know about. I've met several people with similar experiences to your own. In every case, working for us has cleared any blackness in their mind. Incidentally, you will soon realise that there are powerful forces for good that have brought you to us. Now you should also be warned that there are powerful forces for evil that may try to keep you from us. All-in-all, you will encounter a good deal that defies commonly held understandings of reality."

Paul decided not to mention the man at the park bench in his reply, "Okay, I'll buy that for the moment, but what's the training? How can you train someone to sense something that can't be detected in the first place? What would I have to do? How long does the training take?"

"Let's not get ahead of ourselves. We know everything that we need to know about you, and we can offer you work. There's a limit to what I can let you know about our organisation. Despite that, I'd like to give you as much assurance as possible. Firstly, there will be no contract. After all, you can't have a contract from an employer that doesn't exist. We will try to give you some confidence in our good intent and integrity, by paying you for each six months, in advance. Your pay will be according to how much time you wish to give us. Initially, I would like that to be the equivalent of one day per week, although that is entirely up to you. I'm assuming that you would wish to maintain your present business, and that's also what we would very much prefer."

"Okay, that part sounds very good. It remains a most peculiar arrangement, and I do have more questions, but I'll keep them for the moment, so do carry on."

"Thank you. This brings me to the question of your employer. You would continue to be self-employed; you would simply find that you have a new client. It won't be Michael & Co. because, as you know, we don't exist. It will be your own bank. Your bank will become your new employer. I know that you're immediately going to think that's impossible, so consider the experience you've had with us already, and you will realise that we can make that happen. In any case, if you do agree to work for us, the proof will be in the money that arrives in your account, plus the fact that your bank will provide any documents you need to establish that they are indeed your client, and that they are paying for work you have done for them. That work will, of course, be the work you have done for us."

After a brief pause for his words to sink in, Malcolm added, "To continue, you're probably hesitant about what we might ask you to do, and that's perfectly understandable. You needn't be concerned, because being non-existent cuts two ways. If at any time you don't like what we are asking you to do, you can just stop working for us and keep what you've already been paid. Future payments would stop of course, but there would be no hard feelings or repercussions. You will have no contract with us, because we don't exist. Equally, a non-existent company can hardly sue you for breach of a contract that you don't have. In brief, you can leave us at any time without obligation if the work becomes a problem. No-one has ever actually done that, but the offer still remains. Now, perhaps you'd like to think about my unusual proposition, and come back again in a week's time."

"You've certainly given me a great deal to think about. It's the most outrageous set of proposals that I've ever heard, but for the moment I can't quite spot the flaws in it. There is one thing you haven't mentioned. What is your pay rate?"

"Ah, yes, I should have told you about that. If you do decide to work for us, we would pay for your time immediately, in a way that more than matches your possible loss of income, let us say 'by a substantial margin.' Again, if that's not acceptable, you can always take the first payment and walk away. There is another thing I should have told you. Your initial work with us would be training, and as part of that we would provide you with a dog."

Paul blinked in surprise. "A dog? Whatever for? What sort of dog? Where will the dog live? Do I have to look after the dog? You're going to have to explain more about that. What would my wife say if I came home with a dog? ... Oh, wait a minute, I take it the dog's like a drug sniffer. Who will train the dog?"

Malcolm put his hands up in a gesture of submission. "I'm sorry, I did that very poorly. We can provide the dog for your work, and it doesn't have to live with you, though it's actually best if it does. If you do decide that you would like the dog to live with you, we would pay the full cost involved and come up with a credible explanation for your wife, without compromising the confidential nature of our work. I'm assuming that Christine doesn't have any issue with dogs in principle. The ones we use are German Shepherds, otherwise known as Alsatians, and they don't need to be trained. It's rather you who would need the training, and the dog would be helping you with that. We've already been able to train Alsatians to detect the infection once it reaches significant levels. Your experiences have shown us the potential that you have. With the dog's help, you will slowly learn to sense even faint traces of infection. I may say that our dog would be perfectly friendly and loyal, and I'm pretty sure that all our existing Spotters regard their dog as one of the best things about their work for us. Nevertheless, you'd need to bear in mind that, if an Alsatian is going to live with you, it would represent a big commitment on your part, and between us, we would need to ensure that you are ready to make your home suitable – at our expense. One of the few written documents I can give you is a booklet about that." He reached for a slim volume on a shelf behind him and handed it over.

As their meeting ended, Malcolm added one last piece of information, "If you do decide to work for us, I would be your key contact, and I'd provide you with a means to contact me at any time of the day or night."

Paul left, having agreed to think about what had been offered and to return the following week.

Chapter 5 – Intruder alert

Paul woke up early with a very uneasy feeling. Was there someone in the house downstairs? He listened for the slightest sound of movement, but could hear nothing unusual. In the past, he would have ignored the whole thing and put it down to an overactive imagination. Now, after his recent experiences, he was more inclined to check, though he didn't want to put himself in danger. He crept carefully to the bedroom door, opened it very gently by just a crack, and listened for several minutes at the narrow opening.

He was so intent on his listening that he was startled when Chris's sleepy voice said, "What are you doing?"

Putting his finger to his lips, he turned and whispered, untruthfully, "I thought I heard something downstairs."

He continued to listen - there was nothing. Still unconvinced, he dressed quietly and cast his eyes around the bedroom for a weapon. Failing to find anything useful, he was unarmed as he padded softly down the stairs, trying to avoid the creak on the third step. He still felt uneasy, but everything looked perfectly normal. He told himself that he was becoming paranoid as he went round checking windows and doors, only to find that all was as it should be. Remembering information from detective novels, he opened the front door to check for scratches around the lock, though he wasn't really sure that was actually a thing. Anyway, there were no indications that the lock had been picked. His office also looked just as he remembered it, and the vision of himself hunting for signs of intrusion was looking ever more irrational. He was beginning to feel totally foolish as he tried one final test. He logged in to his computer and ran an activity check. Oh! How could that possibly be? That had to be a mistake. No, computers don't make that kind of error. There it was: a failed login at 3.04 a.m. For a moment he froze in shock, then he was a flurry of chaotic activity.

He had little notion what he was looking for as he began searching through his papers, checking his computer leads, and lifting everything on his desk. He ran round the house, rechecking doors and windows. When he finally sat down in bewilderment, Chris came down the stairs to ask what was going on.

"Someone has been in the house," he replied.

She sat down beside him, putting her arm around him. "Are you sure? Everything looks okay."

"I know. I've checked all around the house and in my office. Everything does look okay, but someone has tried to log in to my computer. You should check yours."

As she went to sit at her desk, Chris was saying, "It's hard to see how anyone could have done that. Presumably, you have been checking all the doors and windows." It was a statement more than a question, and Paul was explaining how thoroughly he had been checking, when Chris stiffened. He stopped speaking as she turned to him.

"There's been a failed login here too, early this morning."

They sat in stunned silence. Eventually, Paul said, "We can't go to the police. There's no evidence of a break-in, and no police officer is going to take this seriously. All we could show is that, in the depths of our computers, there is this failed login report. They would dismiss us as crackpots."

With surprising haste, Chris agreed, "No, no, absolutely not, we'll keep this to ourselves, but let's be on our guard. I guess it's a good thing we have strong computer security. Have you checked for hacks recently?"

"Yes, I checked the day before yesterday. It was all okay then, I'll check again now." Paul was assiduous over matters of computer security, and early on in their relationship, he had discovered that Chris was every bit as careful as himself. That had initially surprised him. He hadn't associated that kind of technical awareness with arts graduates. Then he'd remembered her diplomatic and political background and realised that it might not be so surprising after all.

They both found it very difficult to concentrate on work that morning. Paul's thoughts kept returning to his sense of violation that someone had been rummaging through their personal possessions in, what should have been, the sanctity of their home. Why would anyone do such a thing? There had been no theft, so far as he could discover. What could be the possible motivation? More to the point, how could anyone have left no physical signs of their presence? Most people would never have known that anything had happened. Very few people were alert to matters of computer security, and even he didn't routinely check the activity log on his computer. Yes, he did check for hacking as a matter of course, but the activity log, no, he rarely looked at that. Who could have such a great interest in his work, and what kind of organisation could achieve such a stealthy and skilful search? He was settled in his mind that there was no mileage in police involvement because there was an alternative. He did know someone, with powerful connections, who was likely to take this sort of thing seriously. He would talk to Malcolm about the whole affair, and that would be in only a few days' time, so he would leave it until then.

Chris seemed to settle back into work with relative equanimity and slept soundly at night. She made no further mention of the apparent break-in, so Paul didn't either. He had no intention of interfering with her process of putting matters behind her. Paul, on the other hand, hadn't remotely been able to move on with his life. He had uneasy days and restless nights. It was a relief to come to the day when he would go back to Michael & Co.

As the morning dawned, Paul was just thinking that he had better decide whether he wanted to work for Malcolm, when he realised that he'd already come to a decision. It hadn't been a conscious, carefully thought-out verdict. Nevertheless, his decision had been made, and he'd been living for days now on the basis that he had a future with Michael & Co.

Malcolm was as welcoming as ever, but they had hardly sat down when Paul began, "Since we spoke last, I've had a problem at home. Someone has broken in. There was no sign of forced entry, so the only evidence was an uneasy feeling when I woke up and the activity logs on our computers.

They show that someone made failed login attempts in the middle of the night. There's nothing missing as far as we can tell, and I can't think why anyone would do such a thing or how they could manage it without forcing a door or a window."

Malcolm showed immediate concern, "I've never heard of anything like that happening to those associated with us, and as you say, it's a puzzle to know who could manage such an operation or who would want to. I've no doubt that our own organisation could do it if we wished. Needless to say, we didn't. We would have neither the desire nor the need to resort to that kind of tactic. I can't imagine you're in any great danger, or your intruder wouldn't have needed to be so careful, and I think I'll be able to put your mind at rest on that score. I'll explain more about that in a moment, but first, do I take it that you would like to work for us?"

"Yes, I would like to give it a try, if that's acceptable. I can't be sure about a long-term commitment because I would want to see what the work involves. For the moment, I'd like to see how it goes, on the basis of one day a week, if that's okay."

"Certainly, that's exactly what I'd hoped for. We'll be quite happy to pay you for six months. If you decide to leave us before that time is up, there'll be no hard feelings." Malcolm reiterated his previous information about details of employment and mentioned a payment amount that was much more than the average Paul would usually make in a day. Again, there was nothing in writing. Malcolm had more to say about that. "As you'll have realised, we aren't giving you anything in writing, either electronically or in hard copy. We do all our business face to face. Like the old Stock Exchange adage, our word is our bond. I would like you to work in the same way. Please don't keep any kind of record of the work that you do for us. Payment records will be provided by your bank, and it will be as though that is your client. You'll remain self-employed."

Paul indicated his agreement. The arrangement was highly irregular, but he would accept it on a trial basis. He would do almost anything to escape the fate seen in his vision.

"Thank you, Paul," was Malcolm's response, "Now to the matter of your security and, of course, the dog. Your worrying episode at home might make the dog less of a problem to introduce to Christine. From our own research, I realise that my question about your allergies was unnecessary. Your life on the farm would have been impossible if you had been allergic to animals, and that background might make the idea of a pet seem natural to Christine. On top of that, I'd guess that recent events might make the benefits of a large dog seem pretty attractive. As it happens, our dogs are very good for personal security. They are trained to detect 'the infection' in inanimate objects, but they also have a natural instinct to protect their owners and their territory. I really don't expect any security problems to arise from your work with us. Your recent experience is puzzlingly unique in my experience, and I can't imagine why your contact with Michael & Co. would make anyone wish to search your home. However, whatever was going on there, I'm pretty confident that it won't happen again once you have one of our dogs."

Paul could see that the idea of a dog might now be perfectly acceptable to Chris, and he'd be able to broach the concept at home without too many difficult questions being asked. Malcolm arranged with him that the first of his training days would be on the following week and gave him an address to go to for that day, with the promise of seeing him there.

Leaving Michael & Co., Paul almost skipped home. He was in a state of high excitement over the prospect of venturing into something new and unknown. His confidence in Malcolm's sincerity was high, despite the outlandish terms of employment, and he really did like the thought of a dog. It would surely help him to recover something of the joy he remembered on the farm. The break-in at home was turning out to be a blessing in disguise, because obtaining a dog for security would be the most natural reaction in the world.

As he stepped through the front door, his euphoria evaporated in the face of the familiar surroundings. What had he done? Michael & Co. took weirdness to a whole new level. How could he have even entertained the thought of working for them? He could hear Chris chatting in some Middle Eastern language as he slouched through to his office. Slumping into his chair, he reviewed the day's events. What had possessed him to agree to something without written evidence? That went against everything that had been ingrained in him for years: 'never work without a paper trail.' On the other hand, what did he have to lose? He logged in to his bank. There was the amount Malcolm had offered. He clicked for details and found that the payment did indeed come from the bank itself, just as Malcolm had said. That was both reassuring and worrying at the same time. If Malcolm could do that much, of what else was he capable?

Chapter 6 – The battery wrapper

Paul couldn't sleep. He could only keep re-running recent events through his mind, trying to make sense of them. It was true that the periods of darkness in his mind had already reduced since he had contacted Michael & Co. The question was, had he moved from one nightmare, only to find another one that was worse? Malcolm gave every indication of being a good man, but if he was skilled at drawing people into a scam, that's how he was bound to appear. There was some reassurance from the thought that, if this was a scam, it was a very expensive one. Paul had already seen two employees, and there was an office. Small though the office may be, it still cost money to run, and he had now been given another address for his training. If this was all part of a con, it would have to be a very big one. Could they be after his savings? Surely Paul had nothing to be stolen that would justify the financial outlay.

Of more concern was the kind of power that Malcolm was able to wield. His ability to discover personal information was impressive. Paul had provided no information about himself, yet Malcolm was very well informed. Further than that, if his tentacles could find and manipulate Paul's bank account, was anything out of his reach? Then there was the stealthy invasion of their home. Malcolm had appeared to be genuinely perplexed, but it was something of a stretch to imagine that there was another group with the kind of powers that Michael & Co. had at their disposal. And what about the dog? Was that to be a canine form of Trojan horse? Could a dog be a spy? Perhaps Malcolm's dogs came with spyware attached or inserted? Paul immediately began to feel foolish for entertaining such notions. Even so, there remained just the thought that a doggy spy was no more outlandish than the mere existence of Michael & Co.

As he was reviewing events in his mind, there dawned upon him a most unsettling thought. After the intrusion, he had scoured the house to check whether anything was missing. How could he have been so stupid? He should have been looking to see whether anything had been added. Had he been bugged?

It was in the early hours of the morning when Paul succumbed to temptation and jumped out of bed to begin searching again, without any clue as to what he was actually looking for. He was checking behind pictures and feeling round their frames. He was looking under tables and chairs. Before his flurry of activity had gone very far, there was a new concern. If Chris woke up and found him, how would he explain his actions? His search was pointless in any case because if there was anything to find, this was no way to find it. He needed to have one of those bug sweeper devices he had seen in the films, so his best course of action was to go back to bed and investigate more scientifically in the morning, after he had prepared the way with Chris.

Over breakfast he broached his concern with Chris, "Do you think our nocturnal visitor might have bugged the house?"

Chris's response was casual, "I shouldn't think so. Why would anyone do that?"

"I don't know, but then I don't know why anyone should take so much trouble to break in here in the first place, especially since nothing seems to be missing."

"Hmm. I expect you could get hold of a bug detector, if you're worried."

"Okay. I think I'll look into that, and I've had another thought too. The break-in reminded me of when I lived on the farm. Nobody could ever break in there. All the animals would have created such a din that any burglar would run a mile. I was wondering about getting a dog."

He had expected that Chris would start coming up with objections, but she didn't. "That would be a great idea. Let's make sure it's one with a good, loud bark."

Her instant agreement astounded him. That was much better than he'd expected and was the best reaction possible. If Chris was up for it, that was all he needed. Oh! Wait a minute! It wasn't going to be quite as easy as he thought. Chris would be expecting a puppy or a rescue dog. How was he going to account for a fully trained Alsatian? Keeping secrets was becoming very difficult, which reminded him that he had better tell Chris something about his new client too. Maybe he shouldn't mention the name of the company - or had he told her that already? He didn't think so, but couldn't be sure. He would take care not to mention it. If he'd done so already, Chris might forget about it. It wouldn't do to have her investigating who he was working for. It was bad enough that he didn't know much about them, without her asking awkward questions.

He made it his first mission that morning to make some contacts who might know about bug detectors. It turned out that he didn't need special contacts, he could just order one. It arrived the next day. The rechargeable batteries came in a separate package, so he had to insert them and put the device on charge. As he dropped the battery wrapping into a waste bin, he noticed that there was a similar wrapping already in the bin. That was a bit of a coincidence. Then he realised that both Chris and he used batteries in lots of devices round the house, so he thought no more of it.

Paul was impatient to use his detector, but watching the red charging light would do nothing to make it turn green, so he forced himself to work while he waited. Once his detector was charged, Paul began to search the house. He followed the instructions carefully, making sure that all their electronic devices were turned off. Fortunately, Chris was in the home gym upstairs, so he had unfettered access to everything downstairs. After an hour or so of bending and crawling to check low down, then climbing on chairs and tables to check high up, he wondered whether it was himself or Chris, who'd had the most exercise. He had found nothing.

Chapter 7 – Training day

Paul had no clue what his first training day would hold, so he set off with a degree of apprehension. A 20-minute walk brought him to the address, where a forbidding electronic gate, made from thick steel, was set into a two-metre-high brick wall. The security features made Paul think of Fort Knox, the famous U.S. gold depository. He looked up at the camera near the gate and pressed the 'call' button. He listened at the intercom, expecting a response. The only reply was a faint buzz as the gate swung silently open.

Once inside, Paul found himself on a brick path, which curved towards an open front door. Malcolm was coming out of the house to greet him with his usual cheery smile and vigorous handshake. From the outside, the building itself gave every appearance of being a family home set in a large garden that was enclosed by the high brick wall. Inside the house, Paul was led along a wide hallway to a sitting room, where a tall, sandy-haired man in a tweed jacket was standing at the bay window. He was the sort of man who would look comfortable with a brace of pheasants in one hand, a dog trotting beside him, and a shotgun tucked casually under his arm. As he turned in greeting, Malcolm made the introductions, "Paul, this is Piers, one of our dog trainers, and he'll be helping us today."

When they were all seated, with coffee and biscuits in front of them, Paul spoke first by asking Piers about the dogs, "I've been thinking about the difficulties of having one of your dogs at home, Piers. I reckon we can provide the right facilities, but I am aware of the amount of exercise a dog would need, and I'm concerned about the time commitment involved."

Piers was answering in a strong Scottish accent, almost before Paul had finished speaking, "You'll not need to be worrying yourself about that, I'll be making very sure that my dog has a suitable home, and I'll be coming along each day to take the dog for exercise and training. For the first few weeks, you'll be joining me, and that will be the sum of your work for us. I'll be teaching you how to control the dog and keep up her training. At other times of day, you can top up with exercise and play. You can do that yourself, and that would be in your own time."

The way Piers was speaking made it sound as though everything had already been decided. Malcolm hastily chipped in, "This all depends, of course, on how you want to do things. You can leave the dog with us and come here for your own training. We'd much prefer the dog to stay with you, but that's entirely your choice. We'll leave you to think about it."

Malcolm began to explain more about Michael & Co. The company had been founded by a man who was only ever known as Joshua. He had been the first to identify 'the infection,' and he had created Michael & Co. with the sole purpose of combatting the problem. He had financed the operation by finding a set of very wealthy sponsors. That group had all agreed, and then insisted, that their anonymity should be preserved. In setting up the company, Joshua had wanted to provide its employees with every possible support. As time had passed, further sponsors had been found to make that a reality. Paul was given the whole history of how Michael & Co. had learnt to detect and fight 'the infection.' Malcolm was gushing with enthusiasm for how Paul would be able to contribute to the enterprise.

Lunch was a smart buffet, set out in an adjoining room. Paul took the opportunity to find out about Piers' background. He had only managed to establish that Piers had worked with both police and military dogs, when Piers began to quiz him about his intruder, "Do you reckon that any of your business contacts might have had anything to do with it?"

"No, I've wondered about it, but I can't imagine that about any of them. Everything I do is completely open and above board. The idea's inconceivable."

"What about Christine's work?"

"She just tutors students over the internet."

"Aye, that we know, Paul. What does she teach exactly?"

"Her areas of expertise are international politics and languages, so I think she mostly teaches politics and English."

"We're well aware of those skills. The question of precisely what she teaches is a whole different box of kippers, which we have so far failed to open."

"I thought you people knew everything."

"Aye, we usually do, and I don't doubt we'll be getting there before too long. But, enough of that, I've brought some wee toys to show you."

Back in the sitting room, Piers produced a rucksack. He pulled out a diverse set of objects and spaced them out across the floor. There was a glass flask, an evil-looking knife, a black jacket, a small cushion, a spray can, and a handbag. Paul laughed out loud as this last item emerged from the rucksack. Then, seeing Piers' expression, he refrained from quoting "A handbag?" in a voice that mimicked an aristocratic woman of mature years as she expressed shock and incredulity. It was a favourite line from one of the many play rehearsals he had sat through.

Piers cocked an eyebrow as he spoke, "When 'the infection' has caused bad things to be done, items connected with the evil often retain traces of the infection. That's just a fact. I can't say we fully understand it, but there it is. We call that a secondary infection, and it can only be caused by infected humans. The secondary infection itself can't be passed on so, rest assured, you'll not catch anything from these items. Now, let me bring in the dog."

When they were alone, Malcolm said, "Don't mind Piers. He can seem brusque with humans. It's just his way, there's a heart of gold underneath, and when it comes to dogs, he's an absolute wizard. Stick with it and he'll warm to you."

Piers returned with an Alsatian on a leash at his heels, "This is Siete, and she's the dog that we think will work well with you, Paul." Siete was repeatedly looking up at Piers as if she was watching for instructions. Piers led her slowly past each of the six objects. When she came near the glass flask, the dog's ears flattened and she began to whine. There was nothing of the sort near the knife or the jacket, then the performance was repeated at the cushion, the spray can and the handbag. Piers sat down with Siete lying at his feet.

Piers looked at Paul, "What you've just seen is Siete detecting signs of the infection on four of the objects. The knife and the jacket were clean. One came from a butcher and the other is my own. The flask was used to cook up drugs, the cushion was used to suffocate an old lady, the spray can was used to desecrate a graveyard, and the handbag was used to carry an assassination weapon. They were all infected by their users."

"That's very impressive, Piers, but how does this help me?"

"We reckon that you can be trained to do what Siete does. I can't say that it will be a quick process, but we think you could become very sensitive. I've learnt to detect the infection myself. The vast majority of people will never be able to detect it at all, and I will never be great at it. I can only detect the infection on the cushion and the handbag. In contrast, we're expecting you to become much better. We've no clue about what sense the infection can trigger, though it might help you to know that what I sense is close to a smell, maybe like the musty stale smell inside a mausoleum. The point is that dogs can only detect the infection on inanimate objects. We call that secondary infection. We reckon you'll eventually be learning to detect the infection on humans and animals as well. In fact, we're hoping that you will go beyond that and learn to detect the *sources* of human infection, which we call primary infections. For the present, that's a long way down the line."

"Wow! I can't begin to think how any of that's going to work. Let me smell the objects."

Piers passed them silently over to him and Paul sniffed at them. There were smells, but no stale mausoleum was in evidence. Everything smelled just as he had been expecting.

"There's nothing unusual," he announced, "are you really sure this is going to work?"

Piers said, "Aye," at the same time as Malcolm said, "No."

"That's reassuring," said Paul sarcastically, "would anyone like to explain?" Malcolm indicated that Piers should speak.

"I said that my own aptitude for detection isn't very good; I've only been able to develop a low level of skill. You should be encouraged, because to begin with I felt the same way as you. The experiences you've described suggest that you have an exceptional aptitude for this. With training, you can become very good. Just don't expect instant results; it will take work."

Paul turned to Malcolm, who said, "Don't look at me Paul, I can't detect anything. I'm not certain, but I think there's a high chance that Piers is right."

"So, where do I go from here?"

Malcolm took up the running, "I think we should arrange for Piers to visit you next week, with Siete. You could work out between you whether or not you want to have an Alsatian living at home, and at the same time you could begin your own training with Piers and Siete. How would that suit you?"

Paul agreed. He had learnt a lot during the day, but was beginning to see a pattern. Whenever he left a meeting with Malcolm, he had more questions than he had started with.

As he walked home, Paul was in a world of his own, and that world was one of confusion and mystery. The discussion about Chris's work was preying on his mind. They'd never spoken a great deal about her tutoring, and he now realised that he knew virtually nothing about it. He knew she had students from all over the world. How did that come about? Why was it that Michael & Co. had been able to find out all about himself, but so little about Chris? Surely someone offering tutoring should be easy to find! Could her work be something more than he had thought, and might it provide a reason for their intruder?

The more he thought about it, the more peculiar it seemed to be that, after thirteen years of marriage, his knowledge of Chris's work was so slight. It was true that their working worlds were poles apart, and their only point of contact in the realm of employment had been over computer security. The need for security had always been part of his working life, and some would say that he was paranoid about it. He'd been pleased to find that Chris had an enthusiasm and expertise that almost matched his own. Set against that, he could say without exaggeration that his own technical skills were unusually high. How, exactly, had Chris acquired similar skills? He'd always thought that it was related to the background of her aunt's diplomatic work. Now, he wondered whether that was really a sufficient explanation. Judging by the news, politicians and diplomats were not renowned for that kind of proficiency.

This was insane! Was he seriously doubting the person he had been sharing his life with for all these years? Apart from their work, their marriage was virtually all they had; they were totally reliant on each other. Their friends were few, and their family was non-existent. They lived and worked under the same roof, so it was beyond belief that there could be some great sinister secret between them. As he was trying to convince himself that Chris couldn't possibly be involved in anything covert, his line of thought came to an abrupt halt. Here he was returning from what amounted to a clandestine seminar, no - a series of covert meetings. If he could be underhand, so could she.

Chapter 8 – Working with the dog

It was very unsettling to have vague suspicions about the person he lived with and was married to. If it wasn't bad enough to have those doubts swirling about in his mind, the whole concept of primary infections and secondary infections was even more disturbing. He was highly sceptical about the notion that he could turn himself into some kind of drug-sniffing creature. Would he wake up soon to discover that the last few weeks were only a dream? It was much more credible to think that the recent past was all imagination than to believe it was real. The only other alternative was to question his sanity, and that didn't bear thinking about. Only a short time ago, he had never heard of 'the infection.' There had been no mention of anything like it in the news media, and it was extremely hard to believe that, if it was true, it could remain unknown to the overwhelming majority of the population. Okay, it might explain something of his doom-laden experiences, on the other hand, he remembered being taught, 'When faced with a difficult problem, reject any complicated or exotic explanation if a commonplace one is more readily available.' Anyone making a sober judgement would readily conclude that he had a mental aberration. The explanation offered by Michael & Co. would not be given brain space; it would be immediately dismissed as an absurd fantasy.

It had become normal for Paul's mind to slip into overdrive in bed at night. The Michael problem, as he'd come to call it, had no immediate solution. The company didn't seem to present an imminent threat, so he was persuading himself that there was no harm in letting things run for the time being. It was bound to cause problems if he told Chris about what he was doing, but he would have to say something about his new employment before he became totally tangled up in his own secrets. He would talk to Chris in the morning. While he was at it, he needed to say something to prepare the way for the dog. In that regard, he had now refined his cover story, so he didn't anticipate difficulties with that.

Chris herself was another pressing concern in his mind. In the faint street light filtering through the curtains, he was gazing at the latest work in the 'art space.' Mercifully, the screaming man had been replaced with flowers in a vase. On this occasion, it wasn't the picture that had his attention. He had just remembered the real reason why the art space was there. Behind it was a wall safe. It wasn't there through any choice of theirs; it had been there already when they bought the house. The art space covered it up. They both knew that it was a cliché to have a safe behind a picture, but no better solution had come to mind. Paul had never used the safe at all; it was Chris's domain, though he hadn't seen her using it for years, and to the best of his knowledge, it only held a few items of jewellery. Now he wondered, "Was that all it contained?"

The safe was one of those electronic ones with a four-figure code. He supposed that there must have been a time when he knew the code, but if so, it was long forgotten. Chris had probably changed it anyway. Was that an insurmountable problem? After all, there were only 9999 possibilities. If he could get at it surreptitiously for half-an-hour a day, he could certainly crack it within a month - probably a lot sooner. He was working out how to manage that, when he realised that it would take much longer than he had estimated. The system was bound to freeze for several minutes after three failed attempts. Oops! Finding the code by working through all the possibilities would take more than a few weeks, more like two years! The quicker alternative, was to guess what Chris might have chosen as a code. He would have to think about that and look for an opportunity to investigate.

By the time morning came, Paul felt that he had 'Guilty Secret,' plastered in big letters across his forehead. Chris must surely notice the smell of his deceit as it oozed through his pores. He tried desperately to behave normally, but under pressure he couldn't think what normal looked like. How did he walk normally? What did he do with his hands and arms when he was walking in the house? Should he have his hands in his pockets? He always moved without thinking. Now that he *was* thinking, the process seemed to be quite awkward. If he wasn't careful, he would end up with a really silly walk in an effort to look relaxed. Also, how did he call Chris's name without half-choking in an effort to sound casual? In the event, he can't have looked or sounded as peculiar as he felt, because Chris showed no sign of noticing anything unusual. By mid-morning he was calm enough to join her for coffee. It was then that he raised the issue of his new employment.

"You remember I had possible clients locally. Well, I've seen them a few times, and it's looking promising. Although it wouldn't be at regular times, they might well have enough work to occupy me for the equivalent of a day or so each week. They would expect to pay by the hour, rather than by commission, and they're offering a fantastic rate. I'm at the stage when they've already come up with a six-month retainer, so I'm expecting to see them each week."

"I'm sure that'll be a refreshing change for you, so well done! As it happens, I might be going out more often as well, just between students. All my artwork so far has been copying other people's pictures, but I've been thinking of making a few sketches of my own, and I thought the riverside might be a good place to start, especially with some promising weather ahead."

"That's great! I look forward to seeing the results in the art space .... Oh! By the way, I've made some progress on a dog as well. One of my contacts has a ready-trained Alsatian that might be good for us. He's going to come round in the week to introduce us."

"That's really good. I've been wondering how we could manage that. So, you're saying this dog wouldn't need house training."

"No, it's well beyond that stage," Paul replied, "but you do know that it takes quite a time to hand over a dog. It will need weeks or even months to settle in, but before we can even begin that process, we'll need to have a whole list of preparations in place."

"Yes, I quite expected that, still I'm sure it will be worth the effort, so let's hope it all works out."

"Yes, let's. There is one other thing. The guy bringing the dog is a dour Scotsman. He can sometimes be a bit sharp. Don't be put off, he's okay underneath, and he knows all there is to know about dogs."

Paul could still hardly believe Chris's enthusiasm for a dog, but it suited his purpose just fine. Not only that, if Chris was going out to sketch, there might be some time to look at that safe. Up until now, her expeditions out of the house had been at random times and there had been no telling when she would return. In fact, Paul's own behaviour was just as unpredictable. Neither of them needed to engage in regular, weekly shopping outings, or anything of that nature. All such things were delivered. Now that his office was in the garden, Paul himself seldom even saw parcels delivered to the house. From his point of view, post appeared on the hall table, and the fridge magically stocked itself.

On the morning when Piers arrived, Chris was finishing off with a student and could join Paul for the welcome. Jacquie had arrived earlier. She could be heard working upstairs while Piers sat in the living room with the dog sitting on the floor beside him. The dog and the man were both looking around, and Paul wasn't sure whether it was the man or the animal that was studying them more intently. He made the introductions, "Chris, this is Piers and Siete." He saw the Alsatian prick up her ears and turn her head towards him as he said her name.

Piers had no time for small talk, "You'll be expecting some hair in the house once you have a dog living in, so you'll be wanting to decide where Siete will be permitted to go. Once you have decided, you'll be needing to remember what you decided, so that you can be consistent."

Neither Paul nor Chris had an opportunity to respond to that. Piers was pressing on with his agenda. "Perhaps you would show us around. Where will Siete's place be?"

Piers soon made it apparent that he thought Paul and Chris should sharpen up their ideas, but he did indicate that he would be able to source many of the practical items they would need. He inspected the garden, where Paul took his grunt to be one of modified approval. With his scrutiny coming to an end, Piers announced that Paul would be joining him for a walk, and Chris was welcome. Paul suspected that this was a rare conformity to social norms and that Chris wasn't really welcome at all. The issue didn't arise, because Chris declined the invitation, "I'm sorry, I've a student due in a minute or two, so I'll be tied up here. Perhaps another time."

Piers turned to leave. Paul grabbed his jacket and hurried after him with a parting, "See you later, Chris."

Piers kept up a brisk pace with Siete trotting beside him as they headed for the park. Piers was evidently in as good shape as the Alsatian, and he spoke with no hint of breathlessness, "On a walk like this, Siete is going to find a good number of secondary infections. Wherever someone has acted under the influence of the infection, they'll have been leaving traces on whatever they were using. Although the traces will wear off over a month or so, the infection is very wide spread."

Even as he spoke, Siete came to a stop with ears back and a gentle whine. On the ground at the side of the path were several empty gas capsules. Piers bent to stroke and encourage the animal, "Good dog." They all moved on. "Your work here, Paul, is threefold – one is to be learning a whole new language of dog control, two is to learn to look after and handle the dog, and the third is to learn to sense what she was sensing back there. All three are perfectly doable, but they will all be requiring serious time and effort."

The walk to the park was punctuated by similar incidents, with the Alsatian detecting infection on objects such as a public seat and even a waste bin. Paul began to try sniffing when Siete stopped. That was useless. There was plenty to smell, and the waste bin was particularly pungent. In other words, nothing was out of the ordinary. He couldn't understand how the dog could detect anything useful over those offensive odours.

Once in the open area of the park, Piers produced a ball, and they played with the Alsatian. Paul was introduced to a whole set of commands, some were familiar from home on the farm, but several were not. Piers' use of "Watch me," impressed him no end as he saw Siete instantly give Piers her full attention. Under Piers' guidance, he practised some of the basic commands. He was amazed at the dog's quick responses and with the skilled training that must lie behind what he was seeing. A bond was forming, not between Paul and Siete as yet, but between Piers and Paul. Paul's appreciation of Piers' achievement was evident, and they were becoming united in a common purpose, with Siete at the heart of it.

Despite the more relaxed atmosphere between them, Paul didn't learn anything new about Piers himself, except that the many dogs he had trained for the police and the military had always been German Shepherds. A number were used as drug sniffers, and Piers told him a story about how they had been used, "One of my dogs, Rebel, worked with the police as a drug sniffer. Part of his work was to visit schools for his handler to talk about drugs and to warn the pupils about the dangers."

"The children must have enjoyed having an Alsatian in school."

"Aye, most did, but that wasn't a universal reaction."

"Why ever not?"

Piers began to explain, "After he'd been speaking about the effects and hazards of drugs, Rebel's handler would talk about the illegal drugs trade and the dog's work as a drug sniffer. He would emphasise the Alsatian's effectiveness at detecting drugs and then, after his talk, the policeman would stand by the exit with Rebel at his side. The children would file past them as they went off to their classes."

"Were some of them nervous about passing close to a large dog?"

"It wasn't that. There were those who had other reasons for not being happy about the dog. When all the children had left, the policeman would go back into the school hall, where he would pick up all the drugs that had been dropped by the pupils who hadn't dared to carry them past the dog."

Paul was highly amused at that scenario, but that didn't prevent him from being downcast about the prospects of ever sensing the infection himself. His spirits were raised by playing with the lively dog, and he was filled with enthusiasm at the prospect of learning to work with Siete. This was something he could do and was really looking forward to.

On the way home, Paul thought to make a slight change in his arrangements with Piers, "I'm very pleased to have your help each morning, Piers. To keep that going, perhaps we could adjust what we tell Chris. I've only told her that you're a dog expert. During the handover period, it will be perfectly understandable if you turn up every day to take the dog for a walk, but if that carries on for too long without explanation, Chris will eventually wonder what's going on. I thought I might tell her that you're semi-retired, and I've made an arrangement with you to help with Siete's exercise, if that's okay.

Piers understood and agreed at once. As they reached home, he and Siete carried on with a friendly, "Fare thee well, see you in the morning."

Chapter 9 – The bug

As Paul reached the front door, it opened for him, and Chris was standing there, with her finger on her lips. She beckoned him to follow her through to the garden, where she spoke in a low voice, "Could you do another bug sweep please? I know you trust Piers, but I realised when you had gone out with him that I hadn't watched his every move. I know it sounds ridiculous, but I'd be much happier if you could just check the living room and kitchen."

Paul was taken totally by surprise, "Surely you can't imagine that Piers has bugged us?"

"I'm sorry. I know it's not rational, and it's most unlikely. It's just that now the thought has entered my mind it's become lodged there. If you could just double check, then we can forget all about it."

"Okay, if it's going to make you happy, I'll check. Why don't you do it with me?"

"Yes, I'd like that. Can your detector be set on silent? I know we don't expect to find anything. If by any chance we do, it might be best if nobody knew we'd been looking."

Paul replied with some hesitation, "Yes, I can do that."

He retrieved his bug detector from the office, and they crept into the living room, where Paul began his scan in the area beside Chris's computer. To his alarm, his detector lit up almost at once. They rapidly traced the source of the transmission. There was something under the desk! Paul was horrified. Had he truly been duped by Malcolm and Piers? There was no denying the facts; the detector had found something, and as he searched under the desk, behind a wooden ridge, there it was - a disc stuck to the metal bracket.

Paul was about to pull it off, when Chris tapped his shoulder, shook her finger vigorously and mouthed, "No." She beckoned him back to the garden.

"If you remove it, someone's going to know we've found it, so let's think about what to do. First, can we check to see if there are any more?" Back in the house, Paul was now taking the hunt very seriously, but the further search drew a blank. Chris spoke in a normal voice, "I know you've been for a walk today. I haven't and it would be nice to go out together."

As they prepared to leave, Paul was frantically trying to think of alternative explanations for the bug. None of the other possibilities seemed likely, but equally he couldn't imagine why Michael & Co. would bug them. Once they were away from the house, Paul was still shaking with shock, as he began to defend Piers, "I can't believe that Piers would try to bug us." He was about to add that Piers already knew more than enough about him, without any need for bugs, when he remembered, just in time, that Chris didn't know about any of that. He'd have to be much more careful about what he said, so he continued instead with, "He's just a guy who's very good with dogs. There's no reason why he should want to bug us. I mean, what is there to find out?"

Chris seemed much calmer than Paul. "That's all very well, but the fact remains that, after his visit, we have found ourselves bugged. The question is, what are we going to do about it?"

The obvious answer was to go to the police. Paul was pretty sure that bugging people was illegal, but he certainly didn't want to suggest involving the Law. He was surprised that Chris didn't suggest it either. Paul tried a different tack, "Why don't I just remove it and confront Piers with it?" By which he actually meant, show it to Malcolm and ask for an explanation.

Unfortunately, Chris didn't jump at that option either. "Can you find out more about what the bug might be capable of before we do anything hasty? In the meantime, we should be careful about what we say indoors."

Paul heartily agreed with that at least. He'd have to be very careful about what he said indoors, for more reasons than Chris imagined. His big worry was nothing to do with the bug. He had already nearly given the game away about Piers, and his main concern was that he might accidently mention something else that Chris wasn't supposed to know about. He simply nodded as he said, "Okay, we'll play it that way for the moment. I'll take another look at the bug and see what I can find from Google. For the time being, we could have all serious conferences in the garden."

Once they were home, Paul took another look at the bug. He used his phone to take a photo, before beginning his search. It took him only a few seconds to find out what he had been looking at. He confirmed the obvious, that it was an audio bug, and he found its specifications. They indicated that it would pick up voices within 10 metres or so, it had a transmitter range of about half a kilometre, and its battery had a life of 4 or 5 days. He also found that there were laws about its use. The latter hadn't occurred to him, even though it was obvious, once he thought about it.

Back in the garden, he shared the information. Chris came up with an idea, "If that's the case, let's leave it where it is. We'll be careful what we say during the next week, and after that time the battery will be dead. No-one will know that we found it, and whoever left it will want it back. They won't dare leave it for too long, because that would increase the risk that we might discover it. We'll be on our guard, so if Piers, or whoever, tries to retrieve it, we stand a good chance of catching them at it. If we take it away now, they'll find it missing and then they'll know that we've found it."

There is another thing, Paul offered, "If the range is only a few hundred metres, there must be someone, or something, within that distance to pick up the signal. Isn't that a thought? We should keep our eyes open for anything unusual in the neighbourhood."

"There's something else." Chris added. "If somebody is keen enough to bug us, we should make sure we're not being followed when we go out."

"Yes," Paul agreed, "but we'd better not make it too obvious that we're checking." In fact, he was beginning to have an entirely different idea about how to proceed, but that was another secret plan he couldn't share with Chris.

In the few days that followed, there was a whole host of deliveries. They were all the dog-related equipment suggested and supplied by Piers. Paul and Chris did sharpen up their ideas. They worked out most of the practical requirements suggested both by Piers and by the leaflet from Malcolm. There was no problem in sharing the pamphlet itself with Chris. She didn't need to know where it had come from, and dog arrangements were something they could work at together. That would be another thing they would have in common, and those were in short supply.

Strangely, the bug was also something of a uniting factor. Although Paul still couldn't believe that Piers was responsible, he was happy to play along with the possibility, and its existence created a shared secret, which was good for bonding.

Later in the week, Chris did go off to the riverside to sketch. Paul was left with free access to the safe. He'd only thought of two codes to try: Chris's birthday and the date of their wedding. Neither of those worked. He would only have one more try before he was locked out. How long would the lockout last? It was highly unlikely that Chris would come home and go straight to the safe, but it would be a disaster if she did, only to find that the safe was frozen. This opportunity was Paul's best chance to discover how long the lockout lasted, so he should try a third code and hope that the freeze didn't last for hours. His own birthday was a slim possibility. He tried it. As expected, the response was a lockout. Paul began to time it as he sat and racked his brains for any other possible numbers. Drama had been a big feature of their lives, so was there any four-figure number associated with that?

The lockout ended after 10 minutes – that timing was good to know. As it ended, he had a cunning thought. Surely, it was too outlandish, but he had to give it a try. Was there any four-figure number that Chris might have remembered from a play? At first, nothing seemed obvious, and Paul couldn't afford to spend too much time working on the safe.

After several minutes, only one thought had come to mind, and that idea was definitely stretching the bounds of credulity. Both he and Chris had been involved in 'The Hound of the Baskervilles," she as Kathy Stapleton and he on the lighting. There was a possible four-figure number in that story. Sherlock Holmes' address in Baker Street was 221B and that looked very like 2218. It was a crazy prospect that made 'clutching at straws' look positively realistic. All of which made no difference, he had thought of it, the idea was fixed in his mind and he had to try it; there was nothing to lose. He entered the numbers with increasing and totally unwarranted optimism. The safe remained obstinately closed. Guessing numbers was a forlorn hope. Chris might well have come up with a completely random number. If so, he would never guess it; he gave up in despondency.

Chapter 10 – The running man

When Piers arrived with Siete, Paul began to put his new plan into operation. As they were walking and talking, Paul asked, "About the secondary infections that Siete is detecting, what proportion of bad things are caused by the infection?"

"That's a good question." Piers paused in thought before continuing, "I'd say that most crimes are linked to the infection, but not so many of what you might be thinking of as lower level wrong doing. The reality is that our lives are full of arguments and disagreements, and that kind of poor behaviour is too common to get any handle on quantities and proportions. Suffice it to say that at least some of those are linked to the infection."

That was all just as Paul suspected and was exactly the answer he had been hoping for. His plan could work. At the end of their exercise and training that morning, Paul tried the next step, "I was wondering whether Siete might stay with me for the afternoon. She could become more familiar with our house, and I might take her for a walk myself."

Piers responded with some enthusiasm, "As it happens that would be most convenient. I have an appointment for the next few hours, when it would be better not to have Siete with me. As you say, it would be a great idea for her to become comfortable with you, so shall I be picking her up from you at about five?"

"That would be wonderful, Piers, thanks."

So it was that Paul and Chris had Siete to themselves for a while. This all seemed to be a natural progression so far as Chris was concerned. She had no idea that Paul had a further agenda. He had no plans to do much work that afternoon, and they both showed Siete her bed in the kitchen, before the three of them played in the garden. After a while, Chris announced that she had a student appointment to deal with. That had been entirely what Paul had expected. He said that he would take Siete for a short walk. Things were all working out very well.

Once out of the house, Paul didn't head for any of the local parks. The bug in their house had a range of a few hundred metres, and Piers had reckoned that most crime was linked to the infection. That meant that somewhere within half a kilometre there was probably a secondary infection, linked to the criminal activity of listening in to the illegal bug. There might only be a receiver unit, or there could be a person as well. Either way, Paul reckoned that Siete could probably detect the secondary infection on the equipment being used.

Paul set off round the local streets, with Siete at his heels. As usual, the dog detected a series of objects that had been connected with petty crime, or general dishonesty. It was of much more interest that she stopped with ears back and a low whine when they encountered a small, plastic, workman's shelter, which had been set up in front of a green telephone junction box set into the side of the pavement. As Siete was sniffing at the plastic, there was a sudden movement inside the shelter. A short, swarthy man in a grey hoody shot out from the shelter and sprinted down the street. He jumped into a parked, black Mercedes, and it accelerated away with a screech of protesting rubber.

When he'd recovered from his initial surprise and shock, Paul remembered to encourage Siete with approving words, patting, and stroking. Then he looked inside the plastic shelter. There he found a small stool, a sandwich box, and a radio with headphones. What should he do? Could he take the radio away? Yes, he thought he could. This was the scene of criminal activity, so nobody was going to report the loss of the radio. But what would Chris think if he turned up with the radio back at home? After a moment's thought, he realised that there was no cause for concern on that front. He didn't need to mention the infection. He could just say that Siete had sniffed around the plastic shelter, and a man had run off leaving the radio. Siete was the only witness, and she wasn't going to contradict him. Following on from that thought, it seemed best to him if he didn't mention the episode to Piers for the time being.

As Paul reached in to pick up the radio, he experienced a very slight sensation. It wasn't quite a smell, though that was the nearest thing to describe it. Nor was it the musty smell of a mausoleum. It was more like the scent of fallen apples, those that had been lying in the grass for quite a while and had begun to ferment. Could he possibly be beginning to detect the infection?

As it happened, Chris didn't seem particularly interested in the details of how the radio was found, though she did want to know all about the man who had run off. Unfortunately, there was little to be told about him: he was short, at about 170 cm, with a slight build, darkish skin, and dark, medium length hair. He wore a grey hoody, and judging by his turn of speed, he must be fairly young. That was it.

The radio was evidently tuned into the bug in their living room, because there was the piercing squawk of feedback when the two were brought close together. There was the question of whether they should now remove the bug. Once in the garden, Paul said, "There's no point in us being out here. We have the bug receiver, so we know there's no-one to listen in. We might as well go back indoors."

The three of them sat in the living room, Siete being beside Paul's chair. At first, she looked at Paul with expectation, then took to lying at his feet. Paul had to admit to himself that he very much liked the furry warmth of the animal lying quietly there. He began to put his ideas into words, "We've just got to think this through. If Piers was the one who bugged us, which I still doubt, then his game is over. He could still deny it was him. After all, we only have the equipment. There's no evidence to show who was using it, and anyway, it makes no practical difference who put it there. It will now be obvious to our eavesdroppers that we know it's there, so anybody trying to remove it would be taking an unnecessary risk."

Chris was clearly ahead of him and took up the line of thought, "Yes, you're right, it makes no difference who's responsible. The bottom line is that now they know we know; it doesn't matter what we do with the bug."

Paul did have a thought about that; another secret plan that he didn't wish to share. He simply said, "I'll take the bug then and see if I can find anything more about it."

Chris seemed reluctant, but in the end nodded agreement with, "All right."

Chapter 11 – The Hendersons

Chris had been out for a swim at the Leisure Centre. She returned with news, "Zara has moved house to a few doors up the road from us."

Zara had occasionally been mentioned as someone Chris had met in the café at the Leisure Centre. Paul knew no more than that. "Does she have a family?" he asked.

"Yes, there's her husband, Crispin, and a teenaged daughter, Jessica."

"That must have been a sudden move. You haven't mentioned it before."

"There was a problem with their previous landlord. They don't believe in buying houses, so they simply moved, and they've invited us for an evening meal in their new home. I thought it would be really nice for you to meet them and to have some friends close by. Don't you think so?"

"Yes, I suppose so. When would this be?"

"The day after tomorrow. That is okay, isn't it?"

"Well, yes, I don't have anything else on. How much do you know about them?"

"Zara's a personal trainer. I've met her, because she does some of her work at the Leisure Centre, though most of her work is online. Crispin's an opera singer in the chorus at The Coliseum."

Paul's face lit up with enthusiasm. "That sounds interesting. Let's do it! We'd better find something as a house-warming gift."

"I'll pop down the supermarket and sort it out."

"Thanks! Incidentally, do you know their surname?"

"Yes, it's Henderson."

Although Paul was keen to meet these people, by now he regarded everyone with a certain level of suspicion and especially new friends who put in a sudden appearance nearby. He went to his office and made an online search. To his amazement and joy, both Hendersons were found quite easily. Wow! Some people in his life who had a normal existence! Sure enough, there was Crispin Henderson in the chorus of the English National Opera, and there was Zara Henderson advertising as a personal trainer. Could it be that he had come across ordinary people?

Chris suggested that it would be appropriate to 'make an effort,' when it came to dressing for their evening with Zara and Crispin. Paul took that to mean 'smart casual.' He amused himself with a dark polo-neck top and dark trousers; a look-alike for his favourite James Bond in 'Live and Let Die.' It suited his new covert existence, or so he thought. Chris, on the other hand, really had made an effort. She appeared in a shimmering, mid-blue, wrap around dress, tied at the waist, and off one shoulder. With her slim form and dark hair, she would have graced the cover of any glamour magazine.

"You look great, Chris! Do I need to find a black-tie outfit?"

"No, you'll do. Let's go."

Paul picked up the wine Chris had bought as a gift. It was a warm evening, so they set off as they were, arm in arm.

Zara and Crispin couldn't have been more friendly and welcoming. Chris had judged the dress code well. Zara was in a silky red dress, which floated around her from thin shoulder straps, while Crispin had chosen a white formal shirt, open at the neck, to go with his black trousers. Paul guessed that this perfect couple were a year or two older than him. Crispin didn't match his expectations of an opera singer. Paul had somehow assumed that they all had the build of Pavarotti, but the reality was that Crispin would have made a good body double for Roger Moore. He could have pulled off the James Bond look much more successfully than Paul.

There was a brief tour of the house, which proved to be identical to Chris and Paul's house. The feeling of déjà vu was greater still when they found that Zara had an upstairs gym in the same room as Chris's. She explained that, apart from personal use, it was set up for her online training sessions. Zara herself was a great advertisement for the effectiveness of her personal training. She was at least as fit as Chris. The pair of them would have passed as sisters and made a formidable duo.

Paul thought it was peculiar to find that everything in the house was perfectly ordered, with no sign of packing cases, or of a recent move. On the contrary, it was like a show house. "You've organised everything very quickly after your move," he exclaimed, "How did you manage that, Crispin?"

"It wasn't only us, Paul, we had a whole army of family and friends to help us. Two days max. and we were all done."

Army of helpers or not, Paul couldn't imagine how a house move could be done and dusted in two days. "I'm most impressed. That's tremendously good going."

Chris went off to the kitchen with Zara, while Crispin showed Paul to the dining table, where Paul began a new conversation, "Chris tells me you're a singer."

"Yes, I'm with the ENO in the chorus."

"I imagine that means tours and endless rehearsals."

"Not quite endless, although there is a good deal of rehearsal time. It's not just singing either. Most of the shows are stage performances, so there are costumes and makeup and choreography."

"I see. You're obviously not working this evening."

"No, all the shows and rehearsals work on schedules. Some weeks I'm hardly ever at home in the evenings, then equally there are some when I'm often here. Are you interested in opera yourself?"

"I've not much experience of that. Chris and I met through amateur dramatics, and we're still interested in the theatre, but it's mostly plays and musicals that we've seen."

"Well, we have a comic opera on in the next few weeks. That would make a good introduction if you wanted to dabble with a new art form. If you do fancy it, let me know, I might be able to help you to find tickets."

While they were still speaking, Zara and Chris were bringing food to the table and lighting candles. The scene was beautifully set, and Paul admired the lighting effect of the dining table in a pool of candle light, which died away to the subtle dim lights around the edge of the room. Then there was the banquet before him. "Zara, this looks wonderful," he said. She smiled at his appreciation. Her golden hair draped itself over her shoulder and shone in the candlelight as she began to serve.

Once they were eating, Paul commented on what he had been told, "Crispin has been saying that his work schedule often keeps him busy in the evenings, Zara."

"It does, and when he's on tour he can be away for days on end. It all balances out in the long run, because there are times when he's home much more. Fortunately, I mostly work from home, so we can always have someone here for our daughter."

Paul was thinking about how normal this family seemed to be. Then he thought about how normal Chris and he would seem to be as well. Appearances could certainly be deceptive. That thought kept him on the lookout for anything unusual during the rest of the evening.

Chris took up the running. "Is your daughter away, Zara."

"Only for the evening. Jessica's at a sleepover with some friends. She's with a family we know well, so we don't have any worries about her, and it gives us the opportunity for an evening like this. Now, what about you, Paul? What keeps you busy?"

"I mostly work from home as you do, though rather less actively. I'm an insurance broker. Long ago now, I used to work for a large firm in the City then, after a few years of that, I branched out on my own. That was a little scary at first, but in the end, it's worked well for me."

Zara continued, "I've seen you taking your German Shepherd for a walk. That's a beautiful dog. So wonderfully trained too. Where did you find such a fine specimen?"

Paul's senses jumped to full alert; this was dangerous territory. "Yes, we were very lucky. One of my friends has been a professional dog trainer and he sourced her for us." If Zara had seen Siete, she might have seen Piers as well, so he added, "In fact he's semi-retired, but I persuaded him to help me maintain the dog's training. You might have seen him with us."

"Yes, I have. I wondered who he was."

Paul wanted to change the subject. He turned to Crispin.

"How did you two meet?"

"It was back in my student days. I was studying opera and singing in London, and we met in the bar of a theatre one evening, during the interval. I was on my own, and Zara was on a girls' night out. We were briefly together ordering drinks at the bar. You've seen Zara. Who wouldn't want to know more? I took my chance and it paid off. Here we are, 17 years later."

The evening continued happily enough, mainly with Crispin telling humorous stories about the eccentricities of famous conductors, together with a few bitter ones about the perceived failings of the Arts Council. Zara added in tales of minor mishap during online training, but what was remarkable to Paul was that they asked no questions about Chris's work.

Chapter 12 – Who is Malcolm?

Paul was attempting to fully satisfy himself that Michael & Co. was not the source of his domestic bugging. A strong argument in its favour was that Malcolm had discovered so much, with such apparent ease that, surely, he wouldn't have needed to resort to bugging. Bugs were so crude compared with Paul's experience of the company. On the other hand, there was the odd comment that Michael & Co. had, so far, found out little about Chris's work. Might they have finally been reduced to a listening device? He found it hard to believe they would be that desperate, and bugging people really didn't fit in with what he had seen of their style.

Paul decided that he would tell Malcolm about the bug and gauge his reaction. He would use the contact information he had been given to set up a meeting, but before that, he'd have another crack at trying to find out more about Malcolm. He already knew that Michael & Co. was non-existent as far as the internet was concerned. Malcolm himself might be a different prospect. Paul had already tried Googling the name Malcolm McDonald, only to confirm that there was a vast number of hits for people of that name, ranging through footballers and professors, to authors, and even one poor man, who'd had a grafting operation that wouldn't bear talking about in any polite society. He needed to narrow the field somehow – assuming that Malcolm was working under his real name, and even that was a big assumption.

How could he narrow the field? Limiting himself to local addresses didn't help. Although there were plenty of hits in the area, none of the corresponding photos were a match for Malcolm, and many of the hits were without photos, in any case. He sat drumming his fingers on the desk. There had to be something. He tried to construct a mental image of Malcolm, and he remembered his tie. Yes, that was it! Malcolm's tie could be a good clue. Paul had originally thought it might have a military connection, so it was worth searching for military ties. Did any of them match what he thought he remembered? To the best of his recall, it was a relatively simple design, with diagonal stripes of dark blue and red. He thought there was also a light-coloured third stripe in the pattern. As he looked through military ties, he soon struck gold. It had to be an RAF tie.

He tried searching for 'Royal Air Force,' together with 'Malcolm McDonald.' At first, this didn't look any more promising than his previous searches. If truth be told, he was really struggling, and disappointment was gathering fast - until there appeared a single reference in the 'Supplement to the London Gazette.' It was a report of a Squadron Leader Malcolm McDonald who had been awarded the DFC, for gallantry in the Gulf War. There was no supporting picture to be found, and even scrolling through photos of award ceremonies drew a blank, so it was hard to know whether he had actually found his man. The main evidence in favour was the absence of evidence. That conformed with the obscurity he had encountered over everything else to do with Michael & Co. So, when he could find no other reference to this Squadron Leader Malcolm McDonald, it made him think he might well have found his quarry, or as much of his quarry as it was possible to find.

True or not, the RAF officer image was the one that stayed with him as he picked up his briefcase and went to visit 77, High Street. As promised, Malcolm was waiting in his office at the top of the stairs. He was again wearing a dark jacket. Unfortunately, Paul couldn't confirm the pattern of an RAF tie; on this occasion, Malcolm wore a plain, navy blue one. After brief greetings, they sat and Malcolm began, "I gather you have a problem, so let's have the situation report, what's happened?" Paul felt his lips twitch in a supressed smile of elation. After the disappointment of the tie, that reference to a 'situation report' was another indicator of military experience. When it was combined with Malcolm's general way of doing things and some of his other language, Paul was convinced that he had his man.

Paul explained about finding the bug at home after Piers' visit. Malcolm's forehead creased in lines of worry, "That's most concerning. Obviously, the bug was nothing to do with Piers, and I can't think of any individual, or group, who would want to study you covertly."

"I had wondered whether it could be anything to do with beginning to work for Michael & Co. You clearly have very powerful friends, so it had occurred to me that you might have equally powerful enemies, might they be interested in me?"

Malcolm's face showed understanding. All the same, he pointed out a flaw in the thinking, "That's a natural conclusion, but just think some more. As you must have realised, we've been able to find out all about you in pretty short order. Even if I could think of any other group that would be interested in you, which I can't, if they had similar powers to ours, they wouldn't need to resort to anything so primitive as a bug under the desk."

Paul was inclined to agree, but Malcolm hadn't finished, "Then, let's think further about where the bug was placed. There was only one, and it wasn't in your office, it was in the room where Christine works. That's more than a little worrying. Why does Christine merit a bug? I think we mentioned previously that we were having a few problems in researching some aspects of her work. That on its own didn't bother us particularly in connection with your initial work for us, and we didn't try very hard to look further. We don't regard you as a security risk to us, simply because you know nothing that anyone would believe, and in addition to that, our employment of you is entirely deniable."

"Am I in some danger?"

"We don't think so. Perhaps I've given the impression that we know nothing about Christine. That's not the case. We have established that she doesn't appear on any list of disreputable characters, and her record is perfectly clean in every respect. We know all about her history and her aunt. The only short-coming is that we can't confirm exactly what she does. On its own that wouldn't be a great concern. However, in the light of the bug, I'd be relieved to have the dog living with you asap."

Paul smiled, “I must admit that I really like the dog, but that brings me to another thing. It occurred to me that the bug itself was vulnerable to the possibility of further investigation. Chris and I took care not to let it be known that we’d found it, and I did look up its specifications. It turned out that there had to be a receiving unit within a few hundred metres of our house. Piers let me have Siete for an afternoon, so we went for a walk in the neighbourhood to look for the receiver. I thought it would have a secondary infection and that Siete might locate it.”

Malcolm frowned, “I don’t know whether to commend or condemn. For someone who’s worried about being in danger that was rather cavalier, even if it was a very good plan.”

“I wasn’t very worried. Remember I had a large Alsatian with me for protection.”

“That’s true, Paul, and no doubt Siete would have been formidable in the face of hostility, but you need to know that, although our dogs have a natural instinct to defend, they’re not trained to attack. Anyway, putting all that aside, I take it that you found something.”

“Yes, there was a temporary shelter for workmen, which attracted Siete’s attention. We stopped beside it, and Siete was sniffing at it when a man hurtled out and ran full pelt to a waiting Mercedes. The last I saw of him was smoke rising from where he had spun the tyres in making his escape.”

“Can you describe him?”

“There’s not much to say, because I didn’t see his face. He was slim and not very tall. Judging by his speed, he must have been quite young. His hair was dark and his skin was well-weathered. He either worked out of doors, or had an ethnic origin with skin that is darker than either of ours. He was wearing a grey hoody.”

Malcolm was encouraging, “That’s not bad for the brief incident you described. Even though the description wouldn’t give us a photofit, it’s still a good deal better than nothing, so well done!”

"Actually, I think I can do rather better still. Paul reached into his briefcase and produced a plastic bag containing both the bug and the receiving unit. I'm sorry, I didn't think about fingerprints until after I was home, so you'll find my prints on them. Once I did think of it, I was more careful, so I hope my own prints won't totally obscure anything else."

Malcolm was nearly whooping with delight, "That's a jolly good show! I'll see what our technical boys can find from that. As you say, there might be fingerprints. Before you go, would you mind terribly, if I ask you to leave your fingerprints with Annette, across the landing."

At reception, Annette produced a digital fingerprint scanner from under the counter, as though every good receptionist would naturally have one. The scanning was soon done, and Paul was on his way home, refining his cover story for Chris as he went.

Chapter 13 – Fermenting apples

At home, he told Chris that he had left the bug and receiver with a contact who was 'into electronics,' to see what he could make of them. That was another distortion of the truth; an additional lie for him to keep track of. This time, he'd produced a purely fictional contact to cover for what he was really doing. He had been vague and hadn't given him or her a name. But it could become very difficult if Chris took a serious interest and began to enquire further. He didn't think he had made use of anyone else who didn't actually exist, though now he was beginning to doubt himself, and he hoped circumstances wouldn't press him to invent any more characters. There was already an oppressive burden of remembering all the boundaries between the palatable half-truths, that could be discussed, and the whole truths that shouldn't be mentioned.

Mercifully, Piers was a real person, and Paul was pleased to have his daily visits. A large part of the pleasure was that he could be open about some of his secrets. Although, Piers did come to their house, and Paul dreaded that one of them might fail to switch from truth to half-truth when they were within Chris's hearing. If he had to start remembering names and details for a whole set of fictional clients, he feared that would be more challenge and subterfuge than he could cope with.

When Piers arrived the next morning, he announced that he was content with all the arrangements in place, and it would be fine for Siete to stay with them. He would continue to visit daily for expeditions with Paul and the dog. Chris expressed delight, and Paul breathed a quiet sigh of relief. When the unknown man had rushed from the plastic shelter, Paul's system had pumped full of adrenaline, which had anaesthetised his fear. As time had passed, he had become more aware of the danger he had encountered. What if the man had emerged with a weapon to attack him? Or suppose there had been two men. Such thoughts gave him the shakes, and he would more than welcome the additional security brought by Siete's presence.

During the walks with Piers, Paul was now controlling Siete, and on this occasion, they spent time reinforcing the dog's responses to Paul's commands. It was like a whole new language for Paul, and it was galling to see that the Alsatian understood and responded rapidly to some of the commands that Paul himself was struggling to remember. His childhood Labradors had been nothing like this, though now he realised that they could have been if more effort had been made to train them when they were young.

Piers was keen to impress upon Paul the way in which doggy treats should be used. They were fine as part of the reward and reinforcement system for trained responses, but other forms of encouragement were just as valuable. The real point was that treats were to be part of Siete's daily diet, not additions to it. Her food was to be measured carefully, and some of it could then be kept aside for treats. This wasn't the first time that the point had been made, so Piers was clearly determined that it should be fully taken to heart. Alsatians were not supposed to put on unnecessary weight.

As ever, their walk was punctuated by stops as Siete detected the infection, but there was a subtle change coming over Paul. On one or two occasions, he noticed a faint, rather unusual, smell. He called it a smell for want of a better term. There had been a slight whiff of something similar in the plastic shelter where he had found the bug receiver. It was similar to the scent of rotting apples. He mentioned it to Piers, "I'm beginning to think that sometimes, when Siete detects the infection, I might be faintly sensing it too. If I am, it's not the same as the sense you have of it."

"What kind of sense might it be then?"

"I think of it as a smell, as you do, and as I recall, you had described it as the mustiness of graves and mausoleums."

"Aye, that's right. It has to be strong before I'll be smelling it, and when I do it's like the musty smell of a tomb."

"Well, that's not what I'm smelling. If I'm sensing the same thing, it's really faint, but it smells to me like rotting, fermenting apples."

"That's very promising, and if you are smelling it differently, that would be a fine thing for us to know. We'll see how that develops. I'll not be passing that on until we're more convinced that it's the real thing. As it happens, I do vaguely recall that there has been mention of different Spotters having different responses. Confirmation of that would be useful for our understanding."

During the following days, Paul found his sensitivity rapidly increasing, and his sense of decaying apples was definitely the real thing. Before long, he was approaching Siete's level of ability. That was both encouraging and worrying. The worry was that if Paul himself had become a very good Spotter, then Malcolm might think that Siete was unnecessary and was outliving her usefulness by staying with him. In his daily meetings with Piers, he admitted that his ability was improving. He held back on declaring the true extent of his progress, and he'd continue to hold off on that until his next meeting with Malcolm. In the meantime, Paul urgently needed to catch up with contacting his normal business clients. His covert work was in danger of damaging his business, so he had better snap to it. While most people only had to balance the two spinning plates of business work and domestic life, he was trying to juggle secret work in addition to his business commitments and domestic life. That was proving to be a major challenge.

It was during those few days that another disaster struck. He had recently returned from an evening stroll with Siete and was feeling rather pleased with himself. His ability to detect the rotting apple smell had improved in leaps and bounds; to such an extent that he was identifying secondary infections that even the dog had missed. Chris was upstairs in their gym, and Siete had trotted through to her place in the kitchen. When the Alsatian had left him in the living room, Paul encountered the faint smell of fermentation. Where was that coming from? He followed the smell, with his nose in the air like a character in a gravy advertisement, to discover its origin. He must be mistaken! The blood drained from his face and his legs turned to jelly. The source was Chris's computer!

Chapter 14 – Home-help mysteries

Later in the day, Paul was out with Siete. He had already set up a meeting with Malcolm in the hope of finding some answers to the problem of Chris's computer infection. The gears of his brain had been whirring and grinding themselves to bare axles over that. He was trying not to think about it and to concentrate on the problem of the wall safe instead. In that regard, he had run out of obvious code numbers to try, so he was thinking it through again. It was always possible that Chris had chosen a random number, in which case he stood virtually no chance of finding it within any sensible time frame, but he thought it more likely that she would choose a code that was memorable. She was security conscious, so it would be memorable to her, without being obvious to anyone else. If he had been choosing, he would have chosen something mathematical like the product of the first five prime numbers. Once he had thought of that, he lost all focus on his surroundings while he tried to work out the answer in his head. Yes, that was correct, 2310. Correct it may be, but it was certainly useless, because Chris didn't have that kind of mind. Then, inspiration struck. There was a number that would match the requirements; memorable to her and a random number to anyone else. He didn't know what the number was, so that was very much in its favour. He was also confident that he could find it, and that fired his enthusiasm. What had been the birthday of Chris's aunt?

Once he was back in his office, he started to work on it. Firstly, he had to remember her name. She had been Chris's mother's sister. In the absence of any known father, Chris had been brought up with her mother's maiden name, which would surely be the one used by her unmarried aunt. Since she'd been a diplomat, it shouldn't be hard to find out about Dorothea Fairbrother. There had to be some record of her diplomatic service. He doubted that even Michael & Co. could expunge that kind of history, and they'd have no reason to anyway. Sure enough 'Dorothea Fairbrother diplomat' brought up just one encouraging response. It was easy to find a record of her career. Unfortunately, her birthday wasn't part of the information provided. He guessed that there were limits to the information that diplomats were ready to make public. He steepled his fingers in thought. Ah ha! Public information might be limited while diplomats are alive, but less so once they have died. Dorothea was dead. Although she hadn't been a top diplomat, she was sufficiently senior that there was likely to be an obituary, and obituaries do give a date of birth together with the date of death. A few clicks later and there it was - 30th December 1931. He was absurdly optimistic and could hardly wait to try 3012 as an entry code. Wow! What were the chances of that - her birthday was an anagram of the product of the prime numbers he had calculated! Anyway, all he needed now was for Chris to go out for a while.

Perhaps it was a good thing that Chris didn't conveniently leave the house. Paul still did have normal clients, who did need to have work done for them. He pushed the wall safe out of his mind and concentrated on insurance matters. As he worked, he could see Siete out of the corner of his eye. She was lying in the garden and was only disturbed when the trundling of a lawn mower announced that the Lawn Lovers van had arrived. He wondered which of the disparate band of mowers would appear. It was someone he had never seen before – a young woman with flowing red hair, blue dungarees, and big black boots. As she began to cut the lawn, he started to think about his domestic employees. In the light of events, were any of them a security risk?

Paul was confident about the legitimacy of Lawn Lovers. He'd seen their van outside several local properties, and there was no difficulty in finding their contact details. He knew their main address and had frequently observed the van in their drive. However, the sight of a new employee was giving him second thoughts. The secretive group that had been gaining access to his home had an impressive combination of determination, skill, and resources. Perhaps they could plant an employee in Lawn Lovers, just to help with surveillance, bugging, and the like. He would have to give that more thought.

The only other employee was Jacquie. Chris was clearly confident in her integrity, but was she really above suspicion? It didn't help that he wasn't totally convinced about Chris herself. If she wasn't in the clear, then neither was Jacquie. That reminded him of the peculiar circumstances surrounding their engagement of Jacquie all those years ago. Her predecessor, Chloe, had been perfectly likeable and trustworthy as far as he knew then, or now for that matter. Despite her satisfactory work and the fact that Chloe had been enthusiastic to continue working for them, she had been replaced by Jacquie. He knew how they had come to employ Chloe. That was through an agency. Where had Jacquie come from? It was Chris who had produced Jacquie, and it was Chris who had been determined to sack Chloe so as to employ Jacquie instead. He did vaguely remember some mention of an agency being involved, but couldn't recall its name. Thinking back, he didn't think he had ever been told its name – though he had never asked.

His regular work suddenly seemed less important as he brought up his bank records to see how they paid Jacquie. There it was. The bank account details were for an agency called 'Home Support Ltd.' He searched the web to find out where they were based. The result was yet another source of concern. He could find no record in their area of any agency under that name that provided helpers like Jacquie.

This new and disturbing information, or rather lack of information, about Jacquie left Paul in such a state of agitation that he could no longer concentrate on work. He sat in the garden idly playing ball with Siete. Beside him in the bushes his attention was caught by the angry sound of a wasp buzzing, and he turned to see what was happening. The creature had flown into a spider's web, and the spider was crossing the web to its possible prey. He wondered what would happen – the angry wasp was twice the size of the spider. The arachnid was cautious, but in a few minutes the wasp was reduced to helplessness in a mass of fine threads. It was carried away, presumably to make a hearty meal. Paul dismally reflected that this was just how his own life was going. He was becoming ever more tightly entangled in a web of lies and deceit. He fervently hoped for a better outcome than that of the wasp.

Paul needed to clear his head. He collected Siete's leash and left the house by the garden gate. Walking with the dog was always a calming experience, even with the stops for the infection, which he now noticed as much as the dog did. His thoughts remained in a great state of confusion as they were returning home. Then, in the distance, he saw Jacquie leaving the house. She was turning in the direction away from him. It was barely a conscious decision on his part, but he hung back and followed her, keeping as much space as possible between them. The streets weren't busy, so with her green jacket and tightly pinned hair, she was an easy target to observe. There was no need to be close, so he didn't expect her to notice him.

After a short while, Jacquie walked into one of the local public gardens. She crossed the lawn and disappeared into a drive-through McDonald's on the far side. Paul found a convenient seat and watched the entrance through the sparse covering of bushes and the low hanging branches of a tree. There was a steady stream of customers entering and leaving the premises, but Jacquie would be easy to spot among them. As time passed, his puzzlement grew, and an hour later Jacquie hadn't emerged. He could contain himself no longer. He walked to the McDonald's entrance, tied Siete to a post with an instruction to wait, and looked inside. Jacquie was nowhere to be seen.

He went outside, hopelessly looking around for signs of Jacquie. She was such a distinctive figure. How could he have possibly missed her leaving the building?

Chapter 15 – What does Chris do?

Chris and Paul had invited the Hendersons to visit them for an evening meal, and they had successfully overcome the challenge of finding an evening when Crispin was free. They now faced a greater obstacle – preparing an evening meal. Neither of them was very experienced at serious cooking. In the normal course of events, all their meals were ready prepared or semi-prepared. Their hope of matching the spread the Hendersons had produced was zero, but they must at least make a creditable attempt.

After much discussion and looking at menus, Chris had found a promising line of approach. It was possible to order an evening meal kit. The kit would come with all the food that was needed for the occasion, with a step-by-step guide on how to cook it. Given a couple of hours' work they should be able to produce a decent evening meal. They ordered a meal based around Chicken Wellington.

The kit they had ordered arrived as expected, and towards the end of the afternoon, the pair of them set to work in the kitchen. Although the instructions suggested a preparation time of 90 minutes, they both agreed that would be cutting things much too fine, and they allowed well over 2 hours for the project. That turned out to be a good decision, because they spent the first half an hour just laying out the components of the food kit and reading through the instructions, before they began any actual preparation. Despite their lack of cooking experience, Chris and Paul enjoyed the time spent working together with a common aim. There were a few near disasters, due to errors over the timing of some sections of the instructions, but the extra time they had allowed for preparing the meal kept their stress levels low, and there was time for them to take turns in dressing for dinner before their guests were due. The result was that everything was under control, and they were surprisingly relaxed when the Hendersons arrived, holding a beautiful potted orchid in gift wrapping.

Chris received it from them, "Thank you so much. That will make a great centrepiece for our dining table."

Both Zara and Crispin found it a novel experience to be in a home with an identical layout to their own. Though, as Crispin said, "That was to be expected, because everyone could see from the outside that the whole row of houses had been built to the same design."

Zara wanted to see Siete, so the dog was allowed into the dining area, where Zara clearly enjoyed being able to pat and stroke her. While Chris and Zara sat with the dog, Paul turned to Crispin, "There is one difference between our houses. We had an office built in the garden. Come and see."

In truth, there wasn't a great deal to see, though Crispin was impressed with the two large screens attached to Paul's computer. "That's some serious kit you have there."

Paul explained a little about the setup, "In any face-to-face meeting, first impressions count for a great deal. When the meeting is a virtual one, the background contributes significantly to the first impression, so I've carefully arranged what my camera can see." He showed Crispin the view that a client would have during an online consultation. Although there was clutter in the room as a whole, Crispin discovered that any client would see only the clean lines of a smart office.

Crispin and Paul returned to the house to find that Chris and Zara had turned their attention to serving food. Chris was explaining, "Cooking isn't our greatest strength, so we've been cooking by numbers during the afternoon. I only hope that it's turned out to be edible."

Crispin and Zara both assured her that everything looked superb and reiterated their encouragement when they began to eat. Paul was intent on using the opportunity of their visitors to probe for some details of Chris's work. During the meal he asked Zara first, "How do you gather customers, Zara?"

Zara smiled, "There's no shortage. I use the Leisure Centre for some in-person work, and I have an advert on the noticeboard there, which generates a few responses. Then on top of that, there are enquiries from my website and social media information. There's plenty to keep me busy."

As Paul replied to Zara, he tried to include Chris in the conversation. "I expect you know about Chris's online tutoring, but I've never quite understood how she keeps so busy. What's your secret, Chris?"

"There's no great secret," Chris answered, "I don't have to do anything to advertise. I use tutoring agencies, and they produce all the work I can cope with. It's true they charge commission, at the same time they make things easy for me, so I don't mind." She carried on smoothly with barely a pause, "What's coming up in your work, Crispin?"

"I shall be on stage singing as a jolly tar of olden times. That will be good fun, though some of the soloist's songs have become lodged in my head, and I guess that can be irritating for others when I keep bursting into song."

"It's not only that," Zara contributed, "it's the misplaced humour. How would you like to be woken each morning with a cry of 'My gallant crew, good morning?' And it gets worse - there's an expected response of 'Sir, good morning,' which I flatly refuse to supply."

Her expression, and the way she put her hand on his, belied her words and suggested that she didn't really mind at all.

Paul had sensed again Chris's reluctance to divulge information about her work and noted, for a second time, that the Hendersons didn't ask her any more about it. Although Crispin and Zara clearly adored each other, he was beginning to suspect that they might not be the normal couple he had imagined at first. He might have been overthinking it, but their lack of interest in Chris's work could suggest that they knew all about it, and their knowledge included a reality about Chris that Paul himself didn't know. What had been going on between Zara and Chris at the Leisure Centre? He would have to discover more, one way or another.

A day or two later, Paul was out with Siete when he saw Chris leave the house with her swimming gear. He was crossing the park at the time, and he didn't think she had seen him. He knew where she was going, or at least where she had said that she went for swimming, so he followed at a very safe distance. While he was still a few hundred metres from the Leisure Centre he caught a glimpse of Chris going in. When he came closer to the building, he could read the notice outside, which announced, with apologies, that the pool was closed for a few hours. That was interesting. He wondered whether Zara was working in the centre that day, and he thought about waiting nearby for Chris, or possibly Zara, to leave. That could be risky, and he could see little to be gained by it. Anyway, it would be best to be home before Chris; the time she arrived home would be informative in itself, so he would go and wait there.

Chris arrived home at the time he would have expected after one of her swimming sessions, and she hung her towel to dry as usual. Paul searched his brain for a casual comment to test her reaction, "Did you set any records today?"

"No," she replied, "it's more about distance and a steady speed."

That was interesting. She hadn't definitely said that she swam, but she certainly hadn't mentioned that the pool was closed. What had she been doing for the afternoon?

"Did you see Zara, Chris?"

"Yes, she was working there today. We met in passing."

Paul didn't know what to make of that. It could mean nothing at all.

Chapter 16 – The wall safe

The call of Paul's normal business was now urgent, but even as he worked, he could never entirely clear his head of the puzzles that pressed him for solution. Only a short time ago, everything about his life had been depressingly average. Now look at him! If secrets came in packets, he'd have a whole van load. Worse than that, much of his life now seemed to be in the hands of people that 'didn't exist.' Try as he might, he couldn't see a connection between his work with Michael & Co. and all the other secrets that were coming to shroud his domestic life. How had Jacquie, in particular, become involved in all the puzzles? She had been with them for a decade. He had never understood why they had employed her, but that was long before any thought of his work with Malcolm and Piers. He concluded that there must be at least two independent sets of mysteries in his life, though there was an undeniable overlap between them. The infection he had found on Chris's computer provided an obvious link; however tenuous it might turn out to be.

Thinking of Jacquie, he wasn't going to let his failure to follow her be the last word on the subject. All that fiasco proved was that he shouldn't apply for work as a private detective any time soon. Nevertheless, he promised himself that he would find out where she lived, one way or another. He would simply have to improve his performance.

Paul was experiencing pangs of shame over his growing doubts about Chris. Did he really have sufficient solid evidence to justify his lack of trust? All the evidence was circumstantial, and surely there had to be a perfectly innocent explanation - even if he was unable to think of one. He could almost convince himself that his lack of faith was unworthy of him, though that didn't prevent him from listening for any sign of Chris leaving the house. While he was sitting in his office it was difficult to hear small sounds from inside the house, so Paul found himself making excuses to pass through the living room to check on what Chris was doing.

During the following morning, he went to offer Chris a mug of coffee and was just in time to catch sight of her closing the front door, with her swimming bag under her arm. He allowed a few minutes to pass, in case she had forgotten something and returned, then he made for the wall-safe, where he held his breath as his trembling fingers pressed 3012 on the keypad. There was a satisfying beep – the code had worked! All he had to do was turn the handle and open the safe, but was he actually going to do this? Was he really going to be the kind of man who would spy on his own wife?

Trapped by indecision, Paul couldn't summon up the will to open the safe. He paced the room trying to decide what to do. If he opened that safe, he would cross a new boundary in his world of deceit. It would be breaking all bonds of trust between Chris and himself. When they were married, he had promised to be faithful; the idea of opening the small door to that safe didn't feel anything like being faithful. He heard the soft click as the safe timed out and relocked itself. At this moment he knew the code, and he had the opportunity to look in the safe. Such a chance might never come again. Despite the odds, he'd found the combination. Who knew when Chris might decide to change it? If she did, he might never be able to satisfy his suspicion. Opening the safe would be a step of betrayal. Nevertheless, if all he found was jewellery, it would also be a step towards sweeping away his clouds of suspicion.

He paced the bedroom in perplexity. Perhaps he should move further from temptation. He paced the living room instead. Eventually, he gave up, went to his office, and slumped down in his chair. He hated his own indecisiveness and wished that he had never found the code to the safe. In his dejected state, he tried to think about other mysteries, and there were plenty of them to occupy his thoughts.

What was he to do about the new ginger-haired girl from Lawn Lovers? Who was she, and was she a spy? Obviously, he could phone the firm and ask her name, but that would make him sound weird. "Well, that was no more than the truth," he told himself. No! That wasn't fair. Maybe he was becoming a little odd, but he wasn't weird in that kind of way. He didn't go round stalking people. Okay, he had followed one person - that didn't count. He could phone Lawn Lovers, say that the ginger girl's work was exceptional, and he wanted to send a card to thank her. That might sound less perverted. Then again, they might tell her about his call. If she was a spy, she would immediately conclude that he suspected her. Perhaps he could say that he wanted to write a positive review of their work and to include some of their employees by name, though if they had half their wits about them, they would only provide first names. If he were to press the point, that would only draw attention to his enquiry. He could follow her, but that would look like stalking, and he really didn't want to make a habit of following people, so he was stuck. Of course, if he hardly ever saw her, the matter would be resolved – unless Lawn Lovers had several spies working shifts. That simply wasn't credible. He would wait and see.

Since there was nothing he could do about the ginger girl, he would concentrate on a plan to find out about Jacquie. One option would be to raise the issue with Malcolm. He had no doubt that Michael & Co. could find out where she lived and what she ate for breakfast, but he wasn't sure that he wanted them to know more than he did, and he particularly didn't want them to discover that he had been trying to follow her. He should keep everything to himself and work out a way to track her more carefully.

Chapter 17 – An unwelcome revelation

Despite the difficulty he had in concentrating, Paul caught up with his business affairs during the next few days. At night times, his sleep was fitful as his brain teamed with hair-brained schemes to resolve his domestic mysteries. One thing he kept coming back to was the safe. Why hadn't he opened it when he had the opportunity? He resolved not to make the same mistake twice. The chances were that he would find nothing out of the ordinary, and that would be the end of the matter. Obviously, he should do it before that code ended up being changed.

He was on the alert once more for signs of Chris leaving the house. On this occasion, it was easy. She told him in the morning that she planned to sketch at the riverside after lunch, and Paul was filled with the rush of nervous excitement.

That morning, he had his appointment with Malcolm at number 77. Paul had been rehearsing the things he needed to say. That proved to be useless, because Malcolm clearly had an agenda of his own and was all efficiency. He came straight to the point, "How have you been progressing, Paul?"

The speeches Paul had practised evaporated in an instant, "Surprisingly well, in fact I reckon that I'm detecting levels of infection so slight that even Siete doesn't notice them."

"That's splendid news! Not unexpected, but splendid none the less. I thought when we first met that you were going to be very good at this. Although you've exceeded Siete's abilities, she has played her part well."

"Yes, she has, but about that. I'm hoping it doesn't mean that you'll want to take her away."

"No, absolutely not, I've every reason to want Siete to keep living with you."

He had no idea what mix of hormones were released into his system, but a tidal wave of joy and relief flooded over him. Paul didn't know whether to shout or skip round the room. In the event he did neither, though his broad smile spoke volumes. In the lightness of spirit of that moment he knew that he loved his dog. Through all the doubts and fears that threatened to wreck his life, that canine was a devoted and faithful support.

"Thank you. You don't know what a relief that is, though I would be interested to know your thinking."

Malcolm considered for a few moments before replying, "Let's take the infection first. It's a very promising sign that you can detect the infection so easily now, but that's not an end in itself. As we discussed previously, the infections you're detecting are secondary ones. That, on its own, isn't very useful. Those infections gradually wear off without our intervention. To be honest, we don't know how to intervene anyway."

Paul had realised all that before now, and he was already becoming despondent about the prospects for any effective action. He hadn't been going to say anything about his other concern. In fact, he had especially rehearsed not saying anything about it, but Malcolm had an extraordinary way of extracting information without asking for it. "There's something else, Malcolm. I've found a faint level of infection on Chris's computer, and I'm worried about how that can have happened."

"Ah! Now don't rush to conclusions of doom about that. Computer infections are a good illustration of the peculiar nature of the infection. Although it's passed on from humans to inanimate objects, it doesn't require physical contact to do it. The transfer is by bad intent, not by touch, so there are a number of ways Christine's computer could have become infected. It could be through an online contact with an infected student who was up to no good, and if the level is low, that's the most likely source. Having said that, we can't discount the possibility that it was infected by whoever tried to access your computers. Though, since that was a while back, I'd have thought that would have worn off by this time. In either case, the infection should now die away quite rapidly. If it doesn't, we would have to conclude that either an evil-minded student is in repeated contact or, of more concern, that Christine herself is the source of the infection."

Although that thought had been preying on Paul's mind, hearing the words spoken brought him into a cold sweat, and Malcolm must have seen his face become pale, "I had to mention the possibility, Paul, but rest assured, we haven't found any reason to think that Christine has bad intent. In the normal course of events, we wouldn't be looking at her any further. It's only the unusual events in your life that are making us look a little harder, but I'm sure I'll soon be able to calm all your fears. I can't quite do that yet, because we still have a few avenues to explore and, while we are on the subject of exploring, I'm still waiting for the analysis of your bug devices. Our technical people are adamant that they will not report until they have been thorough."

"I see. I suppose that's encouraging." By which, he meant the reassurance about Chris, rather than the lack of bug analysis. Paul also thought about the problem of Jacquie, but he had no intention of throwing that incendiary into the volatile situation. A good part of his reticence was that he suspected the combination of his past actions and his future plans was of dubious legality at best. He didn't think they would be well received. So, Malcolm carried on in what Paul hoped was blissful ignorance.

"We have become side-tracked. You'd asked me about the dog, and there's more than one reason why you should keep her. We don't think that your intruder, or the bugging attempt, has anything to do with your work with Michael & Co. Something else is going on, and that's a mystery. A bigger mystery is that we still don't know what that mystery is, if you get my meaning. The dog will continue to be useful security for you and may well prevent any further incidents. In addition to that, we are hoping that you and Siete will still be able to help each other now and in the future. For example, when she works with you as you try to detect human infection, there's a possibility that we may be able to add to the dog's sensitivity. That brings us to the subject, which I expect you are bursting to know about: how are we going to help you to detect human infection? I'll tell you what we have come up with, but I'm not sure how much you are going to like this plan." Malcolm's face suggested that he was privately amused at what he was about to divulge.

"The first thing we will need is a source of human guinea pigs for you to work on. Some of them must be infected and the rest not. That little problem has been solved with the help of Her Majesty's Prison and Probation Service, together with a drama school. We have a set of prison inmates who are infected. We know they are infected, because they have caused secondary infections on the tools of their crimes. They have volunteered for our programme because it will give them some time away from their normal prison environment. The drama school has both young and mature students, and it will provide us with non-infected guinea pigs. They will be under the impression that their work for us is a component of their studies. The point is that you must be presented with a mix of people, without knowing who is infected and who is not. To achieve that, those from the drama school will be acting the part of prisoners. Neither the convicts, nor the drama students, will know the true purpose of our project. The former will think it's a research project on the factors in early life that lead to criminal behaviour, while the latter will think that it's simply part of their course."

"That sounds very ingenious, Malcolm." Paul decided that two could play at being amused, "Or should I say Squadron Leader?"

Malcolm's smile became more of a grimace, and he raised his hands in mock surrender. "Okay. You've got me. I suppose that's what comes of employing a technically savvy maths graduate. Presumably you have found the Gazette, which is about the only thing we couldn't remove from the public domain. But no, 'Malcolm' will do just fine. We didn't go much for all that rank nonsense when I was in the RAF, far less now that I'm out of it. Anyway, where were we?"

"I think you were about to tell me what part I was expected to play with your assorted band of test subjects."

"Yes, indeed I was. Your work is to interview this merry crew individually. You'll be posing as a freelance journalist, who is researching childhood experiences that tend to result in a life of crime. That should appeal to your sense of drama, because you'll be acting, and so will half the people you interview. The key is that neither party should suspect that the other party is an actor. For your information, the drama students will be very good actors. We have made sure of it. The hope is that you will come to distinguish the real criminals from the false ones by detecting the infection. So, your next project for us is to prepare yourself for playing the part of a freelance journalist. You'll need to work out how to conduct the interviews, and I expect all that will take a week or two. I'll let you know when we are ready to begin the sessions."

It was becoming a routine to think while walking. Paul could see the sense of Malcolm's plan, even if he couldn't see any way that it was going to work. But then again, he hadn't expected to be able to detect secondary infections either, so perhaps Malcolm was on to something. The idea of acting a part was out of the comfort zone of someone who usually controlled the lights, though the way things were going he was spending his whole life acting one part or another, so maybe it wasn't such a challenge.

He did need to make some progress on his home mysteries, and he was determined to look inside the wall safe. Paul ran through the process in his mind. He would supress all hint of moralistic thought and turn himself into an unfeeling robot. With his thoughts and emotions imprisoned, he would enter the code and open the safe, before any objections could burst out of their enclosure.

True to plan, Chris went off with her sketching materials after lunch. Paul tried, with limited success, to shut down his thoughts. He was shaking with the effort as he climbed the stairs. The code was entered and the safe unlocked itself. He only had to convince his hand to turn the handle. The safe timed out and relocked itself. He must act without any further thought, so almost in one action he entered the code and turned the handle. The contents immediately made him wish he had left it alone. There, in full view, was a bug detector – obviously new and exactly the same model as the one he had bought.

He hastily closed the safe and stumbled in confusion back to his office. He opened one of his desk drawers, and there was the bug detector he had purchased. He gazed in disbelief, but as he slowly regained the ability for coherent thought, he remembered the incident of the battery wrapper. When he had opened the packet for his batteries, there had been another one of those wrappers already in the waste bin. It could only mean that Chris had bought and used a bug detector before him. So why did she go through the charade of making him scan for bugs, when she must have done that already? She must have been perfectly well aware that there was something to be found. Why didn't she want Paul to know that she had also bought a bug detector? More than that, why did she encourage Paul to buy a bug detector in the first place, when she had already bought one herself?

Chapter 18 – Jacquie and the convicts

Paul had spent two weeks preparing to play his part as a journalist. His time for Michael & Co. still included daily walks with Piers and Siete, and the reality was that he was well into overtime, spending much more time than the equivalent of one day per week. That didn't dampen his enthusiasm, though it was bound to affect his own business. He should mention it to Malcolm. Anyway, he was as ready as he would ever be when the taxi arrived to pick him up. This was a morning off for Piers, so Paul could take Siete with him, and she was on her leash as they both jumped into the back of the taxi, where Malcolm was waiting for them. Siete laid herself quietly on the floor and Malcolm chatted during the drive.

"The plan is to have two men for you to interview today, next time it will be two women. We've decided that we will always work interviews in pairs, and always with one real convict and one actor. Obviously, you'll see them separately and you won't know which is which. There will be a prison guard outside the room and another one behind a one-way mirror, though I think the presence of Siete should ensure that there are no shenanigans. You'll find your interview room has refreshments prepared. You can offer those to your customers to help in providing a friendly environment, and before you ask, the prison authorities have risk-assessed the whole procedure. They are content with it."

In between Malcolm's pieces of information, Paul did manage to mention the extra time he was devoting to Michael & Co. Malcolm slapped his forehead, "I'm so sorry, I should have worked that out. I'll add to your pay for the current six months and adjust it for the future. Check your account this evening, and let me know if my changes don't seem appropriate."

The destination proved to be a smallish detached house in the Rochester area. The interview room itself was a compact sitting room, with a soft carpet, two armchairs, and a coffee table. Below the large mirror section in one wall was a set of low cupboards. Laid out on them was everything needed for tea, coffee, and biscuits. Apart from the mirror and the fact that the only windows were diminutive and high on the wall, this might have been a small meeting space attached to any smart commercial office.

Paul and Siete left Malcolm in the observation area and settled themselves in the interview room. For this part of his work Paul was permitted to keep records, mainly for the purpose of realism. His plan was to conduct the session using questions from prepared notes on his tablet. In addition, he would use his phone to make audio recordings of each meeting. Everything was as good as he could make it. All that remained was to give the appearance of an experienced journalist by calming his nervous panic.

There was a knock on the door. It was opened to reveal a prison guard, who announced, "Mr Keating, this is Pete," as he ushered in his prisoner. The door was closed, leaving Paul alone with Pete.

Paul made his best attempt at a smile, "Hello, Pete, I'm Paul. Thank you for agreeing to see me today. Please help yourself to a drink and biscuits."

Paul had already poured his own coffee, so he sat and watched as Pete poured his. Pete was a small man, probably in his forties, with short dark hair. He was dressed in a navy sweatshirt and jeans. Once he was seated, Paul briefly explained that he was researching information about the early life of those who had been convicted of serious crimes. Pete was nodding. He'd clearly been told all this before. Paul placed his phone on the coffee table saying, "I hope you don't object to a recording. It will help our conversation if I don't need to keep taking notes." There was no objection, so he continued, "Could you tell me about the offence that landed you in prison, Pete?"

The reply came in a surprisingly cultured voice, "Certainly, I worked in the City in a large financial institution. The pay was okay, but my prospects for promotion looked slim, so I devised a system for creating certain transactions that would end up with money being paid to myself. Of course, there were checks in place that were supposed to stop me doing that. A second person had to review and authorise all transactions. I dealt with that obstacle by stealing another employee's login details. When he went off for coffee, I would log in as him and authorise my transactions. I did take measures to conceal what I'd done, so it was very unlucky that someone noticed them, and I was caught."

"You say you worked in the City. Was that always your ambition?"

"Not exactly that, but it was a fairly obvious career choice. At school, I'd always been good at maths and with computers. I was in the chess club, and out of school time, I played online computer games with friends."

"So, you're saying that you were a typical school boy."

"No, not quite, I was suspended a couple of times for hacking into the Staff intranet. To begin with, I only did that for the challenge, to see if I could do it. When I succeeded, I thought there would be no harm in a few adjustments to my reports and grades. It would all have been fine except for the dinosaurs on the Staff who kept paper records of everything, and then wondered why the computer records no longer agreed with them."

Paul already had Pete summed up to his own satisfaction. Here was a guy who thought he was good with technology, but was nothing like as good as he imagined. No wonder he had been caught. Paul found himself becoming genuinely interested in why Pete had taken to a life of crime, so much so that he almost forgot the real reason for the interviews.

Further questions served to reinforce Paul's initial assessment. Pete had always felt poorly treated as a child. His talents were always overlooked in favour of others. His reaction was to progress by cheating. He was almost always caught. Amazingly, that never dented his belief in his own skills. His reasonable academic record earned him employment in the financial world, where his work in the city had been his opportunity to make it big.

Paul shook hands with Pete as he showed him to the door, before sitting down to review the session. The key point was that there had been no odd smells, but then Pete might have been a drama student.

The second interview of the day was with Lance, who was very different from Pete. Lance was big, and most of his body mass was muscle, or so it seemed from his tight tee-shirt. Although he too wore jeans, that was about the only similarity between him and Pete. Lance had a scar down one cheek, and when he spoke, Paul felt that he was making a great effort to keep coarse language in check. Paul fervently hoped that the guards outside the room were on the alert, and he was very pleased to have Siete in the room with him. He kept looking at that scar. Was that from a knife fight or courtesy of the make-up department of a drama school? He couldn't quite be sure, though he didn't fancy taking a close look to check.

Paul wasn't surprised to discover that Lance's offence was GBH - for the second time. When Paul asked about his early life, Lance told him about living on the streets in a deprived area of North Kent. His parents had a tempestuous relationship. When his father finally left them, his mother had engaged in petty theft to feed her drug habit. Social services never did catch up with Lance, and he roamed the streets with a gang who became his security. He soon realised that his status in the gang could be improved by big muscles and an aggressive nature, so he worked on both. His story was desperately sad - if it was true of course. True or not, there were no unusual smells. Paul decided that he valued his fingers too much to shake Lance's hand, so he simply showed him out with thanks.

The same taxi took Paul and Siete back home, again in the company of Malcolm. They spoke about the two interviews with no reference to the infection, or otherwise, of the candidates. They chatted as though both of the convicts' stories were true, and they arranged to meet at '77' to review progress.

Paul was delighted that the whole process was efficient from a time point of view, because he had particular plans for the afternoon, which involved the mystery of Jacquie. This time he would be fully prepared.

As he had hoped, Jacquie arrived shortly after lunchtime. Paul waited for an hour and a half before taking Siete out for a walk. He'd already identified a space in the park where it was possible to observe his own house through a screen of trees and bushes. There was a convenient seat where he could sit and look occupied on his phone. After a while he saw Jacquie leave. She set off in the opposite direction to that of the previous disaster. There was a chill in the breeze, and as he followed at a very safe distance, Paul saw Jacquie tie a yellow scarf round her head. That was as good as a tour guide holding a bright umbrella to guide a party of sightseers. Following that scarf should be easy. Jacquie was walking briskly as though she had another appointment. That also made her easy to follow, though if she was going to another cleaning engagement, it wouldn't help him very much.

They reached the busy High Street, where the yellow scarf stood out like a beacon among the subdued coats of the shoppers. Nevertheless, Paul closed the distance as Jacquie disappeared into a shopping arcade. Paul and Siete hurried forward and took the same turn. He needn't have rushed. There was Jacquie looking into a shop window only about 50 metres away.

"Please don't let her look round," Paul thought. He was in luck and she moved on. When he passed the shop, she had been interested in, he saw that the window was filled with men's wear, and he wondered why that had caught her attention. Was she married? He had never thought so. Anyway, he couldn't think about that now, and the concept of a shop window being used as a mirror didn't occur to him. Jacquie was leaving the arcade at the far end, so again he had to hurry after her to peep round the corner at the end of the precinct. Fortunately, she hadn't gone far and could be seen descending the steps of a pedestrian underpass, which crossed another busy road. As her head disappeared from sight, he ran forward and saw her going into the tunnel. There were only a few people in the underpass, so Paul was afraid of being spotted if he turned into the tunnel too soon. He wanted to peek cautiously round the corner, but other pedestrians would wonder what he was doing. As he reached the entrance, he bent down to fiddle with Siete's leash, using that move to glance into the tunnel. Jacquie was reaching the far end, so he moved rapidly after her, only slowing as he came to the steps out. In fact, she had already cleared the steps, and when his head reached pavement level Paul could see her turning right into an alleyway. That could be a problem. With just Paul and a dog in a deserted narrow street, Jacquie was sure to become aware of them.

His fears were unfounded, because the alley proved to be a short one leading into a park. Jacquie had already disappeared from sight and Paul had no qualms about hurrying to find out which direction she had taken. That was easy, there was the bright yellow scarf crossing the grass. By this time, Paul had quite lost his bearings, and he was mildly surprised to realise that he was in the same park as before, when he had lost Jacquie in McDonald's. Unfortunately, that was exactly where she was headed again. Paul did not want a repeat of the previous experience, but he had never worked out what had happened on that first occasion, and he was struggling to know how to prevent a repeat performance. Those fears were unfounded, because Jacquie walked past the fast-food restaurant in favour of a Tube station. Now, he heartily wished she had used the McDonald's. The Tube station would be a total nightmare! Paul and Siete broke into a trot. Only the yellow scarf could save them now.

Once in the Underground station there was no sign of Jacquie, and to make matters worse, there was more than one underground line at this station. As he searched the concourse and looked beyond the ticket barriers in disappointment, the truth dawned. He had been played. She must have spotted him at the outset, and that yellow scarf had been no fortunate accident. Jacquie leading him to the path across the gardens just about summed it up – she had led him right up the garden path. On the other hand, it did confirm his suspicion that Jacquie was more than a home help.

At home Paul's dejection was cheered by the sight of his bank account. Malcolm had made good in a way that was more than generous.

Chapter 19 – A fateful decision

Paul was becoming increasingly concerned about his own state of mind and about his relationship with his wife. For one thing, all the secrets in his life were affecting his judgement. He'd become a different person from the ex-geek who had married Chris, and he could hardly believe some of his own recent actions. There was the stealthy investigation of his own wife, and then, what had possessed him to follow Jacquie? That situation had become a disaster area. She obviously knew that he had tried to tail her. What would be the repercussions? There had to be a high chance that she would tell Chris. Paul could of course deny it and say that he was merely walking the dog; Jacquie must have imagined that he was following her. But then, Jacquie might point out the convoluted route involved. On second thoughts, perhaps she was less likely to tell Chris than Paul had imagined. After all, why would Jacquie take such an odd route if the person behind her was someone she knew well? That was a most peculiar course of action. She clearly did have something to hide, so she would surely remain silent.

His breaking into Chris's safe was another matter altogether. That still dominated his thoughts. It was as though he was developing a split personality. There was one Paul who enjoyed being with his wife. That was the Paul who had loved cooking with her and who thrilled at her touch, the one who no longer worshipped her from afar, because he could now delight in her presence. Then there was a second Paul who was suspicious of what she might be involved with. No, it wasn't only suspicion, it was worry. This second Paul was worried that the marriage of the first Paul was in danger, and that concern was entirely understandable. What really disturbed him was that he could change so easily between the loving first Paul and the suspicious second one. In his suspicious persona it was as though the other version of himself had simply been switched off.

The fact remained that Chris was keeping secrets from him. If he could satisfy himself that they were innocent secrets, then suspicious Paul could be consigned to history. He was desperate to know what Chris was up to. There was her reticence about her work. Was it all that she claimed, or was that part of a guilty secret? He began to wonder whether he could bug some of her tutor sessions to find out.

Chris was out, so Paul began to examine her work desk and computer setup. He already knew that bugging devices could be very discrete. Was there a way for him to listen in to Chris at work? One problem would be that she used headphones. It might be possible to hear her words, but would that be sufficient? He would only have half of the conversation. In addition to that, if he could listen in, he wouldn't understand the language, so he would need a translation of any recording he made. He couldn't allow someone else to listen to a recording; who knows what they might hear, and how would he explain the recording in the first place? This already seemed like an intractable set of issues, but there was yet another problem: Chris had a bug detector in her safe. Did she run bug sweeps as a matter of routine? He wasn't ready to take that risk.

Paul wondered idly about the possibility of placing a device inside Chris's computer to record both sides of a conversation. It didn't look as though it would be possible to insert anything into the headphones. He would have to find out if there was technology that would detect audio signals before they reached the headphones. He was just pushing connecting leads aside to see how the computer could be opened when he heard the front door. Chris had returned! He hurriedly stepped away from the workstation and almost ran through the kitchen to reach the safety of his office.

That was a lesson to learn. He had nearly been caught examining Chris's computer. What would have happened if he had been in the middle of dismantling it to insert a bug? He needed to think about all this much more carefully. He made a mental list of all the problems. Chris had a bug detector, she taught in languages that he didn't understand, she listened with headphones, and he didn't know about the legality of buying or using a bugging device. Paul worked on each problem separately. As he found possible solutions to them individually, an overall plan gradually evolved. It was far from perfect, but it wasn't bad, and he thought it stood a good chance of working.

Later in the afternoon, Paul relaxed by taking Siete into the garden for a game of 'Find the treats.' The game had reached the stage when the food could be made very challenging to find. The Alsatian was sitting patiently waiting for him to finish hiding a selection of her favourites, when the rumble of a lawnmower could be heard as it was unloaded from a van in the road. The ginger-haired girl appeared at the garden gate, with the machine. All the treats had been concealed, so Paul gave Siete the 'Find' instruction and the enthusiastic dog shot across the garden to the first treat. Paul called to the girl, "Could you hang on a second please?" Siete took only a short time to find all the food, and Paul beckoned the girl to come through the gate.

She was smiling with delight as she pushed the mower on to the lawn. "That looked fun. Isn't your dog clever?"

Paul agreed before commenting, "I don't often see you here, do I?"

"No, I'm a student at the college. There are spaces in my timetable, so I can fit in some part-time gardening work. Lawn Lovers is ideal, because I'm studying horticulture."

"I'm surprised that Lawn Lovers can slot you into their timetable," Paul replied.

"That part's easy, I'm on a work share with my grandad. He should have retired years ago, but says that the gardening keeps him fit. I expect you've seen him. He's beginning to struggle with the work, and although it's only part-time, even that has become more than he really wants. He had the bright idea of arranging for us to have a part-time job share. Lawn Lovers was happy enough with that, and it works out very well for both of us."

"Well, that's a new one on me, and I'm pleased it's worked out for you. Anyway, I won't hold you up any longer."

That had all sounded reasonable, and Paul concluded that she probably wasn't a spy. He was fairly sure that her grandfather must be the elderly worker who used the lawn mower like a walking frame. The whole story rang true.

Chapter 20 – The red flag

In preparation for his next meeting with Malcolm, Paul had been reviewing his project of interviewing convicts. The problem was that everyone he met had smells associated with them. They ranged from the faint ones that might arise from the soap they used or from their latest cooking, to some that were quite aggressive in their intensity. His sense of smell had become acute, and he could be almost overwhelmed by clothes impregnated with tobacco smoke or people who overused perfume, but Paul wasn't trying to detect ordinary smells. The infection didn't produce a scent. It was just that the sensation it did produce in the brain was very similar to a smell. He didn't know how it was sensed, he only knew that it wasn't through his normal scent receptors, so sniffing, for example, didn't help. But whatever infection sensors his body used, Paul had already learnt something about how they worked. When he had first been trying to detect secondary infections, ordinary smells had dominated his senses. That changed once he had a faint whiff of the infection. Then, he'd been able to focus on that sensation, and his infection sensors had rapidly seemed to become more sensitive. Maybe it was more likely that his brain had become increasingly adept at distinguishing their signals from his normal sense of smell. Anyway, he would expect the same thing to happen with human infection. He'd become very sensitive to secondary infections, and he had expected that human infection would be stronger and easier to detect. It was odd that he hadn't detected anything other than ordinary scents from his first two clients. The more he thought about that, the more of a conundrum it seemed to be. Secondary infections had proved to be common. They originated with people, so he would expect human infection to be common as well. In fact, he must be encountering it frequently in everyday life, yet he hadn't detected it from anyone he had met or passed in the street.

During the meeting with Malcolm, Paul expressed doubts about his work, "If we assume that I'll become able to detect human infection, and that is a very big assumption so far as I can see, I still don't see how that would move us forward."

"You're right, Paul. In itself, detecting human infection would be of limited value, however the real mission is to go a step or two beyond that. It would help us a great deal if you were able to detect the sources of human infection. Those are primary infections. If they could be detected, then we would stand a chance of limiting the whole chain of human infections and the bad things that result from them. I know that seems to be a distant prospect from where you are now but, be assured, there are those – not very many it's true – who have successfully trodden this path before you. I'm very optimistic about that possibility. During the last few weeks, your progress has been amazingly rapid, so don't be downhearted."

This did indeed sound encouraging and Paul was heartened by the thought that he might achieve far-reaching good, but Malcolm had news of his own, and not all of that was good, "I've finally received the test results from the bugging apparatus you found. There were two sets of fingerprints apart from your own. We don't know whose they are, though one set was recognised by the system as being involved in an unsuccessful terrorist incident last year."

"That's worrying. Why would any terrorist be interested in me? Am I at risk of being blown up?"

"I don't think so. If they had wanted to blow you up, they would have left a bomb, not a bug. Nevertheless, someone is taking an unhealthy interest, so I'll look into increasing your security."

"That's good to know. Can I ask you about the bugging device?" Paul needed it as part of his latest plan, and he had thought of a suitable excuse to cover his real purpose. "May I borrow it back? I'd like to check how much it was picking up from its place under Chris's desk. Could it pick up conversation in my office, for example, or in the bedroom?"

Malcolm seemed hesitant. "Alright, but only for a few days. I'll arrange for Annette to have it ready for you when you go. Now, there is another thing. You should know that I do have some indication of where the interest in your home is coming from. You'll remember that we had a few issues in researching Christine's work. But, before I say more, I need you to sign the Official Secrets Act."

Paul couldn't believe what he was hearing. His surprise and confusion were clearly evident as Malcolm was producing a document. He would have been even more worried if he had realised that this was the first time Michael & Co. had asked him to sign anything. Malcolm tried to reassure him, "Signing this doesn't put you under any new obligation, it's just that I have something to tell you that is confidential and could be related to national security. All of us, including you, are bound by the Official Secrets Act. I have permission to tell you something, and it would be illegal for you to pass the information on, whether or not you sign this. At the same time, I don't want to burden you with a secret that you would prefer not to know, so if you don't wish to sign, that's fine, but you'll understand that I wouldn't then be comfortable to tell you what I've found out."

There were enough mysteries in Paul's life as it was. One more secret to add to his existing horde was as nothing compared to the prospect of solving one of the mysteries. There was no way that he was going to pass up the opportunity to hear what Malcolm had discovered. It didn't occur to him that he might hear something that he would much rather not know, so he scanned the document and signed.

"Thank you. I must emphasise that the information I'm going to tell you is confidential. You must not share it with anyone, though I don't think that will be a temptation. It relates to Christine. As you know, we were able to research her background, and everything was just fine, though it was a little odd that details of her work were sketchy. In the light of events, I looked harder and I came up against a red flag. A red flag means that one of our secret services has an on-going operation connected with Christine. I don't know the nature or extent of the connection, nor do I know anything about the operation itself. What I can be sure of is that it has nothing to do with Michael & Co. or your work for us."

Paul's hope of having a mystery solved was dashed. This new piece of information only served to increase his worry about Chris and to deepen the mysteries surrounding her.

Chapter 21 – More convicts

Malcolm again arrived in a taxi for Paul's second set of convict interviews. On this occasion, Paul was observing the route they took as he listened to Malcolm informing him of developments, "Since yesterday, I've been thinking about security for you. I know you have Siete, and she should alert you to any intruders, but the fingerprint report from the bug you found does raise worrying questions. I don't like the possible link to terrorism, so it would be good to enhance your security. Unfortunately, the situation is made complicated by the red flag that was triggered by Christine's name."

Paul didn't know how to respond to that. Any normal person in his position, who had no secrets of their own, would be bound to ask Malcolm how it was that terrorism had become a threat as soon as he began to work with Michael & Co. The problem was his belief that the bugging episode wasn't connected with *his* work, either for his business or for Michael & Co; it was much more likely to be linked with his wife's secrets. Malcolm was clearly thinking along the same lines. So, what should he say?

Paul didn't want to admit that he had already become suspicious of Chris's activities. He especially did not want to say that he had been making covert investigations of his own. It would be better to act the part of a husband who couldn't imagine ill of his wife, but a husband like that would surely express some doubts about Michael & Co. On the other hand, he was confident that Michael & Co. wasn't where the trouble lay, and if he cast too much suspicion on the company, Malcolm would begin to wonder why he was still working for them. Paul could only venture a neutral reply, "So, what are you thinking of doing?"

"Well, I don't know what the red flag is about, but I do know that great discretion is called for. I don't want to end up causing a bun fight between ourselves and the Secret Intelligence Service. I remain convinced that there's no threat to you as a result of your work for us. All the same, you are employed by us, and if there is a threat to you from persons unknown, I'm not going to leave you unsupported."

"I'm grateful for that, but you must admit that it's a big coincidence to have these issues arising as soon as I began work with you."

"I do accept that and I, too, could hardly believe it was unconnected. However, I've examined everything about your relationship with Michael & Co. extremely carefully, and I can't find the slightest hint of a way in which we could have started all this. I can only conclude that it's an almost incredible coincidence; you have become tangled up with something else altogether at the same time as meeting us. On reflection, it may not be the coincidence of timing that we imagine, because it's quite possible that whatever is going on now has a long history, and you might have only recently become aware of it. The point is: I am persuaded that the mystery is nothing to do with us, which means we don't know the extent of any danger that may or may not exist. On a more positive note, I am confident that Michael & Co. can put up a strong defence against most hazards."

Paul heartily agreed that any danger wasn't because of Michael & Co., though he wasn't going to say so. He was less certain about the support that Malcolm could offer, but he wasn't going to say that either. He would be pleased to accept any help on offer.

They reached Rochester, where Paul saw that they were driving away from the town centre. He began to understand that the location of the house they were using had been carefully chosen. It was at the end of a quiet leafy lane, close to the river Medway. He thought they must be on the southeastern side of the river. He couldn't remember whether that made it 'Man of Kent' or 'Kentish Man' area. It was of more relevance that in this location neither of those species, nor any other, was likely to take much notice of a few cars arriving.

Paul's first interview was with Ashley. He was a little taken aback by her smart blue, knee-length skirt, and bright floral blouse. That wasn't what he'd expected from someone serving a prison sentence. The pixie cut of her mousey hair completed the picture of a well-to-do young lady. No, on closer inspection she was older than she looked – 40 perhaps. His first impression was of either a very unusual prisoner or a very bad actor.

After the introductions, Paul began the interview proper, "Ashley, could you tell me how you ended up in prison?"

As she spoke, it was very hard to think of her as a convict. Her accent sounded like the product of an expensive education, although her tale of criminal activity also sounded convincing.

"I made a career," she began, "of separating elderly people from some of their valuables. I would choose a neighbourhood and study it to identify a suitable victim. I was looking for someone who was retired, who was living on their own, and who might be lonely. It shouldn't be someone who had carers, or others, who might drop in unexpectedly. Once I was happy with my choice, I would ring on their door during daylight hours. Mid-afternoon was my favourite time. I always had an excuse prepared for asking them to let me in. It was a good idea to vary the excuses, but one I liked was to have a shopping bag with me and to be all tearful. I would say that I was miles from home. I'd lost my phone and my credit cards. Could I please phone my boyfriend to come and get me?

"Once I was in the house, I would make the phone call, and then ask if I could wait there. They usually said 'Yes,' so I would ask them about their photographs. Old people always have photos, and they love to talk about them. I was doing them a service really; they just didn't know they would be paying for it. It was almost certain that they would offer me tea, and as they went to make it, I would ask if I could use the toilet. That would give me a few minutes to look around in other rooms for anything small and valuable – jewellery or cash for preference. Anything I found would be slipped into my bag. When they were returning with the tea, my boyfriend would arrive outside. I would make my apologies and hurry out with my booty."

Paul didn't know what to make of her performance. He revised his first impression. This woman could certainly act, though he couldn't tell whether she had a life of crime in which she played the part of an innocent or was an innocent who was now playing the part of a criminal. Of course, that was the whole idea of the project. Out of genuine interest he asked, "How often did you do this?"

"Most days, but we took care to change our target area. As I said, some time was spent in research. So, all-in-all the work kept me busy. I was only caught by bad luck, when one piece of jewellery turned out to be more valuable than I had thought. It was recognised when I tried to sell it."

"Where were you brought up, Ashley?"

"On the Isle of Sheppey. It was only me and my mother. Dad had no work, though that didn't prevent him from being drunk more often than not. He used to hit my mum, but he hit other people too and went to prison for GBH. Mum couldn't find work either, so she stole what she could, which wasn't much."

"Did you look for work when you were older?"

"No, I knew there wasn't much about for the likes of us, so I planned for a better future than my life with Mum. I learnt to speak nicely, and made plans to steal without aggravation. I didn't really do much harm. No-one was going to starve from what I did, and it worked a treat for a long time. I suppose I always knew that I would be caught in the end, although I always thought that would be sometime in the future. One day it wasn't."

Paul couldn't detect any smell of fermenting apples, though there was the faintest, rather pleasant, hint of citrus from Ashley or her clothes. An illuminating interview, but not helpful for his purpose.

Ashley was followed by Tiffany, who was a slim figure in her mid-twenties; blond, with a ponytail, and wearing a black track suit. She was quite attractive to look at, but that all changed when she opened her mouth. Tiffany, or Tiffy, as she preferred, certainly hadn't learnt to speak nicely; swear words punctuated her every sentence. Between the profanities, Paul learned that she had spent most of her childhood in a care home. The main good thing she had been taught was not to use drugs. Surprisingly, she had followed that advice. She'd also learnt that there was money to be made from drugs, so as soon as she was free from the restrictions of social workers, she joined the illegal drugs industry. She rose through its illegitimate ranks to become a major supplier – until the day when the Drugs Squad visited and found her, sitting on the floor of her flat, packing large quantities of drugs into smaller packages.

Paul asked about her school. That had been in Tunbridge Wells, which was the area where she had ended up supplying drugs. From her replies, she must have been the despair of all her teachers. She always regarded education as an evil designed to ruin her childhood. Lessons were intended to be frustrating and boring. It became clear that the more her teachers had tried to provoke her into learning, the more she had made them targets for abuse. She'd had no intention of studying, despite the fact that she did have some natural ability. Even without any effort on her part, her brain held some of the maths she had been shown, and that became the only part of her education that contributed to her career as a drug dealer.

Paul found Tiffy to be much more wearing than Ashley had been. The coarse language was like sandpaper rubbing on his ears, so he was delighted to see the back of her. Unfortunately, there was still no scent of rotting apples.

Chapter 22 – The mystery of the monument

Paul frequently used some of his time lying in bed to review his experiences of the day. Though the prisoner interviews had been interesting, it was frustrating that his real mission there hadn't progressed. He was very good at detecting secondary infections, so why couldn't he detect human infections? Siete had shown no sign of detecting them either, but that was expected. He'd been told that the dogs could only detect secondary infections. Oh! Of course! He had been looking for the wrong thing. He'd assumed that human infection would produce the fermenting apples experience. In a flash, he saw that was obviously wrong. If the two infections created the same sensation, then both he and Siete would have recognised them immediately. There would be no need for the prisoner interviews at all. He should have been looking for a different smell.

In his recent interviews the only unusual smell had been a slight waft of citrus, but that had been from Ashley and her floral blouse. He'd already concluded, without careful thought, that the obnoxious Tiffy was the criminal out of that pair. Although the first two interviews hadn't produced any peculiar scents, maybe it was worth seeing all four candidates again with a focus on oranges rather than apples. He would ask Malcolm about that.

Testing the bug in his temporary possession was also something to think about. He hadn't told Chris that he had the apparatus again, because his plan was to bug her with it. That was going to need careful planning to reduce the risks to an acceptable level. Good grief! How had he come to this? Wrong question. He hadn't come to this; he had been *brought* to this by the actions of others. It was not his fault. The bugging plan must be carried through. The growing number of mysteries in his life were not of his own making, and he could not leave them without resolution. The bug could be planted easily enough, with a new battery, but if he left it for very long, Chris might find it. Actually, he couldn't leave it for very long, because Malcolm would ask for it to be returned, and even a short period of time would be a risk as he now knew that Chris possessed a bug detector. Perhaps she used it daily, for example when Paul was out with Siete. That was the one remaining problem in his plan. How could he sabotage Chris's bug detector without raising suspicion? He fell asleep trying to solve that problem.

With a start, Paul was awake. His brain must have carried on working because he saw how he could sabotage Chris's bug detector without her realising it.

Next morning Paul was in his office with his own bug detector. He turned it on in silent mode, disabled the auto turn off, and left it running. After an hour or two the battery was flat. Now all he needed was for Chris to leave the house. He was impatient to put the rest of his plan into operation, but time was passing frustratingly slowly. In desperation, Paul was forced to engage in his insurance work to help the time to pass while he waited for what he really wanted to do.

At lunch time Paul tried to spur things on, "How's your sketching coming along, Chris? Will there soon be a new entry in the art space?"

"My initial effort didn't work very well. Sketching real scenes isn't the same as copying paintings, and my first attempt was coming out all wrong. I had to abandon that one and begin again. The second try looks more promising, so far."

"I'll look forward to seeing it."

"Hopefully, you won't have to wait too long. I'll pop out this afternoon to work on it for a while."

True to her word, Chris did leave the house with her sketching equipment. As soon as she had gone, Paul fetched his bug detector and made for the bedroom. As he climbed the stairs, he was worrying that Chris might have already stymied his plan by changing the code for the wall safe. He moved the picture and held his breath as he entered 3012. It worked! There was Chris's detector, identical to his own. Well, not quite identical; his one had a flat battery. He swapped them over and closed the safe.

Back downstairs he wondered where to place the bug. Should he use the location under the desk? If Chris did sweep for bugs, he didn't think she would bother to crawl under the desk to make a physical check. Of course, she wouldn't be able to sweep for bugs at the moment - she had a flat battery. She would have to charge her detector before she could use it. Would she crawl under the desk in the meantime? Paul thought that, in the first place, it was unlikely that Chris swept for bugs every day and in the second place, if she did, and she found that her detector needed charging, she probably wouldn't immediately crawl under the desk. So that was a chain of two unlikely things. He didn't intend the bug to be in place for very long anyway, so he placed it under the desk and retreated to his office.

Paul retrieved the receiver unit from his desk drawer and connected it to his computer. He set the system to record and arranged for a visual display of the signal received to be displayed in one corner of a computer screen. During the afternoon he worked in his office, and he saw the signal change with the sound of Chris returning home. She evidently had a student scheduled, and Paul could see the audio signal of her speech as her session began. He regretted that he hadn't found a way of recording the signal she was hearing as well as the sound of her voice, but he hoped that one side of the conversation would tell him all he needed to know.

After her tutor session, Paul heard Chris working in the gym upstairs. He wasn't going to press his luck, so he slipped into the living room and quickly removed the bug. All that remained now was to listen to the recording.

Back in his office, Paul disconnected the receiver unit and placed it in his drawer, together with the bug itself. He could always explain his temporary possession of those with the same story he'd told Malcolm. The only really incriminating evidence was the recording on his computer, but there was no reason for anyone else to look at that, and he didn't intend to keep it for very long.

With his headphones on and his pulse racing, Paul listened to Chris's tutor session. It sounded as though she was speaking Russian, so he didn't understand a word of it. That didn't dismay him in the slightest as he was fully prepared for the session to be in a foreign language. He opened the translation app he had acquired, set it for Russian, and played the recording into it. As the recording played, the translation scrolled across his screen.

To begin with, the conversation sounded innocent enough. There was talk about tourist sites in London, as though Chris was advising someone about the best places to visit and helping them to plan an itinerary. Then there was one thing that struck Paul as odd. Chris was speaking about a church Paul had never heard of – 'St Hugo's at the gate.' The discussion wasn't very clear because he could only hear one side of it, but there was something about a monument to Giacomo Rucellai. The really peculiar thing was that they seemed to be talking about the size of the monument and the amount of space there was in it. If Paul had guessed correctly, they were discussing the possibility of hiding something in the monument. He couldn't fathom why anyone would want to conceal something in a church monument. Was that sinister or just weird? Either way, it didn't sound like part of an ordinary tutor session.

Chapter 23 - Assaulted

The next morning, Piers didn't arrive at the usual time. That was unheard of, he was always very punctual. There wasn't much Paul could do about it as he didn't have any method of contacting Piers directly. He could enquire through Malcolm, but that would seem excessive. Malcolm wasn't responsible for Piers' domestic arrangements, and there were any number of perfectly ordinary occurrences that could have upset Piers' schedule. Paul took Siete out for exercise on his own.

As they made for one of Siete's favourite play places, Paul was thinking about his performance as a spy. The dog kept identifying secondary infections as they went, and Paul still needed to encourage that part of the Alsatian's training, so there were the usual pauses in their journey. By this time, of course, Paul could detect the infections more quickly than Siete, and his successes didn't need the same reinforcement. Now there was an idea – a pocket of treats for himself. More seriously, it did occur to him that there might be a hitherto untapped use for his skill. So far as he knew, covert operatives sometimes used dead-letter drops to pass secret messages between them. Presumably, if the operatives were on the wrong side of the law, the drop sites were likely to be infected. Paul would now be able to 'smell' such secret locations if they were in regular use. Wouldn't that be handy?

Paul played and trained with the dog, and had forgotten about Piers' failure to arrive until, as he was setting off for home, his phone buzzed. It was Malcolm. Piers was at the local hospital, and would Paul please meet him there. Malcolm would give no details over the phone. Siete and Paul trotted home. The Alsatian would have to be left there as the hospital staff were not going to be keen to have the animal on their premises.

At the hospital, Malcolm was waiting with an explanation. Piers had been attacked in the street early that morning. He had ended up in hospital with a knife wound and a collection of other more minor injuries. There was nothing life-threatening, but he wouldn't be going home that day.

There was a great deal of waiting to be done. A nurse on reception explained that doctors and nurses were attending to Piers' wounds. After that, there were police officers waiting for interviews with Piers, and they were also intent on obtaining a DNA sample. This could all be expected to take a considerable time. Pangs of hunger drove Malcolm and Paul to go in search of hospital food while they were waiting. It was mid-afternoon before they were finally permitted to visit Piers to discover what had happened.

They soon saw that Piers wasn't a very good patient, and they found him even less good at parting with information, though Paul suspected that they were hearing more detail than he had given to the Police. They pieced together the full story from Piers's terse responses.

He'd been out early in the morning, for reasons he didn't disclose. In a quiet street, he'd been confronted by two men, who both wore hoodies and had scarves pulled across their faces. One was brandishing a knife while the other, larger man, was wielding a baseball bat. They had threatened him, and insisted on him handing over his wallet and phone. He had handed them to the batsman, really to see what they would do next. He'd been calmly assessing his predicament, and concluded that, if it came to a fight, the bat was the greatest threat. That man was big, and if he made a successful blow to Piers' head, it would likely be terminal. The knife was large, but wasn't being held in a very professional way, and its holder looked nervous. He would be hesitant in its use and, hopefully, less effective.

Piers' guess was that they would try to run with his valuables. One would be faster than the other, and that would be their vulnerability. They wouldn't expect pursuit, and he would stand a good chance of catching one of them – probably the batsman. But then he saw in the eyes of the big man, in the set of his jaw and in his firm grip of his bat, that his guess had been wrong. This man was preparing to launch an attack, and his mission was murder. What the aggressor didn't know was that Piers was already preparing to receive his attack. As he swung the bat, Piers didn't try to jump backwards or duck, as expected, to avoid the swing, and the villain's eyes flashed with surprise as Piers stepped forward inside the path of the bat. That proved to be the last surprise the attacker had before he found himself whirling round Piers' body into a sickening crunch as his head collided with the pavement. The man with the knife had been obstructed by the falling body of his companion. Unfortunately, he still had the wit to lunge with his knife, and he caught Piers with a slash to his briefly exposed side. Although the wound drew blood, it didn't seem to slow Piers' reaction. That cost the assailant a broken wrist, the loss of the knife, and a solid stamp as Piers' boot scraped down one of his shins and crushed his foot. He had retreated with a limping gate to leave Piers standing alone on the field of battle.

A passing woman had seen the end of the conflict and called 999. Piers nodded in acknowledgement to her as he kicked the weapons out of the reach of the prone man and checked him for life signs – breathing, but unresponsive. He rolled him into the recovery position, rescuing his own property in the process. Amazingly, he could already hear sirens. He sat and tried to staunch his own blood flow as he waited for rescue and, no doubt, interrogation.

Apart from the knife wound, which was a long shallow cut, Piers himself had caught a slight blow from the bat, and he had a few bruises from the flailing limbs of his attackers. The limping attacker had made good his escape, while the other one was in a coma in the Acute Assessment Unit. The latter couldn't be interviewed for obvious reasons, and the hospital staff had little idea if, or when, that state of affairs might change. The police had satisfied themselves that Piers had been the victim, not the perpetrator, of the crime. That had been fairly obvious from their observations at the scene of the crime, and Piers' story had been confirmed by the woman who had phoned for help. Piers had been able to give a description of the man who had limped off, though in the near future, his various wounds alone would mark him out as guilty.

Neither Piers nor Malcolm was able to come up with any reasonable motivation for what had happened. Piers was adamant that this was no standard mugging. He was convinced that their demands for his phone and wallet were simply to make the event look like a badly managed mugging. In reality, he was sure that assassination had been their plan from the beginning. From their point of view, they should have brought more men.

There wasn't very much more that any of them could do that day. Piers would have to stay in hospital overnight for observation, and Malcolm would need more information before he could come to a good assessment of what had happened. Piers claimed that there was nothing Paul could do to help him, so he had better go home, though Paul suspected that was because Piers really wanted to be left alone to talk with Malcolm. Paul arranged to meet with Malcolm during the next afternoon.

When Paul came to leave the hospital, he encountered a new problem. There was a police cordon at the entrance, with reporters and TV camera crews all clamouring for information. Paul retreated to find Malcolm, but he'd evaporated without trace. Paul didn't want to run the press gauntlet, so he followed signs to the maternity unit where, to his relief, he found another exit. He was in a worried state as he left the hospital. Of course, he was concerned for Piers, but he was also scared for himself. This had been an attack on somebody close to him, a man he saw every day. If Piers' impression of an intended murder was correct, were there people after him as well? He would certainly be avoiding lonely backstreets and alleyways for quite a while.

At home, Paul told Chris what had happened, and she was full of sympathy for Piers, "Paul, that's dreadful. Are the doctors sure that he's going to be okay?"

"Yes, they're only keeping him in for observation, and he's just frustrated at being cooped up."

"Should we take something for him tomorrow?"

"I did ask if he needed anything." Paul was about to add that he was sure Malcolm would take care of everything. He stopped himself just in time. Chris didn't know about Malcolm, or any connection between Michael & Co. and Piers. Paul kept on safe ground by adding, "He said that he didn't need anything, and I reckon they would need a straitjacket to keep him in beyond tomorrow, in any case. I can't imagine that he'll be here to walk Siete for a while, but I'll check up on him once he's home." That sounded like the kind of thing Chris needed to hear, though Paul had no notion how he could fulfil such a promise; he didn't know where Piers lived, and had no contact information for him. Perhaps he could sort something out with Malcolm the next day.

Chris didn't raise the question of their own safety, and she must have assumed that the event was a random mugging. Paul did nothing to change that impression. After all, so far as Chris was concerned, Piers was just a man who was good with dogs.

Paul had other issues on his mind. What was the business with St Hugo's-at-the-gate? He had plenty to keep him busy in research of that. And who was Giacomo Rucellai?

Although Paul hadn't previously heard of St Hugo's, he discovered that the church was outside the line of the ancient defensive wall of London. Having survived the great fire in 1666, it had been less fortunate during the Second World War. Nevertheless, a substantial proportion of the original building had been incorporated into the post-war rebuilding. The church was well-attended and held regular services throughout the week. Indeed, it was something of a tourist attraction because of its ancient crypt and its organ recitals. Although the building was said to contain several historically significant monuments, Paul was unable to find details of any names associated with the memorials. He did establish that the church building was open during normal office hours, and that it was even possible to book guided tours. So, despite the alarm of the day's events, he had pretty much decided that he needed to plan a visit to St Hugo's. He would like to see the monument to Giacomo Rucellai. Perhaps it would shed some light on the strange conversation between Chris and her supposed tutee.

Chapter 24 – Revelations from Piers

Piers had extracted himself from the hospital, and the only outward evidence that he had suffered from a serious assault was that he moved more cautiously than usual. He was now seated with Malcolm in the office at number 77, together with Paul, who had been provided with a third, less comfortable, chair. They were discussing the attack.

In his usual mysterious way, Malcolm had come up with more information, "The police are telling everyone that this was an attempted mugging, pure and simple. They gleefully add that the muggers met with more than they had bargained for. The press and media are practically hyperventilating with excitement over the story; they're like hyaenas fighting and squabbling to tear the last scraps from the rotting carcass of events. To begin with, they were complaining vociferously about their failure to secure photos of Piers. That was until they realised that it only added to the mystery of the whole episode."

Paul remembered the press pack at the hospital, and the headlines that were everywhere. He showed his surprise, "How did you fool them? Surely, they're bound to come up with something in the end."

"That did take some effort," replied Malcolm with a grin, "We wrapped Piers in a few more bandages than were strictly necessary, stretchered him out of A & E straight into an ambulance and took him on to another hospital. There, we unwrapped him in the ambulance and ferried him away in a car. Our drivers returned the ambulance to the original hospital. Once the journalists realised that he'd gone, they all tried to find the home address of Peter Warren – that was the name we persuaded the police to accept. We produced an address as well, and when the reporters discovered that it was a military base, they all rushed off there with their camera crews. Naturally, when they arrived, they were faced with a military guard and soon found themselves being moved on without learning anything. The story of 'muggers assaulting a mystery military ninja' will do the rounds for a few days, then it will die for lack of information."

"That's some story," Paul exclaimed, "so you won't be famous, Piers."

"That's exactly how I like it," Piers answered drily.

"Now to more serious things," Malcolm announced, "We all know that this wasn't an ordinary mugging, so I've been searching for a better story than the one the police are promulgating. There's sufficient DNA to give us a lead to the escaped mugger. Unfortunately, it doesn't tell us who he is, and it's somewhat surprising that he hasn't been found at medical facilities, looking for treatment. I suppose that shouldn't be a total surprise because his DNA links him to a group who used to smuggle weapons, drugs, and anything else they could find that was both illegal and valuable. He might prefer to suffer in secret rather than be incarcerated for the foreseeable future."

"You say, the group *used* to smuggle," said Paul.

"That's right. All the key members of that gang were arrested and are currently locked up with no release date on the horizon. Our escapee was only part of their hired help, and he wasn't caught at the time. Be that as it may, our mission for this afternoon is to attempt to make sense of what has happened. Paul, you might be wondering why you are with us. The answer is straightforward. You've been closely associated with Piers, so we want you to know anything that we know. Do feel free to chip in." Malcolm looked around expectantly, "So what do we know?"

Piers answered, "The smuggling group was known to us as FourCo, because they were sending and receiving gear across four continents – the two Americas, Europe and Africa. You'll have worked out that I was involved in an MI6 operation to catch them. Our roles were compartmentalised, so I don't know who else was on the team. What I do know is that my work with a dog was key to apprehending the whole gang."

Malcolm was acting as chairperson of the gathering, "I think that's the only, rather tenuous, connection we have.

Piers told me about it this morning, and I've made enquiries. The only information I could find that might be significant is that it has become unclear whether the whole of the FourCo operation was actually rounded up."

Piers looked puzzled, "Why, what's happened? There would have been a few underlings, like yesterday's man who escaped, but we were confident that we had scooped up all the serious players above them."

Malcolm looked thoughtful, "Yes, that is the impression that MI6 had, but more recent events have cast doubt on it. Some of the supply lines that FourCo were using still seem to be in operation, and that's making us wonder whether the top man was ever caught in the net."

"If that's all history," Paul questioned, "how would it affect us now?"

"I don't know," Malcolm answered, "but I do have a theory. If the top man is still active and is rebuilding FourCo, it occurred to me that he might try to track down some of those who brought about his fall, and he might be intent on revenge. Piers, could it have been an attempt at retribution?"

"Aye, that's not an unreasonable theory. It fits the small amount we know, and I'm coming up empty for any better idea."

"Thank you. In that case I think, to be safe, we should work on the assumption that we do have an unknown weapons and drugs lord who is looking to be avenged. I reckon we should react before anything else happens."

Piers nodded, "I would like to think that I can take care of myself, Malcolm, but realistically I have to agree with you. If revenge is the name of the game, then next time there will be more men who are better armed, or a sniper. So, what's your plan of campaign?"

Paul watched and listened as Malcolm answered, "Well, we're good at not existing, so I think it's time that we removed you from existence, Piers. Perhaps initially, we'll use the country estate and then reallocate you from there. For you, Paul, that means that Piers will drop out of your life. You could tell Christine that he's gone back to Scotland following yesterday's incident. I can't see why FourCo should be interested in you. Even so, we'll maintain a discrete presence. How does that sound?"

Paul agreed. After a short pause, Piers looked sad as he spoke, "I can't say that I'm overjoyed with the idea, but I can't disagree with your plan either so, yes, that's what we should do."

Malcolm took his role as chairperson seriously, "Any other business?"

Piers' situation had driven it out of his head, but the question reminded Paul that he did indeed have other business, and he answered, "Yes, please. I might have made some progress with the convict interviews. It's only an idea at the moment, but it might be helpful to see the first four people again. I wouldn't need extended sessions with them; a few minutes with each should be quite enough to know whether I'm on to something. Would that be possible?"

"I can't see why not," said Malcolm, "It would probably take me a couple of days to arrange. Shall we say two days' time?"

"That would be great, thank you. Let's hope it pans out."

The meeting ran to a close, and Paul said farewell to Piers as he shook him carefully by the hand, "I can't thank you enough for all that you've done for me. Siete has transformed our lives at home, and it has been a great pleasure to see you each day."

Piers had recovered his composure, "You just look after that dog properly. I may yet be seeing you around."

All that was left for Paul now, was to go home and explain the sanitised version of events to Chris. It wasn't going to be quite as simple as it had been made to sound. TV and newspaper headlines couldn't be ignored. There was the matter of the false name, not to mention the fact that Piers had successfully demolished the attack of two armed men, leaving one in a coma. His abilities might take some explaining, so Paul needed a long walk to sort all this out in his head.

Fortunately, Chris was working when he arrived home, so he just waved the dog leash and mimed that he was taking Siete out. Once out of the house again, he settled to some serious thought. Paul had seen the press scrum outside the hospital. He could tell Chris about that and say that Piers didn't want to be hounded. He could add that Piers had given a false name to put them off the scent.

Now, what about the military base that was given as an address? Perhaps he could link that with Piers' self-defence skills. Paul didn't know whether Piers had been in the armed forces or not, but he had acquitted himself with considerable skill. In any case, Paul could make up whatever he liked to account for that expertise, so long as he remembered what he had said. Neither Piers nor anyone else would be around to deny it. Okay, he would say that Piers had been in the Commandos when he was younger.

He could say truthfully that Piers had helped to bring down a gang of international drug dealers, and that some of them were looking for revenge. Consequently, Piers thought that he should make himself scarce. He had been in lodgings, so he had paid off his notice and caught the first train for Scotland, where he had discrete friends.

That was the tale he told Chris in the evening, and he rounded it off with, "Piers said to say 'Goodbye' for him and to tell you how much he has enjoyed being part of our lives." To invest it with a convincing parting shot, he added, "And he said to take good care of Siete."

Paul had thought he might have to explain how Piers could use the military base as an address, but Chris didn't ask, so he didn't need to invoke the tale of Piers having friends who remained in the armed forces. So it was that, with barely a "Fare thee well," Piers disappeared from their lives, and a beautiful Alsatian was the only lasting sign that he had ever existed.

Chapter 25 – The security advisors

Chris had finished her first teaching session of the day, and she was taking a coffee break with Paul. They were discussing the assault on Piers and bemoaning the fact of him moving away. Chris was interested in his background, "What a good thing that he was so good at self-defence! Did you know he'd been in the Commandos?"

"No, not until yesterday, when it all came out. I knew that he'd had some kind of connection with the police and the military, from his talk about training dogs for them, but he never spoke much about his past."

"The attack on Piers has brought things close to home, and it's made me think about how we would manage if it happened to one of us. What would you do, Paul?"

"I don't know. I would probably just hand everything over. Though I mostly have Siete with me when I'm out. I would think that she would make most muggers look for a different target. But never mind me, what would you do?"

"Don't worry about me. I would just run. They'd have to be amazingly fit to catch me." Paul knew that was no more than the truth though, as it turned out, he didn't know the half of it. They'd moved on to commenting on the TV reports, when the doorbell rang.

"I'll go," said Paul.

There was a man holding a warrant card on the doorstep, with a woman beside him. "Good morning, Mr Keating, I'm Detective Sergeant Pearson, and this is Detective Constable Tuli." The woman added her warrant card to the display. "May we come in?"

Paul ushered them into the living room, announcing, "It's the police, Chris." He indicated seats for their visitors before asking, "What can we do for you, officers?"

It was Pearson who answered, "D.C. Tuli and I are part of a team that specialises in home security, and we've been asked to offer advice on your security, if you would accept it."

"I take it you have come after the Piers incident," said Chris.

Paul stifled a gasp. The police had been told it was Peter, not Piers. Fortunately, it didn't cause a problem. D.S. Pearson answered, "I don't know anything about that. We were simply asked to visit you – no special reason was given. What we would like to do, if it's alright with you, is look around and make suggestions. Naturally, it would be entirely up to you to decide whether or not you wished to follow them up."

Chris and Paul readily agreed, and they toured the house with the two officers. Doors and window locks were examined and mostly pronounced to be good. That wasn't the case for the door in the kitchen, which led to the short covered area between it and Paul's office and also opened out into the garden. D.C. Tuli took the lead on that, "You might want to consider improving the locks on the kitchen door and on the door to the office. I realise that there's an issue of convenience if you're going in and out a lot, but we could leave you some information to look at."

They came to the garden gate that gave access to the path along the side of the house to the road. It was regarded with obvious dissatisfaction. "If I was you," the sergeant said, "I'd like to see a higher solid gate here with a secure locking system."

"We do have gardeners who would need access," Paul offered.

"You could give them a key, and that's the cheapest option. Alternatively, a key pad system would be better, because you wouldn't have keys passing between all and sundry, and you'd be able to change the combination regularly."

They retraced their steps back to the living room for final comments from D.S. Pearson, "Your security's generally pretty good, and your German Shepherd is a real bonus, but I would recommend an alarm system. I'd also strongly recommend reviewing your garden gate. We'll leave you information about all that and about door locks. You can study it at your leisure. If you want to go for all the bells and whistles, you could think about automatic lights outside, both front and back, and the possibility of cameras, also front and back. They don't come very cheaply, though they would enhance security. Now, before we go, do you have any questions for us?"

There was really nothing more to be said, other than the thanks and goodbyes. Chris and Paul were left to think about all the advice they had been given. Paul was dismayed at their own short-comings, "Why did it never occur to us to have an alarm system in the house? That was such an obvious thing to do, especially after the bug planting episode, but also, as I should be fully aware, we could save a little on our house insurance. We should look into that straight away."

"What about the garden gate and the door locks?"

"Let's look at the pamphlets they've left, and we'll check out more information online. We can think about our options after that."

Chapter 26 - Reflections

During the trip to revisit the convict interviews, Malcolm was eager and upbeat, "Do you really think you're in sight of success with this, Paul?"

Paul was trying to dampen the enthusiasm, "I don't know. I've had an idea, and it might work. Then again, it might not. I do think it's worth a try, but I can't say better than that." Paul turned the conversation to the matter of security, "We had the police on the doorstep yesterday, wanting to give us security advice."

"Ah, splendid! I'm glad they arrived so promptly. What did they have to say?"

"They recommended all kinds of things from a stronger gate, through alarm systems and better locks, to security cameras and automatic lights."

"In the circumstances, I'd suggest that you do everything they've recommended."

"But that would cost a fortune."

"No, it won't," Malcolm countered, "You'll shortly receive a special offer, for you personally, via your business. It will essentially offer you that complete package for the cost of just the alarm system and a new gate. The cover story will be that a startup security company would like a well-known insurance broker to be impressed with their work."

"That sounds fantastic. Thank you very much."

"It's in our interests to look after you. Your skills have enormous value, and we need to look after them. I've been trying to find ways of enhancing your security without upsetting those who have raised a red flag against Christine. The attack on Piers helps us because it gives you an obvious motive for beefing up your home security, so no Secret Service hackles should be raised."

At the interview house, Paul made arrangements with Malcolm, "I'd like to see Ashley first, followed by Pete, then Lance and finally, Tiffany. Can that be managed?"

"Yes, the house is bulging with prison officers keeping convicts in isolation, so let's do it."

Ashley was shown in, wearing an even brighter blouse than before, but with what looked like the same skirt. Paul explained that he'd like a little more information about her life as a child. As she began to speak, Paul wasn't really listening; he was trying to sense citrus. Yes, faintly, there it was. Once he had the scent, he concentrated on it and, to his delight, the smell became stronger. He smiled at his success – at entirely the wrong point during Ashley's story. "That's not funny," she snapped, "my mum was in hospital for nearly two weeks."

"No, I'm sorry, it wasn't that," Paul hastily improvised, "I was impressed by your ingenuity in progressing from that life."

She still looked annoyed, "You're forgetting that I'm in prison."

Paul was impatient to move on, so Ashley was thanked and dispatched back to her guard.

The experience had been very promising. Paul still didn't know how he sensed the citrus sensation, but he did know how to concentrate on it. He was in a state of high excitement as Pete arrived. For Pete's interview, Paul asked to be told about tales from school. As stories were told, he concentrated on the citrus scent. There was nothing. His feeling had always been that Lance was the real criminal. This was confirmation – he hoped.

As Lance entered the room, Paul began to concentrate immediately. He physically staggered as he was assaulted by an overpowering sweet smell of citrus. He didn't need, or want, any more time with Lance. He apologised for bringing Lance all this way for one brief question. Lance wasn't put out in the slightest, "Any excuse that gets me out for a bit is fine by me." Paul asked him if he was still in touch with his mother. He wasn't, and Paul sent him on his way. Definitely no hand shaking with Lance.

There had been an interesting development during that brief conversation: Paul seemed to have a volume control. When he had concentrated, the citrus sensation had strengthened, but he had also found that he could reverse the process. How useful! The final check was Tiffany.

"Hello, Tiffy, take a seat." She swore at him with abuse as she sat down. He ignored the abuse and calmly asked her about her life in the Care Home. The result was a stream of profanity about every aspect of it, the food, the staff, the other girls, and so on. Paul tuned all that out, and turned up his 'citrus volume control,' as he had already named it. There was nothing. This girl really was an actor. As she left, he shook her hand warmly, and tried to give her a knowing look. She put her tongue out, but he could have sworn that she was supressing a grin.

Paul couldn't wait to report back to Malcolm. His words gushed, "It worked! It really worked! It was better than anything I could have imagined. I can control my sensitivity! I have a volume control!"

Malcolm was smiling widely, "Slow down, Paul. I take it we're done here. You can give me full details in the car."

On the way home, Paul began to explain, "First to satisfy you, Malcolm, Lance and Ashley were the real criminals."

"That's right, Paul. Now tell me exactly what has been happening."

"It's very simple really. Human infection doesn't smell the same as the secondary infections on objects. As you know, secondary infections create an impression of fermenting apples, with a slight sense of rot and decay about it. By the way, Piers senses that as a completely different smell. Anyway, human infection is different. It's a sweet smell, like ripe oranges. That's why I didn't detect it to begin with. I was looking for the wrong thing. It also explains why your trained dogs don't detect it. They have never been trained for the smell of human infection."

"You mean that it might be possible to train dogs to detect human infection"

"I would say that's a possibility, but there's something else. Not only could I sense human infection this afternoon, I could also control my own sensitivity to it. I learnt a nasty lesson about that. When Lance came into the room, I had turned up my sensitivity to a high level without knowing what I was doing. You know the blinding flash you get if you are looking straight into a camera flash when it goes off. Well, imagine that kind of thing as a smell, except not as a brief flash; more as a rolling wave. It was like a physical attack. I don't want too much of that, so I need to spend some time practising my volume control."

"That's wonderful, Paul. I thought we were going to spend weeks or months on prisoner interviews. Your ability has obviously developed beyond anything we had wildly hoped for. Let's meet tomorrow afternoon to work out where we go from here."

After the taxi ride, Paul took Siete out for a walk straight away. He wanted to experiment with his new found skill on other people as they passed him in the street. He turned up his citrus control to 'casual interest' level rather than to 'intense concentration.' Sure enough, a significant number of pedestrians registered in his consciousness as they came close. His ability to sense the infection was most encouraging, but the number of people turning out to be infected was most discouraging. What were they all up to? He began to appreciate the enormous value of being able to turn his citrus volume to the 'off' position. Without that ability, he'd be surrounded by the smell of infection all the time. Perhaps he could find a volume control for the smell of rotting apples as well. He should definitely work on that.

Oh, no! He needed to sit down. He was feeling nauseous with understanding and apprehension. What was he going to find at home? Was Chris infected? Suspicion was one thing; certainty would be unthinkable. He was on the verge of discovering something that he might well rather not know. Suppose he found himself sleeping with the sweet smell of citrus!

As he entered the house, he carefully turned up his citrus volume. There was nothing, but Chris was out. He turned the volume up slowly to 'intense concentration.' That was beyond the level that had resulted in Lance's odorous assault. To his horror, there was the faint smell of citrus. He opened all the windows and the back door. There was no rational reason to do that, because he knew very well that the infection didn't produce a real smell, so no draughts made any difference. The smell would not be cleared by open windows. He sent Siete into the garden. The background scent was faintly present everywhere in the house. It couldn't be infected objects – that would be a smell of fermenting apples. He stepped out of the front door into the street. There was nobody in sight, yet the citrus scent was still with him. He turned his volume control down slightly and the scent disappeared. Paul went indoors to think, but he didn't like the thoughts he was having.

In the street there had been no human or animal anywhere near him, and yet he could detect citrus if he really tried. The idea of Chris being infected had been unthinkable. This might be a great deal worse. Was he himself infected? He sought comfort with the thought that he might be wrong. After all, he had only recently acquired this detection skill, and he might be receiving false readings. Then there was the faintness of the citrus sensation. Lance's infection had been overpowering. This very faint infection might be almost normal. Perhaps, it was normal. If he became sufficiently sensitive, he might find that everyone had an extremely low level of infection. Maybe there was no cause for concern. Nevertheless, he was pleased that he was meeting Malcolm again the next day, and he hoped that much-needed reassurance would be available from that quarter. Until then, he would leave his citrus control alone and think about other things.

Paul worked on his insurance broking for a while. During the course of that, he received the offer Malcolm had spoken of, the one about a comprehensive security package for an amazingly low cost. It was couched in precisely the terms that Malcolm had explained.

After the evening meal with Chris, the couple were sitting in the living room discussing their security advice. Paul explained that he had a promotional offer, from a company called Pad Safe, that looked extremely good. It meant that everything suggested by the police could be installed without vast expense. They had nothing to lose by it, because the firm were only going to take any payment at all on satisfactory completion of the whole project. Paul calmed Chris's suspicions about too much of a good thing, with talk about a startup company wanting to create a good impression in the hope of drumming up business. He pointed out that he had done exactly that to grow his own business, so it would be good to give others the same opportunity. In the end, they agreed that Paul should enquire further.

Chris wanted to discuss something else, "I was thinking it would be nice for us to go out for a show. We haven't done that for a long time."

"That would be great. I guess we could leave Siete for a few hours, if we gave her plenty of attention during the day."

"Oh, we wouldn't need to leave Siete alone. I know someone who is absolutely itching to spend time with her. In fact, we would be able to make a full evening of it."

"Who is this mystery person?"

"Zara, of course. She was totally smitten when she came here and is longing to see Siete again."

"Well, if you think she wouldn't mind. What would Crispin do?"

"Zara will certainly not mind. She'll be delighted, and Crispin is away on tour. We could buy in an evening meal for her, and she will have the time of her life."

"Okay, that sounds ideal. You ask Zara, and let's find out what shows are on."

Paul sat scrolling theatre shows on his phone and calling out suggestions, but Chris said that she had a student to deal with. She moved to her desk, where she sat with her back to the long wall of the room, at the far end from where Paul sat. It made sense to have her computer screen and camera facing the wall, so that online callers didn't have a view into the room.

Paul was still searching theatres on his phone when Chris began to speak - Arabic perhaps. He looked up at Chris briefly, then his gaze strayed along the wall. There was a framed photograph, from long ago, mounted there. It showed a golden sunset over the meadows of his grandparents' farm. From his shallow angle of view, he couldn't see the picture very well because it was masked by reflections in the glass. He idly noticed that he could see the area around Chris's work station in the reflection. If he moved his head a little, he would be able to bring the reflection of her computer screen into the middle of the picture frame. He had no great interest in her computer, it was just a simple experiment in basic science. That changed in an instant. What was going on with Chris's computer screen? Where was the tutee? He could see the screen clearly. There was no student visible on it. Surely that was one of the Windows wallpapers he could see filling the screen. Was she working without video? Was her own camera turned off as well? Why would she conduct a tutorial session without video? He couldn't ask her directly, or she would think he was checking up on her, but he did think it was odd.

Chapter 27 – What Joshua did

First thing in the morning, Paul contacted Pad Safe and made an appointment for a home visit. Then he was off to see Malcolm at number 77, where he outlined his fear of personal infection. He wasn't sure what to make of Malcolm's cheerfully enthusiastic reaction, "Congratulations, Paul, that's your greatest leap in progress to date."

Paul's face was blank with confusion, "You did hear what I said, didn't you? It's a disaster! I think I might be infected."

"Yes, I heard. That's not a disaster, it's a success."

"You really are going to have to explain that."

"Okay, Paul, it's like this. As you know, there are primary sources of infection. Humans can easily be infected by them. Apart from that, people can also infect each other to a lesser extent. The result, over the years, is that the infection has spread widely, and pretty much everyone is infected to a greater or lesser degree. You only detected your own infection when you tried hard. You will find a similar level of infection on many other people. Now that your abilities have become so very acute, I've no doubt that you would detect the faint infection on our actors, for example, as well as the strong infection on the criminals. Be that as it may, the whole business of the infection *is* a disaster of the first magnitude. However, there is a 'but.' Actually, there's more than one 'but,' though we don't need to think about more than one of them at present. The immediate information for you is that we can do something about human infection, though our procedure only works on those who understand that they are infected."

"That sounds most peculiar. Why can't you just do whatever it is to everyone? Incidentally, I hope it doesn't involve surgery."

"No, no, nothing like that, Paul. The procedure is perfectly simple and completely painless. You'll remember that the infection isn't a virus or anything of that nature. We don't truly know what it is, and all the key information we do have comes from our founder, Joshua. We know that the infection largely affects the human mind and stimulates it into all kinds of destructive thinking. Joshua understood all about it in a way that nobody else has since, and it was he who devised all the treatments we have. As far as you're concerned, we have a special plunge pool at our country estate. It's filled with water plus a combination of various salts. Don't ask me what they are. There is a recipe, though I have no notion about what it is. The point is that we can use it to remove your infection. You only have to do two things. One is to submerge yourself briefly in the pool, and the other is to mentally reject the infection as you do it. What I mean is simply that you must have in mind a desire for the infection to be removed. The combination of the pool and the thought will be effective."

"Well, I've never heard anything like that. How can it possibly work?"

"We don't know. You shouldn't be surprised about that because we don't understand the infection itself, so it would be a strange thing if we knew how the cure worked. We do know that simply jumping into the pool doesn't work. The infection works on thought processes, so perhaps it's not ridiculous that thoughts should be part of the removal procedure. You might be thinking that the thought process should be enough, but in practice it isn't. You need both the pool and the inner desire. Now, if you'd like, I can book you in for an overnight at the estate for your cure. Your cover story for Christine could be an insurance conference, and I think I can promise you a very pleasant and informative stay."

Paul paused for thought. Such was his abhorrence of the infection that his answer was never in doubt, "Yes, of course, please do." Then he continued, "You told me about Joshua early on, but at that time I didn't really absorb all the information. Perhaps there's more you can tell me now."

"Yes, surely." Malcolm went on to explain how Joshua had identified all the sources of infection, including the ultimate single source. He had always claimed that the ultimate source was too dangerous for anyone else to tackle, so he had refused to reveal its location. There have been all sorts of wild speculations that it might have arrived on earth with a meteorite or with fragments from a passing comet, but nobody really knows. This ultimate infection was capable of generating other primary infection sources, sprinkled all over the world. Again, it wasn't understood how that worked. It was as though spores were being thrown out at intervals and landing in random locations. If that was the case, the spores themselves had so far defied detection. Primary infections could have dramatic effects on humans and animals that came into contact with them. Those creatures could then pass on the infection in a lesser way. Some locations of primary infection were known. Unfortunately, there were likely to be many that hadn't been discovered. Whether or not their location was known, they were all capable of triggering evil activities."

At this point, Paul interrupted. "Do you mean this is still going on? Is there an ultimate source somewhere that is still spewing out venom? Didn't Joshua do anything about it?"

"I'm glad you raised that, Paul. Joshua did do something about it. His actions were decisive, but their results are complicated. You might have thought that the ultimate infection could be sealed in as you might seal a leaking nuclear reactor. Unfortunately, that was impossible. What was possible was to damage the source so that it would eventually stop working, and that's exactly what Joshua did. The result is that the ultimate infection now has a limited life. Regrettably, that doesn't stop it spreading its horrors as we speak. There is some good news about that. Despite the fact that the infection still spreads, its potency has also been dramatically reduced by Joshua's work, and he left us methods for sealing primary sources. If we can find them, we do know how to seal them, and that renders them impotent immediately. Joshua also left us the plunge pool arrangement for removing personal infection. I hope you can see that, although we do have a battle on our hands, we are not without weapons."

"I see, and I also understand now why you were so interested in the effect the screaming man picture had on me. The vision in my mind at that time, does match the reality you're talking about."

"Quite so. I could see then that you could become a powerful ally in our cause, though I'll gladly admit that you've been far exceeding all that I thought possible. So anyway, we'll book you in for the country estate. It's a little way south of Bedford, but we'll fix transport for you."

"That's fine, thank you." Paul wanted to mention his other progress, "I received the security advert. from Pad Safe, and I've asked for a visit. I've discussed it with Chris, and I think she'll be persuaded to go along with it."

"Ah, yes. I heard about your follow-up. There are a couple of brothers who will pop round – Matt and Mark. I think you'll like them. They are the ones who would do the work, and I'm sure they would do it well."

Yet again, Malcolm had left Paul with more than enough to be thinking about. On this occasion, Paul's thoughts were mainly happy ones. There was his enormous sense of relief that, although he was infected, it wasn't a sentence of personal doom. The prospect of a cure was most welcome, even if he would once, not very long ago, have regarded the whole procedure as being well beyond weird. After his recent experiences, his definition of weird was changing. His vision in the picture had prepared him for a complete revision of his world view. The information about Joshua, for example, would have been pure fairy tale to him a few months ago, but now he believed it without question. His new view did make sense of much that was there for all to see; much that few people thought about. And he was looking forward with anticipation to his 'conference' on the country estate.

That afternoon, Mark and Matt arrived. If Paul hadn't known they were brothers, he would still have realised within a matter of seconds. They weren't twins, but if he had been told they were, he would have accepted that too. Both were of medium height with blue eyes, shortish, light brown, curly hair, and bright smiles. "We're from Pad Safe," they announced, "Mark and Matt." They offered firm handshakes to accompany their words. Paul never did work out which was Mark and which was Matt. His vision of a sweet packet blocked all such considerations as he mentally labelled them M&M. Their Pad Safe introduction was unnecessary, since it was emblazoned across their dark blue polo tops, which went with their workmanlike black cargo trousers.

Chris was in, and available, so the four of them inspected the property before sitting in the living room for an informal meeting over coffee. Paul was delighted to see that M&M had made a favourable first impression on Chris. They oozed honesty, competence, and efficiency.

One of the M's outlined the possibilities, "The gate would be the biggest piece of work, though we could do that without affecting your routine in the house. You'd probably want to keep the dog out of the garden while we did that. Everything else would be fairly easy. There would be some electrical work. The cameras, the recorder unit and the alarm box would all need mains supplies. We don't see any great problems with that, and we'd conceal the leads, otherwise there would be a risk of malefactors trying to cut them. Not that it would do them much good because all the units work from onboard batteries; the mains only provides charging. Everything would be Bluetooth. We noticed that you have a box in the gym for your kettlebells. We'd suggest inserting a false bottom to that so that the receiver unit for the cameras could be hidden there."

Chris asked about the cost. The other M replied with a figure that matched the combined cost of a budget house alarm system and a solid garden gate. He then added, "We are not looking for any upfront payment. You just pay us the total once you're entirely happy with our work. While we're working, you're more than welcome to come and inspect what we are doing."

An agreement was made, with the unheard-of result that M&M said that they would be able to begin work on the next day. Chris was almost open-mouthed with astonishment. All those connected with any kind of trade usually suggested vague times a few months ahead. She wasn't going to argue with this offer. Paul sensed Malcolm at work, and he wasn't really surprised at all.

Chapter 28 – The memory stick

M&M were working on the garden gate. Paul caught occasional glimpses of them through his office window as he worked. Siete was lying under his desk gnawing a toy.

When he had finished the work for one of his clients, Paul thought about St Hugo's. He'd like to find the church and look for the Rucellai memorial. Taking Siete with him might not be a good idea because he wasn't sure that she would be welcome in a church. He'd have to leave her at home for several hours while he made the journey to St Hugo's and back. The obvious answer to that problem was to find a time when the dog could be left with Chris. Unfortunately, that meant he would need an excuse for his trip. More fictional clients would have to be invented, and he could say that he was planning to meet them at their office in the City. As a precaution, he'd use the Underground system rather than the buses because he felt that the Tube offered greater anonymity to cover his tracks.

Although he was confident in the honesty of M&M, Paul locked the house when he took Siete for a walk, and he left them working in the garden. Chris was already out sketching, so he chose a route that would take him along the river bank to find her. To his untrained eye this looked like a particularly good afternoon for artists. The tide was in, the sun glinted on the ripples in the water, and the buildings on the opposite bank glowed with the warm light.

There was Chris in the distance, facing down river with her back to him, and there was someone sitting near her. Paul was sure that he hadn't been spotted; the sun was behind him, and both Chris and her companion were looking the other way. He walked closer. He didn't recognise her friend, but thought she was in conversation with him. Paul preferred to remain unseen as he observed them, so he moved off the river bank and into the trees.

The man with Chris was considerably older than her. Paul was already thinking of spies and secret meetings. He was watching for a newspaper or a brown envelope to be exchanged, but he saw nothing sinister. After a few minutes, the man moved off. Paul moved in straight away and allowed Siete to approach Chris ahead of him. She said, "Hello" to the dog as she stroked Siete's head and turned to face Paul, "I didn't see you there, hello."

Paul glanced at the back of the departing man, "Who was that?"

Did he detect a hint of a delay and momentary fluster before she answered? "I've no idea. He just stopped to ask about my sketch."

Chris had covered the sketch, and Paul asked if he could see it. "Not yet," she replied, "I'd like you to see it in a finished state when it's as good as I can make it. That won't be long now, and then you can take a proper look. I might even finish this afternoon if I stay on for another hour or so."

"Okay, then. I'll see you later. Hopefully, your sketch will be in the art space."

Paul took Siete away from the river bank and headed back the way they had come, in the direction of the Leisure Centre. His failure to spot any espionage at the river had reminded him about his dead-letter box idea. If Chris was exchanging any physical materials secretly, there might be a dead drop on the route between their home and the Leisure Centre. Paul resolved to search the route straight away while he knew where Chris was.

At the Leisure Centre, Paul engaged his infection sensors for the fermenting apples effect. Following his discovery of a sensitivity control for the citrus sensation, he'd found a similar one for secondary infections. Siete had no such control, so her stops for detection always punctuated their outings. On this occasion, the pair of them walked with sensors aquiver. At each pause for detection Paul examined the area for any signs of a space where objects, or messages, could be secreted. Waste bins were a common source of infection. The design of modern bins didn't make for a natural hiding place, and Paul had no intention of trying to rummage through them by reaching through the slot intended for posting rubbish. No self-respecting spy would leave things actually buried in a bin, would they? He did check the area around the bins. The route took them close to the local war memorial, where there was a patch of lawn and a wooden seat.

The seat itself was infected, so Paul sat on it facing the memorial with its wreath and the few poppy crosses that were always there. He tried to be surreptitious as he felt under the seat. "Yuk! Bad idea," he thought as his hand encountered sticky goo and grime. However, there was something else there - small and hard, and stuck with blu-tac or similar. He retrieved a small memory stick. It was one that would slot into his phone, and he nearly plugged it in without thinking, but there was a problem to think about. Was he ready to attach an unknown device to his phone? Would it contain malware and cause serious problems? On the other hand, if he took the device away, would someone come looking for it? He looked around furtively. Had he been observed at the seat? The longer he stayed there, the more likely he was to be observed, so he stood up and walked towards home. There'd been quite enough excitement on this walk, and his only thought was to reach the safety of his office, with the memory stick in his pocket. He would examine it on an isolated computer and then decide whether to return it to its location under the seat.

In Paul's office there was a laptop that he kept offline. It wasn't in electronic contact with any of his other devices, so he plugged in the memory stick. As far as he could determine, there was no malware and no encryption; it only contained a set of documents. He began to read. They contained lists. Each item in the list was labelled, but each label was followed by a paragraph of code. Paul couldn't begin to decipher the information in the paragraphs, though the labels themselves were enough to be troubling without looking any further. C-4, M112, PE-4 and M183 all stood out as recurring labels. Paul recognised C-4, and soon established that the other three also referred to high explosives. The memory stick must contain information about explosive materials. Whether it said who had them, where to get them, how to use them or something else, really didn't matter; this was serious stuff. Judging by its hidden location, it was almost certainly connected to something highly illegal.

What should he do with his find? If he took it to the police, they would want to know who he was and how he had come by it. If the information on the stick was as serious as he imagined, an enquiry would be launched. His own recent activities might not stand up to a police investigation. Worse than that, Chris might well be investigated too. He didn't want that for fear of what might be found, though he desperately hoped she wasn't guilty of anything. Finding the device on Chris's route to the Leisure Centre didn't constitute a real reason for thinking it was anything to do with her. At least, that would have been true if it were not for the host of other events that raised doubts.

Dead-letter boxes had to be very rare. Even with his enhanced detection methods, the probability of him locating one must be microscopic. Given that he *had* discovered one, the chances of it not being linked to his existing suspicions were equally miniscule. Nevertheless, what he'd found could be a matter of national security. He couldn't do nothing, but he was struggling to think of any course of action that wouldn't create a trail back to him. Anywhere he tried to hand it in, his details would be requested. Even if he avoided that, he might be recognised, and there were the almost ubiquitous video cameras that would capture his image and enable his movements to be tracked. He wished that he had never looked for a dead drop!

In the end, he decided to wipe the memory stick of fingerprints and to post it anonymously to MI5, including a note with the location of the local war memorial where it had been found, together with the suggestion that the contents might have security implications. In his paranoia, Paul wore gloves for the whole procedure. He hoped there was no truth in reports that he might be traced through glove prints. Paul kept a copy of the files he'd found, with the idea of giving it to Malcolm. Then he breathed a huge sigh of relief as he rested more easily in the conviction that he was performing his public duty without drawing attention to either himself or Chris.

Chapter 29 – Under attack

Paul's schedule for the day was a busy one, the first appointment being a hurriedly arranged meeting with Malcolm. Paul produced his copy of the files on the memory stick he'd found and gave a redacted version of how he'd found it. He made no mention of searching for a dead-letter box. Instead, he explained that Siete and he had been practising their combined skills in the detection of secondary infections. In the course of that, the USB stick had come to light under the bench at the war memorial. Paul explained how worried he had been when he found all the coded material and the apparent mention of explosives. Malcolm was pleased with the find, "That's good work, Paul. I'll ensure that the information reaches the right quarters straight away, and I'm sure that the coded material will reveal all its secrets to our cyber sleuths, in short order."

That was really the whole business of the meeting. Malcolm's response added to Paul's relief that he'd dealt with the matter well. Malcolm confirmed that all was in place for Paul's brief stay at the country estate. In that connection, he also mentioned that two other Spotters, Gabrielle and Stephen, would be there for the removal of their infection.

The next mission of the day was to investigate St Hugo's. Chris had happily agreed to stay with Siete for the rest of the day. The condition was that Paul should be home in good time for their evening out, when Zara would take over the dog sitting.

Paul took the Tube, as planned. After only one change of trains, he was in the vicinity of the ancient London walls. He knew that the area had an unsavoury history. In times past, it had been a place to be avoided by the upper classes, but now the reverse was true; the upper classes were falling over themselves to move in. A short walk brought him to St Hugo's and its surrounding graveyard. The church building was open to visitors though, contrary to expectation, Paul found himself with only a couple of other people inside. One was an elderly lady praying in a pew near the front, and the other was a youngish man lighting a candle in front of a statue, which might have been of St Hugo himself for all Paul knew.

The church was large, in Paul's limited experience. He took it all in from a stand point at the back, beneath the tower and steeple. There were many rows of wooden pews in front of him. Beyond those was a raised area with choir stalls and an altar covered with an ornate green cloth. The main seating area of pews was flanked by stone columns. Between the columns and the external walls there were side aisles without seats. In these side aisles there was an abundance of monuments and memorials on the walls of the building and in the spaces between the columns. Paul's search for Giacomo Rucellai could take quite a while. As he looked more carefully, Paul could see even more memorials around him, under the tower, as well as in the distance behind the choir stalls.

Paul looked briefly along the aisle to his left and saw that it was terminated at the front of the building by the decorated pipes of an organ. When he looked down the right-hand aisle, he saw that it led to a carved wooden screen with a central open gate. Beyond the gate was a chapel area, where there was a second altar with a flickering oil lamp hanging over it. Paul decided to begin his search on this side of the building. Many of the inscriptions were a mystery to him. The only Latin he knew was 'Veni, vidi, vici,' and he wasn't too sure what that meant. Actually, if he was being pedantic, he had also come across 'QED,' which some of his maths lecturers had written with a triumphant flourish at the end of their mathematical proofs. He knew that it stood for something in Latin, but could only remember the student translation of 'Quite Easily Done.' Neither of these phrases appeared on the memorials, but fortunately the names of those commemorated could usually be spotted without the need to translate the rest of the writing.

All concerns about the difficulty of finding the relevant monument proved to be unfounded. His search was rewarded when he was only half-way along the aisle. His objective was on the outer wall where, for Paul, the air was heavy with the scent of rotting apples. A particularly impressive 3D sculpture contained the name he was looking for, and Paul's infection senses announced that someone had already been there experimenting with malicious intent. The memorial was in the shape of a large stone arch defining a room or chapel where a carved man, presumably Giacomo Rucellai, was kneeling at a prayer desk. The floor area within the monument was at shoulder height, and it projected from the wall sufficiently to create a space behind the stone of the prayer desk. Paul reached into it. There was plenty of room to hide something in the monument if that was what Chris's tutee was planning. Nobody would ever reach in to check, except that was exactly what Paul was doing now. He realised that he might be committing sacrilege and hastily withdrew his hand. Too late! He had been spotted. He turned to find that a teenaged girl was studying him. She gave him an evil look and ran for the exit to the building. There was nothing reverent about her actions. As she ran, she was calling loudly for Oleg and Yuri to come.

In alarm, Paul hunted frantically for somewhere to hide. In his search for concealment, he hurried through the wooden gate to the side chapel. There was a space behind the altar, and it might be better than nothing. As he crouched down there, he saw that it would be possible to crawl under the altar cloth and into the altar itself. He promptly did so and laid himself down. Once he had arranged himself in comparative comfort, he tried to calm his heavy breathing and think. This was an absurd thing to be doing. A few moments ago, he'd been an innocent tourist – almost. Now look at him! If anyone did find him here, he shuddered to think what might happen. In the event, he was right to hide; that girl had been calling Russian names, and the look she'd given him suggested the possibility of violence if her men found him. The church was empty by this time, so there would be no-one to witness his fate. He dared not try to leave; the risk of encountering Oleg and Yuri was too great.

The building wasn't quiet for long. The girl had returned with both men, as he could tell from the footsteps and the raised voices. She must be showing them where he had been. The men began to search the church. Paul was rigid with fear as one man entered the chapel where he was concealed. He closed his eyes and held his breath as he prayed. Holding his breath was a mistake, he was going to have to breathe, and his next breath was now bound to be a gasp. How long would it be before he was forced to give himself away with a gasping breath as an alternative to passing out? The searcher approached the altar, and Paul could see his dirty trainers under the hem of the altar cloth. The man was moving round to look behind the altar. He would only need to lift the cloth a little for Paul to be revealed. Not only that, Paul was going to have to take a noisy breath very soon, and it would certainly give him away.

Something distracted the searcher, and he hurried away from the altar. Paul could breathe again as he heard more feet entering the building. The addition of low voices suggested that it must be time for a service, so the searchers would have to give up in the face of a growing congregation. They weren't the only ones with problems! If Paul didn't move soon, he would be trapped. How long did services last? Discovery still didn't bear thinking about, and nor did the excuse he would have to come up with if he was late home – "Well dear, I was laying under the altar of a church during a service." There was no part of the truth that he could tell Chris. After all, he was supposed to be meeting clients in an office. Sliding out from under the altar Paul gained the safety of the side chapel. It would still be a great risk to try leaving the church on his own; Oleg and Yuri might be waiting outside with evil intent. His best option was to leave with the congregation, but when would that be? He dusted himself down, silently blessing the conscientious church cleaner who had swept under the altar as well as round it. In the main part of the church, Paul took an empty space in a pew and glanced at his watch. He would be okay for 45 minutes or so, but much longer than that and his evening would be doomed.

A few minutes later a priest and his assistant entered and stood behind the altar. Everyone came to their feet, and the service began. Paul was entirely unfamiliar with the proceedings, but he copied the rest of the congregation as best he could. There was some standing, sitting, and kneeling, at various points. That was easy. On the other hand, people sometimes crossed themselves, and he couldn't get the hang of that. Incense was being wafted by the priest's acolyte as the priest himself read from the Bible and arranged wine and wafers on the altar. Things were progressing with merciful speed. There were no hymns, and before long, everyone processed to the priest at the front to have a wafer dipped in wine placed in their open mouth. Paul spotted just in time that one was supposed to bow or nod to the altar on leaving and re-entering the pews. After not much more than half an hour, Paul was able to leave with the congregation. He could see no sign of hostile Russians outside, so he walked briskly to the Tube station and safety.

All was well on the home front. Zara arrived with obvious enthusiasm at the prospect of spending time with Siete. Paul and Chris left her with food supplies for the evening. Their plan was to take the Tube to Waterloo for a performance of 'Witness for the Prosecution' at the former London County Hall. Chris never seemed to carry anything that wasn't strictly necessary, and Paul didn't think she even possessed high-heeled shoes. They walked the streets, free of encumbrances, arm in arm. The whole area around the London Eye was a glow of light and colour, and they found the Jubilee Gardens were alive with couples and groups laughing and chatting as they enjoyed the warm evening. Chris had booked a table for them at an Italian restaurant close to County Hall, and after a splendid meal of Pollo Madeira, they were ready to take their seats in the former London Council chamber.

The auditorium for the play was as much of an experience as the play itself. The seats were virtually armchairs, so Chris and Paul sat in comfort, and imagined themselves as members of the council that had debated and made their decisions in that very place until they were disbanded nearly 40 years previously. The chamber made a splendid setting for the court-based drama that unfolded.

The evening was thoroughly enjoyable right up until the time, late at night, when the couple were almost home. They were using a pedestrian shortcut between houses when they heard footsteps behind them and saw a stocky man with a large, ugly knife step out of the shadows in front of them.

He pointed the knife in threat as he spoke, "You're gonna need to come ...." He didn't finish the sentence.

Paul never could work out precisely what happened next. There was a blur of movement beside him as Chris launched herself. Before he could focus properly, she had performed a somersault and was standing facing him. Their assailant was on his back with his knife arm held in a lock with Chris's leg, and he heard a crack accompanied by an agonised cry. Was that a breaking bone? The knife was on the ground. Chris released her victim and kicked the knife out of reach. Paul turned, expecting to find accomplices behind him, but he could only hear running feet; the alley itself was empty. Despite the fact that he was beginning to feel light-headed, he managed to say, "We should call the police." He looked back at Chris. She was already on the phone.

Paul sat on someone's garden wall to recover. It seemed to him as though only seconds had passed before three men in uniformly dark clothing arrived. They silently removed the prone man and his knife, leaving Paul and Chris alone in the silence of the dark alley. "We should get back to relieve Zara," Chris said in a matter-of-fact tone.

Paul rose unsteadily to his feet. "What just happened there and where did that Ninja stuff come from?"

"We'll talk about that later," Chris replied as she took him by the arm, "Let's get home first."

At home, Chris spoke with Zara and told her briefly what had occurred. The two women were full of sympathy for Paul, who remained traumatised. He was vaguely aware that the two of them didn't seem enormously disturbed by the incident. Chris was certainly not in the state of shock that he was experiencing.

By the time Zara left, Paul was beginning to think more clearly, though physically he was still trembling all over. Chris sat with her arm around him and he sought additional comfort from Siete sitting between his legs with her head on his knee. As he ruffled her head and ears, he was replaying the assault over and over in his mind. Eventually, he asked, "How did you do that Chris? Did you break his arm?"

"I simply put him out of action. When I've been at the Leisure Centre, I've been taking some self-defence classes, as well as swimming. It's all a matter of practice and confidence. You get to the stage where response to attack is almost a reflex action. I just did what I'd been practising, and fortunately, it worked."

"It was stunning. I was just frozen to the spot. I can't get over what you did."

"Perhaps you need some lessons too. I could fix it with Zara. She's my instructor."

Paul didn't sleep that night. He knew a cover story when he heard one. He should do by now because he'd produced enough of them himself. Chris's efficient gymnastics in disarming their attacker was not the product of a few self-defence lessons at the Leisure Centre. What she had done could only be the result of years of high-level training. Clearly there was truth in the claim that Zara could give instruction in self-defence, but why did that information not appear on her website? Regardless of that, it might be a good idea to take up the offer of lessons from her. Paul remembered his first impression when he'd seen Chris and Zara together. "They were a formidable pair," had been his initial thought. Now he realised what an under estimate that was turning out to be. The two of them had made every effort to comfort him after the assault. The mere fact that they had taken everything in their stride and were in a position to offer comfort was itself quite worrying.

Then there was the issue of the police response. How did they arrive on the scene so quickly? It was odd that the police hadn't escorted them home to conduct interviews. Would the police arrive first thing in the morning? Were the men who had arrived actually policemen at all? Their dark clothing matched his image of an armed response unit, but there had been no 'Police' signs on their jackets.

Chapter 30 – New friends

The police did arrive in the morning. A female sergeant and her male assistant took statements from Chris and Paul. Paul went along with the story that Chris had been taking self-defence lessons and had used her training to incapacitate their assailant. There was no mention by the police officers of anyone's arm being broken in the process, so Paul and Chris didn't allude to it either. The visit only took about 30 minutes, and it gave every impression of being a box-ticking exercise.

This was the day for Paul to visit Malcolm's country estate, and he was taking Siete with him. The alternative was that Chris would have to take the dog for walks. Although she'd been with Paul and Siete together, she still didn't know about the infection or the Alsatian's detecting abilities. When Siete stopped periodically, Chris was left under the impression that this was the normal behaviour of a dog finding an interesting smell. She'd interpreted the reinforcement of Siete's behaviour as encouragement for the animal to move on. Paul couldn't leave Chris to exercise the dog herself. For one thing, she might realise that something unusual was going on, but she would also fail to deliver the appropriate reinforcing approval of Siete's performance. In short, the dog would have to go with Paul. He'd explained that by pointing out that he evidently needed the protection of a dog more than she did, given her Samurai skills and a home that now bristled with security features.

An unmarked car arrived promptly at 9.30 a.m. for 'Mr Keating and dog.' Paul picked up one overnight bag for himself and another for Siete. They both set off in style for a new adventure.

The car skirted the centre of London and crossed the Thames via the Blackwall tunnel, before continuing north to join the dreaded M25 motorway. After a short westerly interlude, they could again travel north on the M1. Both motorways were free-running, which their driver thought could only be due to divine intervention. Within a couple of hours, they had passed signs for Milton Keynes and were turning off on to country roads. Before long, they were driving through elaborate guarded gates to follow a long drive, in parkland, to a large mansion, where Malcolm was waiting to greet them, "Welcome to our country estate. I trust you had a pleasant journey. Let me show you to your room, and then I'll introduce you to our other guests."

Paul and Siete followed Malcolm from the cavernous entrance hall up the grand staircase. The place was like a palace, and Paul was feeling distinctly regal when Malcolm opened the door to a vast ensuite bedroom, which featured a large four poster bed, complete with deep red curtains. There was also the most luxurious dog bed he had ever seen. Malcolm showed them the bathroom and explained the emergency procedures. Then he took them back downstairs to a huge lounge.

The focus of the room was an enormous fireplace decorated for the summer with a single large log. Well-padded easy chairs and sofas were placed in groups round low tables, and two of the chairs were occupied by a man and woman of about Paul's age. On the table beside them there were glasses of drink, and an Alsatian was lying on the floor in front of them. All three of them rose as Malcolm began the introductions, "Paul, this is Gabrielle and Stephen."

Hands were shaken all round, with Gabrielle announcing herself as Ellie and Stephen shortening his name to Steve. The two dogs made a remarkably restrained doggy greeting and soon seemed to satisfy themselves that friendly relations were in order. It occurred to Paul that the animals might have met before. Malcolm directed Paul to a table of drinks and nibbles, at the side of the room, before leaving the trio to chat. Paul helped himself to apple juice and crisps, before joining the others. The three of them sat down, with their two dogs lying side by side in the middle of the group.

Ellie's neck-length, brown hair framed her round face. Her radiant smile was one of delight, and the round frames of her spectacles could do nothing to conceal the welcome in her hazel eyes. Steve had the kind of golden skin that one might associate with life in a Mediterranean country. His brown eyes and dark, curly hair completed the impression. Like Ellie, he radiated uninhibited pleasure at meeting his fellow guest.

Ellie and Steve had a great deal in common with Paul, but a major difference was that they worked together, so Paul explained that, in contrast, Chris wasn't even aware of his work for Michael & Co. Steve and Ellie rapidly covered their evident surprise and spoke of the way they had found Michael & Co. in Birmingham. They were both part-time solicitors, and in search of something more, they'd been together when they investigated the small notice on a maroon door, numbered 77, just like the one Paul had found. Their contact person, Sania, performed the same function for them as Malcolm did for Paul. Like Malcolm, she was staying overnight at the country estate.

Paul remembered his early meeting with the stranger at the park bench and told them about it, "When I was thinking about investigating Michael & Co., I had a peculiar encounter in the local park. A total stranger initiated a conversation, and he almost seemed to be threatening me with the dire consequences of making hasty decisions."

"I believe that something like that's quite common." Ellie spoke in a soft voice with just a hint of a French accent, "Our experience wasn't quite like yours. In the early days, various casual acquaintances made suggestions that we were keeping secrets from each other. It felt like an organised crusade to drive us apart. Fortunately, we told each other what had been said and immediately established that nonsense was being pedalled. We had the distinct impression that there was a co-ordinated, but very subtle campaign to stop us working for Michael & Co. Obviously, it didn't work."

"Do you think there was any sinister intelligence behind that? Could the infection be capable of evil planning?" Paul enquired.

"We wondered the same thing," Steve responded, "and we asked Sania about it. Her comment was that it was a serious possibility. There was plenty of circumstantial evidence in support of the notion, but she'd never been able to reach a definitive conclusion."

"Well, after the stranger at the bench," Paul added, "I've been surrounded by physical aggression. Our house was bugged, our dog trainer was attacked in the street, and only last night Chris and I were faced with a knife-wielding mugger on our way home from the theatre."

Ellie was a picture of concern, "That's awful! What happened?"

"Well, it turned out that, unbeknown to me, my wife is a secret Ninja. Though she was unarmed, she flew at the guy with the knife and gave him a serious beating. I think she broke his arm. We reckon he had some friends coming to help him. They ran off when they saw what had happened."

Steve and Ellie both looked thunderstruck. "That's a horrible experience," Steve said, "what a mercy you weren't hurt! We've never had anything like that. The only opposition we've found has been in the form of sly comments, nothing remotely physical."

"Yes, Malcolm's been puzzled by the things that have been going on as well. Actually, I haven't been able to tell him yet about last night."

Ellie smiled wryly, "If he's anything like Sania, he already knows. Sania always knows everything."

"Yes, you're probably right, Ellie, Malcolm is like that too."

The three of them discussed their dogs. Steve and Ellie had a male German Shepherd called Doce. They had come to delight in their dog, just as Paul loved Siete. On one occasion, Doce had found a gun that had been used in a bank robbery. The police had been full of appreciation for the amount of work that had saved them. Fortunately, they never questioned why the dog had persisted in searching through a large pile of rubbish until he found the weapon.

Paul envied Steve and Ellie. The only secret they had to keep was their work with Michael & Co., whereas he was keeping a multitude of additional secrets from everyone he knew. He longed to be free of that burden, but he could see no way of escape.

Five heads turned and two sets of ears pricked up as the lounge door opened. A middle-aged woman, wearing a golden sari, spoke from the doorway, "Hello, Paul, I'm Sania – Gabrielle and Stephen's contact." She spoke with the careful precision one might expect from a voice coach or a news reader. "Would you all like to come through for lunch. Do bring the dogs, we have water available for them and a space they can explore." As she turned to lead the way, Paul could see that her black hair was woven into a thick plait that hung down between her shoulder blades.

A sumptuous buffet lunch was laid out in the dining room, where French windows opened out on to an enclosed garden consisting of a large lawn edged with shrubs. It was sprinkled with dog toys and with paths that invited canine investigation. The dogs were released into it, and they both scampered off without hesitation.

Over lunch, Ellie, Steve and Paul continued to discuss their experiences with the infection. They soon found that the fermenting apple and citrus sensations were factors in common. Like Paul, Steve and Ellie had interviewed convicts to develop their ability to detect human infection. Their training was more efficient in that respect because the two of them could interview one convict - or actor. They reported the experience of interviewing an attractive young woman who became totally repulsive as soon as she opened her mouth. They were absolutely convinced that she was a drug dealer and had been celebrating the fact that she was in prison. Once they were able to detect the citrus, they were gob-smacked to discover that she was one of the actors.

Paul was intrigued, "I had one exactly like that. A fair-haired girl called Tiffany."

Ellie became animated, “That’s her! We saw the same person! What an actor she was!”

“She certainly had me fooled,” Paul answered.

After lunch, they were all invited to explore the estate with their dogs. For once, they could be assured that there would be no infections for the dogs to detect, so they could simply enjoy the environment. They were to meet back in the lounge for afternoon tea when information would be given about the rest of the day.

Chapter 31 – The plunge pool

After a wonderful afternoon with Siete running free in the parkland surrounding the house, Paul made a resolution – he would raise his level of fitness. An easy way to do that would be to jog when he took Siete out for exercise. He envisaged that a fringe benefit might be that they wouldn't need to stop every time they passed an infection.

On his return to the mansion, the Alsatian was released into the garden, and Paul headed to the lounge for tea. Sania and Malcolm were already there in conversation. As Paul was helping himself to tea and a plate of sandwiches Ellie and Steve arrived to join the group.

Once everyone had moved on from sandwiches to cake, Sania called for order, "I assume you would all like to know the programme for the evening." There were three nods of agreement. "Well, as we speak, the plunge pool is being heated for you. There is no reason why your dip should be uncomfortable, so we have been spending the day warming it up to a pleasant temperature. It should be ready for us in an hour or so. The procedure in the pool is quite straight forward. You can wear a swimsuit or any clothes that you don't mind becoming wet. The pool area will have plenty of towels, and there are also changing cubicles."

"The pool itself is over 2 metres deep, but there are handholds, so there is no need for concern if you are not confident with swimming. All you will need to do is to lower yourself into the water so that you are fully immersed for a couple of seconds. If you are using the handholds, that means holding on to the ones below the level of the water. For the procedure to be successful you must desire the infection to be removed. That works a little like throwing a coin into a well and making a wish, though in this case you are the coin. As you duck under the water you must wish for the infection to be removed. The combination of your thoughts with Joshua's concoction in the water will be effective. You may be reassured that the water itself is harmless to your body, and it will not damage any clothing you wear. I do not recommend that you drink the water, but it will not cause any harm if you do. Are there any questions about all that?"

Steve replied, "That all sounds straightforward enough."

Sania continued, "After the pool, you will have time to change for dinner and, what we hope will be, a very pleasant evening together. Tomorrow morning after breakfast, your drivers will be ready to take you home. Now, before all that, we have some time now to talk about primary infections. Malcolm, would you like to explain?"

Malcolm nodded, "Yes, thank you Sania. As you know, there are primary sources of infection scattered across this country and over the whole world. Where they're active they can infect humans and even animals. The infection operates to distort thought processes, and it may cause those who are strongly infected to engage in highly antisocial behaviour. Our first problem is to find the primary sources. We'll be able to take you to some that we already know of. Naturally, they have been neutralised, which will make them harder to detect, but we believe that with your experience so far, you'll still learn to detect them. Once you're able to detect those sources, you'll obviously be able to find the locations of others that we haven't yet identified. Clearly, it would be most inefficient to have you roaming the whole country in your search for new sources. Instead, we'll try to narrow down the field of investigation. We hope to do that by concentrating on small areas that are hotspots of crime and antisocial behaviour. There are almost certain to be primary sources in those districts. Given that an active source will be easy for you to detect, in comparison with the neutralised ones you will have practised on, we are confident of success."

Paul could see a problem with this, "If these primary sources are as infectious as you say, Malcolm, won't we become reinfected by approaching them?"

"That's a good question, Paul, and I'm pleased to assure you that, no, you won't be infected again. Today's pool dip offers a high degree of immunity. Having said that, I'm afraid there is a different problem. Although you should be able to detect and neutralise primary sources, that's going to be an unending task. You might think that eventually we could find all of them, but unfortunately new ones are cropping up all the time."

Steve was indicating a wish to speak and did so when Malcolm made a gesture of invitation, "So, for all our efforts, do we actually end up achieving anything?"

"Oh yes, Stephen, indeed we do. Every source neutralised will effectively prevent an enormous amount of damage being done to people, property and to society as a whole. It's disappointing that we won't be able to stop all bad things from happening, but we will prevent many of them, so we will do a great deal of good."

Ellie had a question, "Once we have identified a source, how do we neutralise it?"

"That is simplicity itself. We use a more concentrated form of the solution in the pool that you're about to use. All we have to do is to spray the infected area. You'll know when that's been successful, because the smell that you sense will quickly die down to the low level expected from a neutralised source."

Malcolm turned to Sania and she took charge again. "If everyone is happy, please collect anything you need, and we will meet in the entrance hall."

After a few minutes they were all gathered, and Sania led them to a door beneath the grand staircase, where a flight of simple stone steps led down to the basement. The air became warm and humid as they descended to a circular pool of water that glowed orange from the lights beneath its surface. The pool itself was about 3 metres across, and the stone circle surrounding it was broken only by steps, with a handrail, leading into the water. Ellie, Steve and Paul used the changing cubicles, and the three of them emerged in swimming costumes. They made an informal queue at the steps with Ellie in front.

Sania gave the final instructions, "One at a time please, as soon as you are ready."

Ellie lost no time in descending a couple of steps and then jumping into the water. "Hey, this is great! It's like a spa bath," she exclaimed. With that she dived under the water to resurface a few seconds later and to climb out of the pool, dripping. She wrapped herself in the towel that Sania was holding.

Steve was next and he, like Ellie, was superbly confident in the water. Paul was quite pleased to be going last while the others would be too busy drying themselves to inspect his performance.

Once Steve was clear of the water, Paul used all the steps to enter the pool. He didn't need to use the hand holds, but he did want to hold his nose and close his eyes as he ducked under the water. Beneath the surface he remembered to wish himself uninfected before bobbing back up and climbing out of the pool into the waiting towel. In the water he had felt a slight tingle as though something was happening to him, although, with the heightened emotions of the occasion, that could have been pure imagination, or perhaps it was just the salts in the water.

Michael & Co. hadn't stinted on the evening meal. The dogs had already been fed, and they were happily relaxed in the lights and the warm evening air of the garden. The humans were seated in candlelight, that produced flickering reflections in the polished wood of the circular dining table, while serving staff, in black and white uniforms, catered to their every need. The meal was standard English fare of roast beef, but there was nothing standard about the way this meat had been prepared. It came in thick, medium roasted slices that melted in the mouth. Paul had no clue about how they achieved such a texture with beef - the effect was superb.

During the meal, Paul reflected that it had only been the previous evening when he'd sat with Chris in the Italian restaurant on the South Bank. As wine and happy conversation flowed now, he observed the contented couple on his left and Malcolm, as he chatted with Sania, to his right. He was immensely reassured to know that such people were his colleagues, but at the same time there was a great ache in his heart. How he wished that Chris could be sharing in this evening with him.

Lying in his four-poster bed that night Paul reviewed his day. It had been a lavish experience. Why had Michael & Co. gone to so much trouble and expense? It was true that he would return home with a spring in his step. Secretive though the organisation may be, he was now even more impressed that here was a group with power and influence. Perhaps that was the point. His stay had been designed to give a glimpse of effortless competence and clout. He would leave knowing that he could do some serious good in the world, and that he would be supported with strength and authority.

In the morning, Paul left Sania with a warm handshake. Looking her in the eyes he saw there, behind a reserved exterior, a friend who would assume a casual mantle of effective command in any situation and who would always have his back. There was a group hug of farewell with Steve and Ellie. In less than a day he'd developed a strong bond with this couple. Their common cause and experience would keep that bond alive, even if he didn't see them again for decades. Malcolm joined Paul and Siete for the ride home.

Chapter 32 – Disaster in Acton

On the next day, Paul was planning to visit his first neutralised source of primary infection.

During the journey home from his 'baptism,' Malcolm had informed Paul about the Aldgate Pump. For centuries, this ancient water supply had been an informal marker for the beginning of the East End of London, an area that had been a hotspot for crime, degradation, and disease in olden times. The pump itself had been identified as both a primary source of infection and as one of the underlying causes of all the historic problems. It had been neutralised many years previously, but it would be a good place for Paul to begin his efforts to sense primary infections.

Paul had been hard at work in the afternoon after he had returned home from his 'conference' and again on the following morning. By lunchtime, he was keen to visit the Aldgate Pump. Siete was always eager for an outing, and the two of them set off together in the afternoon. They travelled using buses, so as to avoid problems with a German Shepherd using the escalators of the Underground system. At the end of their bus rides, they were close to the pump. After only a couple of minutes' walk from the bus stop, there it was – a decorated stone obelisk on the pavement in front of a Co-op. The column itself was only 3 or 4 metres tall, although an iron lantern structure on top added another couple of metres to the height. Set into the side of the stonework was a disused metal water spout in the form of a wolf's head.

After a cursory inspection Paul tried sensing for citrus in the way that he would for human infection. This met with some success. The wolf's head was the source, but it wasn't only citrus he could smell; there were other scents in the background. He tried to concentrate on those background smells and that was like changing from spotlights on one small part of a stage to floodlights illuminating the whole set. With growing intensity, the citrus odour was surrounded by the gorgeously intense aroma of a whole basket of ripe fruit.

There was an almost irresistible cocktail of rich, sweet, intoxicating perfume, and Paul felt drawn into its inviting embrace. He would not succumb, guessing that the arms of that embrace were as malevolent as they were sweet.

That had been easy, and now that his senses were tuned-in, he wondered how far away he could walk without losing the effect. He walked along Aldgate and found that he could still detect the scent at the Tube station, which had to be the best part of 200 metres away. That was most encouraging. If he could locate a neutralised source from 200 metres, he would surely be able to find an open source from a very satisfying distance. In fact, he had better practise the adjustment of his sensitivity. Failing that ability, he might well pass out if he came close to an active primary source. Paul spent about forty minutes in experimentation with distance and sensitivity before catching the bus towards home.

There were a few days before Paul's next scheduled meeting with Malcolm. He used the time to bring his insurance business up to date. Chris asked perfunctory questions about his day away, clearly expecting no real content to his answers beyond an opinion about the food and accommodation. Happily, for Paul, she seemed to assume that the rest was boring insurance stuff. Paul thought it wise not to mention the four-poster bed or the candlelit dinner.

Finally, at number 77, Paul reported on how easy it had been to detect the primary infection at Aldgate and said that he was keen to detect and seal new sources. Malcolm was equally enthusiastic, especially when Paul added that he might be able to detect active sources from as much as a kilometre's distance. "In that case," he suggested, "I do have a possible source for you to take a shot at. Recent reports suggest that there might be an infection somewhere between Acton and Ealing Common. Do you fancy trying to find it and neutralise it?"

"I certainly do. What's the spray gear like?"

Malcolm delved into a briefcase beside him and brought out an ordinary spray can. "This is it. You use it just like spray paint, except that it won't leave any mark or lasting residue. Shake it up and spray it on. You've seen the wolf's head at Aldgate. It wasn't very large, and it was about the size of the infection you should be expecting to find. If you spray over a source until the scent dies down, that's job done. One can of spray should be good to deal with about ten sources."

Malcolm handed over the spray and chuckled, "Oh, one other small thing. The spray is harmless, so don't think that it's any good for self-defence. If you try spraying someone with it, they'll think you are basically spraying water. I suppose it might work as a weapon if you spray them in the face to disorientate and then hit them with the can, but you're probably in trouble if that's the best you have."

Paul could hardly wait to go to Acton, but for appearances' sake he would have to be based at home for several days. He couldn't invent clients in the City every day. By the time several days had elapsed, Paul was in a state of high excitement. He left Siete at home and took the Tube to Acton Central. His plan was simple: walk towards Ealing Common and see what happened. Apart from a small deviation, that was an easy matter of walking west. At first, he was worried that his senses would be saturated by the aromas wafting from all the coffee shops and restaurants in the area. That, of course, was a pointless concern. Detecting the infection didn't use his ordinary sense of smell, and after five minutes' walk, the scent of the fruit basket was in the air. He passed a busy roundabout and negotiated a few road junctions. By now, the scent was becoming much stronger and Paul was furiously attempting to make himself less sensitive. Without his previous practice he would surely have been rendered unconscious with the power emanating from the infection.

He followed the perfume trail into Twyford Crescent Gardens, to one of the public benches. The infection had to be lurking at the far end of the seat. Paul retrieved the spay can from his shoulder bag, shook the can and began to spray the end of the seat. A lady with a shopping trolley walked by, studying him. “I’m just cleaning the end of the seat,” he called. She moved on without comment. The smell died down, and Paul felt that he could breathe again, though he knew that was irrational. He packed the spray can and continued through the gardens to the next exit.

Paul was preoccupied, thinking about the first real piece of good he had done and how easy it had been. He didn’t notice the white van parked near the exit from the gardens, and he hardly had time to react at all when the van door slid open, two men jumped out, grabbed him, threw him into the back of the van and drove off.

Chapter 33 – The captive

Paul was pushed face down on to the metal floor of the van. One of his captors was sitting on his back, holding him down, while a voice filled with threat said, "Don't struggle, Paul, or we'll have to hurt you, and we don't want to do that – yet." Paul couldn't struggle anyway; the man pinning him down was far larger and stronger than he was and could have been a clone of Lance, one of Paul's convict interviewees. In the dim light of the van interior, he saw that both the men with him wore greasy overalls. Then he saw no more as a black canvas bag was pushed over his head.

Paul and his guards were shaken and rocked by vigorous acceleration and braking. Sharp turns caused loose objects to slide across the floor of the van. His captors probably didn't care about that, but for Paul these were missiles hitting him from all directions. The ride was a short one, and Paul soon found himself being pulled roughly out of the van. With one of his abductors on each side, he was firmly marched on to an area of rough ground. He could tell that much by looking down through the open mouth of the bag. It gave a view of the small area around his feet as he stumbled over broken bricks and tussocks of grass. They reached a building, where he was pushed through an open doorway into a room, in which their footsteps echoed. Judging by the echoes, it had to be a large room, and he could see its dusty concrete floor. He was man-handled across the room and through another door to a much smaller room, where his kidnappers shoved him on to a metal chair. As one of them pulled his arms round the back of the chair, the other took his mobile phone. Paul winced as plastic ties were applied to hold his wrists tightly together. Looking down, he saw hands at work as they fixed cable ties to his ankles to hold each of them firmly against the front legs of the chair. Not a word was spoken by the captors. Paul thought that silence was probably his best policy as well. Footsteps moved away from him, a door was slammed shut, and he heard it being locked.

Paul was left alone, but he could hear his gaolers conferring outside his cell:

"We've gotta get a shift on. The boss says we've got about a day before they find this place, so you get him here quick. I'll get some of the crew ready to pick up the pretty little bitch."

"Yeah, well go careful. You know what she did to Ron."

"She won't be doing anything to anyone this time, and she may not be quite so pretty by the time I've finished with her."

"Just remember the boss wants her intact."

"A bit of damage will be inevitable, won't it."

"Go on, get going."

Paul heard them leaving the building. It sounded as though he didn't have long to make an escape, which threatened to be very much easier said than done. His wrists were held very tightly, so trying to wriggle a hand free was extremely painful and seemed hopeless. What about the bag over his head? He tried to push it up using his shoulders and his chin. The trouble was that the wrist ties restricted his shoulder movements. He bent his head forward in the hope that the bag would fall off, but he couldn't bend far enough. If he could just lift his hands over the back of the chair, that would do the trick. Try as he might, he couldn't manage it; the back of the chair was too high. He tried flicking his head forwards in an attempt to throw the bag off. That did achieve a little more. He lifted his head back to flick again then, as he raised his head, the bag dropped back into place. Eventually, he devised a system of jerking his head forward and then gently rolling it back again to make another forward flick. This was probably going to give him a whiplash injury, but finally it worked and he could see.

His chair was in a small room with rough brick walls. The only light came through a small panel of wired glass in the door ahead of him. Paul needed to get out of the chair. His feet were touching the floor, and he found that small jumping movements would shift the chair slightly, though each little jump caused a sharp pain as the ties scraped his wrists. Despite the agony, he gradually manoeuvred the chair backwards towards the rear wall. His idea was to lean the chair back against the wall while he tried to slide the cable grips round his ankles off the bottom of the chair legs. The danger was that he would lose control of the chair and that it would go crashing to the floor with him still attached. That would make his situation even worse. He pushed with his toes and leaned backwards. Yes! He had the front chair legs off the floor. The tie on his right ankle was a little less tight than the other one, so he slowly eased it off the chair leg. Once one tie was off, it was easy to use his free foot to release the other one.

At last, he could stand up and lift his arms over the back of the chair. Now that he could walk, Paul looked through the wired glass panel in the door. The room beyond was an ancient workshop. There were all kinds of implements lying around. If he could only open the door, there would be a fair chance of cutting his hands free. He gave the door a good kick and nearly fell over in the process. Kicking was surprisingly difficult with his hands tied behind his back. He looked around the small room for something that would serve as a lever. There were two or three long iron bars on the floor, but none had an end thin enough to use as a crowbar. Then he spotted exactly what he needed - a broken hacksaw blade lying in the dust. He squatted down with his back to it and felt behind him in the dust to pick it up. He only hoped that it would be long enough for his purpose and soon discovered that it was. As he attempted to saw through the wrist tie, he was cutting himself nearly as much as the plastic, and he could feel blood running down his hands. He was slipping into a state of total despair and disappointment when the tie suddenly broke. He was free! The remainder of his plan was to smash the door with the metal chair. He went to work with a will. Glass broke and woodwork splintered. Before long Paul was surrounded by debris, the door was knocked loose on its hinges, and he could force it open.

He stepped through the door, only to be greeted by a large man leaning against the wall, watching him, "Congratulations, Mr Keating, I was about to come and get you, but didn't want to spoil your fun." This man was wearing a balaclava over his head and face, with holes for his eyes and mouth. He spoke between puffs of a cigar. Paul assumed that this was the boss. One of the original captors was also in the room laughing. The boss pushed Paul forwards on to a chair in front of a work bench. He pulled up a second seat and sat on it beside Paul, then turned and gestured to his underling, "Give me his phone."

The boss turned the phone on and draped an arm over Paul's shoulder as he spoke gruffly, "Now Paul, you've got a choice. You can tell me which of your fingerprints unlocks this phone, or I can try your fingers one by one and break each one that doesn't work. So, which is it to be?"

Paul instantly extended the second finger on his right hand and unlocked the phone. The boss held his cigar in his mouth while he worked the phone. He held it to his ear with one hand, took his cigar in the other hand and blew a cloud of smoke into Paul's face as he replaced the hand with the cigar back over Paul's shoulder. The trail of cigar smoke now drifted over Paul's nose, and into his eyes as the boss spoke into the phone, "Hello, Mrs Keating, I've got your husband with me." He brought the phone close to Paul's mouth. "Say 'hello,' Paul."

Paul said nothing. "Aaaah!" His neck exploded with pain as the boss stubbed his cigar into it.

"Now, say 'hello,' Paul." Paul complied.

The boss spoke into the phone again, "Your husband is relatively undamaged for now, but if you want him to remain that way, this is what you're going to do. Eventually, I will be wanting a substantial sum of money to return him in working order. That will take you a while to organise, so we'll begin with his accommodation costs for tonight. Go to your bank before it closes and extract £1000 in cash. Put it in an envelope and go to the alley where you assaulted my men.

You'll find a dustbin there, labelled with number 33 on its lid. Drop the envelope inside and return home. Needless to say, we will be watching, and you had better be alone. If we see the faintest hint of police, all bets are off. I expect you to comply by 4 p.m., so you'd better get a move on."

As he was finishing the call, Paul yelled, "Don't do it Chris, they're trying to grab you! Aaaah!" There was excruciating pain as the cigar was stubbed on the other side of his neck.

"That was stupid, Paul, but at least you have symmetrical burns now." The boss placed the phone on the work bench so that he could chat with Paul as he pressed on the burns with one hand whilst smoking with the other, "Don't get your hopes up, the cavalry isn't going to come riding over the hill. We'll be long gone before they find you. Come on." He was pulling Paul to his feet when a dog barked nearby, and the whirr of an approaching helicopter could be heard. The boss swore and rushed to the window, where he swore again more effusively, and shouted, "Get out, Stu, we're not being paid enough for this!" With that, the two men ran, and Paul was left alone trying to sooth his wounds.

Shortly, there were voices outside, "Mr Keating, are you there?"

"Yes, I'm okay. They ran off when they heard you coming."

"We're coming in. Keep your hands where we can see them." Two policemen with guns came through the doorway, sweeping the room with their weapons. They checked the room and shouted, "Clear!" before lowering their firearms. These people really were police officers; it was written in bold letters across their clothes. They instructed Paul to stay in the room with them while the surroundings were being secured.

"How did you find me so quickly?" Paul enquired.

"I was hoping you wouldn't ask that, sir," one of them answered, "We were worried about you after the knife attack, and decided to keep an eye on you. One of our plain clothes lads thought it would be a good idea to follow you today to make sure that you came to no harm. He saw you being bundled into the van and called for reinforcements. At that point, we didn't know exactly where they'd taken you - until one of the miscreants was kind enough to use your phone to contact your wife. Incidentally, you might want to know that we brought her with us - she's outside, waiting with your dog."

Paul was delighted for the few seconds before he had a very worrying thought. He had been followed! How on earth was he going to explain what he was doing? What about the spray can? That would take some explaining as well. But where had it got to? Okay, he remembered – it was still in the van. His captors had taken it, so they'd done him one favour at least. All he needed to do now was to come up with a credible cover story for his behaviour. The alternative was that his whole construct of secrets and half-truths would come crashing down into a rubble heap of exposed deception. He had about two minutes to think of something that was at least half-way convincing. How was he to explain his presence in Acton of all places? The prospect of a credible explanation wasn't promising, and his throbbing neck wasn't helping his thought processes.

A policeman spoke from the doorway, "It's all clear, sir, we can leave now."

They emerged from the building, and there was Chris waiting for him. He rushed into her arms and they both shed tears of relief. Siete showed her pleasure by trotting in circles, wrapping them in her leash as she did so. Chris voiced her concern, "Are you alright? What did they do to you?"

"Yes, I'm okay. They burned me on the neck with a cigar, but it could have been a lot worse."

"I was sick with worry about you, and you were so brave trying to warn me."

A woman in a purple tracksuit was approaching them, "Sorry to break up the reunion." She showed a warrant card and said, "I'm D.I. Lister. We have a car waiting for you both." She looked down before adding, "And the dog."

Paul looked round at where he had been held. It was an enormous deserted building, maybe an old hotel. He guessed that once there had been well-kept grounds around it, but now nature was encroaching, and any former glory had long since departed.

D.I. Lister led the little group through wire fencing, marked copiously with 'No Entry' signs, to a waiting vehicle. Siete leapt into the boot, where a dog guard was fitted. Paul and Chris sat hand-in-hand in the rear seats. Paul wondered where they were being taken to - his second unknown destination of the day.

Chapter 34 – The safe house

This journey was a far cry from Paul's trip in the white van. He didn't know much about cars, but he did recognise a powerful BMW when he was travelling in it. There were no features to mark it out as a police car so, to a casual observer, they would look like two well-to-do couples on an outing with their dog.

D.I. Lister explained the plan, "Our first objective is to have Mr Keating's burns sorted out at a medical centre. Then, with your permission, we'd like to keep you out of the hands of the gang that have now assaulted you twice. We have access to a safe house not too far away, and we'd like you to stay there for a day or two while we round up those who intend you harm .... If you're imagining a small house with steel doors and bars on the windows, you can stop worrying. This place is a posh detached house on a private estate. There's loads of space, and every convenience; think of it like an up-market holiday home. I'll be staying with you, and I'm looking forward to the comfort. Our driver is D.S. Philips, and he'll be staying with us too."

"I'm sure that will be great," Chris replied, "You'll be happy with that, won't you Paul?"

"Sure." Paul's burns were quite painful, and treatment for them would be very welcome. He wasn't really thinking beyond that.

After only a few miles, the car turned into a private drive that took them to the forecourt of a smart medical facility, where a uniformed nurse was waiting to treat and dress Paul's burns. The cream she used was effective, and he felt much better once the constant sting was subdued. He then began to think about the idea of a safe house and couldn't see any objection to it. During a stay with the police officers, he might be able to elicit more information about who had kidnapped him.

When the brief medical treatment was over, they drove on towards the northern outskirts of London. As they travelled, Chris asked Paul the question he had been dreading, "How did you come to be in Acton?"

He answered with the best excuse he'd been able to come up with, "I used to have a good colleague when I worked in the City. He retired early, and I was going to look him up to ask if he wanted to do some freelance work for me. The stupid thing was that I didn't have any contact details for him. He wasn't on any of the professional sites, but I'd been to his house once, and I thought I knew where he lived – in Acton. When it came to it, I couldn't find the house, so it ended up being a wasted journey. That was before the hooligans in the van turned it into something much worse."

Chris made no comment as she held his arm and stroked his hand.

Paul was paying attention to the route. He noted that, though they hadn't reached the M25 ring road round London, they were already in leafy lanes with expensive-looking houses. They turned off into a private estate with a barrier and a security guard. Their driver spoke to the uniformed man on duty, the barrier was raised, and they were waved through. The estate itself consisted of a series of large green spaces, which were meticulously maintained and were planted with trees and shrubs. There were connecting roads between them, and each grassy area was surrounded by a circle of detached houses. D.S. Philips swung the car into the drive of a comparatively modest house, where they slowed as they came to a double garage door that was already rising to allow entry. They drove in, and the garage door was closing behind them as they all left the car.

A door inside the garage opened into a utility room containing laundry appliances and a large freezer. Beyond that was a spacious modern kitchen with a central bar table and stools, where D.I. Lister pointed out a dog bed for Siete. She also commented that police dogs sometimes needed to stay, so appropriate food was on hand. There was a door from the kitchen to the garden. The latter could be seen through the kitchen window, which was above the sink and double draining board. Through the glass, Paul could see a substantial orchard, surrounded by a tall laurel hedge, so he let Siete out to explore among the fruit trees.

D.S. Philips put on the kettle while D.I. Lister took Chris and Paul through to the leather sofas of the lounge as she said, "I'll show you everything else shortly, but before that, let's be comfortable for a chat. Is coffee okay for both of you?"

"Yes, great," they chorused.

"White?"

"Yes, please," Chris answered for the two of them.

The detective called out, "Two white coffees please, Sam. I'll have my usual black one."

"Now to business," she continued, "the sergeant answers to Sam, as you've heard, and you can call me Polly. We're going to be together for a while, so is it okay if I call you Paul and Christine?"

Paul nodded, "Yes, that's fine." His wife answered with, "Just Chris is good for me."

"Thank you. Paul, could you tell me exactly what happened to you today?"

Paul ran through the story of the abduction, describing his assailants as best he could. He remembered that the boss had called one of his men 'Stu,' and also that the attacker in the alley had been referred to as Ron.

Polly asked about any other conversation between his abductors. Paul recalled that they had spoken as though their real objective was to capture Chris; he had only been a means to an end. Polly allowed that piece of information to pass without comment. Paul added that when the boss was about to make a run for it, he'd said something about not being paid enough. It sounded as though they'd been hired for the abduction.

Sam brought coffee and a biscuit assortment on a silver tray, and he sat down with them. As they drank, Paul took stock of their guardians. Sam was a tall, burly man with short brown hair. Paul had already gained the impression that this was a deceptively quiet person, who didn't miss much and was good at his work. He was probably under 30. Polly was a few years older. Her purple track suit and pink trainers made her look like a girl out to have fun. Nothing could be further from the truth, he thought. Beneath the plain clothes disguise she was sharp and incisive. Physically, she looked stocky and tough. Paul should take care not to be taken in by her baby blue eyes, short blond hair, and innocent expression.

Paul wanted more information, "You mentioned rounding up the gang, Polly. Does that mean you know who they are?"

"Yes, we've had an eye on them for a while. What you said about them being hired muscle fits with what we thought. We'd rather hoped to find out who was paying them, but no luck on that so far, although we will soon be having words with the one you called the boss. That's Paddy Brewer. His real name is Patrick, and he's not remotely Irish."

"It was fortunate that you arrived so quickly." Paul said, "Another minute or two and we would have gone."

"That was largely thanks to our man who took it into his head to follow you. Then again, we had resources. The powers that be must be very keen to catch this whole gang of misfits. Either that, or you have friends in very high places. You saw the car that Sam was given to collect Chris, and we even had helicopter support. We don't get all that every day of the week, and nor do we get premises like this. Anyway, enough of that, let me show you the rest of the house."

On the ground floor they were shown a dining room, a toilet, and a study. Upstairs, Chris and Paul were shown to a double bedroom with an ensuite bathroom. "You'll find plenty of clothes in the drawers and wardrobe," Polly explained, "I suggest you use them, and wash your own clothes ready for when we're done here. There are three other bedrooms. Sam and I will use one each if, and when, we get to sleep. At least one of us will always be awake downstairs if you need us. There'll be another officer arriving soon to help us with that."

"It's about time I fed my Alsatian. Could you show me the food?" Paul asked.

"Yes, of course. I'll show you the food for us humans as well. Follow me."

Polly took them back to the kitchen and showed Paul a cupboard with dog supplies. For the people, there was a well-stocked fridge and a vast selection of frozen meals in the freezer they'd spotted on the way into the house.

Paul fed Siete before he and Chris went to change in the bedroom. They searched through the clothes stores and found no lack of choice. Chris took their own clothes to the washing machine while Paul explored the food supplies. Polly and Sam were both in the kitchen, and they soon had a group agreement on a 'sweet and sour' meal for four from the freezer.

After the meal, Paul asked whether they were allowed outside. "The garden is fine," Polly told them, "but we would sooner that you didn't leave the property for the moment. Although the security guards are pretty good, we wouldn't want to rely on that. If there's anything you need that isn't in the house, we can make arrangements."

Paul had kept back some treats for Siete, so he went with Chris to play 'hunt the treat' in the orchard. The dog never had a care in the world, and the animal's enthusiasm was infectious. By the time they went to bed, Paul was calm and relaxed, even after the traumas of the day. That didn't prevent him from reviewing his experiences as he cuddled up with Chris in the comfortable bed.

His latest cover story was barely plausible, and he was surprised that it had been accepted without comment. Was there a reason for that? He thought about the tales that had been told to him during the day. How credible were they? Was his rescue really brought about through a detective who happened to follow him all the way to Acton? Then there had been the motivation for the kidnap. He had told Polly that the gang wanted to catch Chris. Surely there should have been follow up questions along the lines of 'Can you think of any reason why they would want to do that?' It also occurred to him that he'd never been asked whether he knew of people who would wish him harm. Why had these questions not been asked? He was beginning to doubt everyone. Were Polly and Sam actually ordinary detectives? Another plain clothes officer had arrived while they were playing with the dog. That made three police officers, a powerful car, and a posh house. Then there was the medical centre where he had been treated. There had been none of the waiting he would have expected from the NHS, and none of this matched his impression of the resources normally available for police work. He knew that Chris had secrets. Were all these things connected in some way?

The stay in the safe house turned out to be short-lived. Before lunch the next day, Polly informed them that the whole kidnapping gang were in police cells and that Paul and Chris could be taken home.

Chapter 35 – The great reveal

Though it was good to be home again after all his adventures, there was plenty to be done. Paul arranged to report back to Malcolm the next morning. Unusually, this was to be at the house he thought of as Fort Knox. The steel gates and high surrounding wall made it look like a high security store from the outside, though inside was a totally different story.

Paul's afternoon was a combination of business work and exercise with Siete. All was returning to normality, except for his growing mountain of secrets, which was becoming increasingly oppressive. He craved an open relationship with Chris.

On the next morning, Chris left early for the Leisure Centre. A short time later, Paul took Siete with him to his meeting with Malcolm when he would need to explain all about the Acton affair, which was precisely the subject that Malcolm began to address, "I was sorry to hear that you've been in the wars. I hope your injuries are improving."

Paul had learned not to be surprised at Malcolm's information-gathering skills. "Yes, thank you," he answered, "the treatment has been amazingly effective."

"Good show. Now perhaps you would tell me the story from the beginning."

"In Acton I found masses of smells from all the restaurants and coffee shops. Despite that, I soon began to sense the infection above all that - from as much as a kilometre away from the source. As I followed the scent trail, it became stronger and stronger until it was painfully oppressive. The infection proved to be at one end of a park bench, but I sprayed it, and the whole sensation reduced dramatically. As I was walking out of the gardens, two men grabbed me and bundled me into a white van. I'm sorry that I lost my spray can in the van."

"Don't worry about that, Paul. They are easily come by, and to anyone else it will be a useless water spray."

"That's good to know, but the whole episode has made me wonder again about whether the infection is intelligent.

Within a minute or two of neutralising an infection, I was attacked."

"Yes, I understand your concern. As I said before, we've had the same suspicions. Regrettably, we haven't been able to reach a firm conclusion on that. In this particular case, I'm pretty sure that the neutralisation and the attack weren't connected. I'll be able to explain that shortly, but first tell me what else happened."

Paul gave the same information and description of events that he'd given Polly, except that he added, "I'm very puzzled by the police reaction, or rather lack of reaction, to one part of my account. When I pointed out that the attack was really aimed at capturing Chris, there were no questions asked about that. I can't understand that at all. Surely, they should have been asking if I knew of any enemies, for example."

"Okay, Paul, I'm in a position to explain a few things to you. I haven't been able to do that up until now because this refers to matters that I wasn't aware of myself until the time of your kidnap. I have finally been able to break through the barrier of the red flag against Christine, and you're going to need to prepare yourself for a shock."

Paul felt numb with trepidation as he wondered what was coming, but he had to know what was going on. He took a deep breath. "Alright, go on."

"There has indeed been a Secret Intelligence Service operation involving Christine and her work. That's why I couldn't find out exactly what she does. In the light of recent events, the bosses of SIS have decided to talk to me. In fact, they've put me in touch with the agent in charge of the operation, and we've been able to have 'full and frank discussions,' as they say. Better still, the head of the SIS operation would like to speak with you too and explain personally about some of the things that have been going on around you. I'll introduce you now. Malcolm walked to the door and opened it, then roared with laughter at Paul's flabbergasted expression when Chris walked into the room and sat demurely on Paul's knee.

Malcolm was wiping tears from his eyes, "I'm sorry, Paul, I couldn't resist the dramatic moment once I found out about this. Christine herself has been in charge of an intelligence operation based at your home."

While Malcolm recovered his composure Chris spoke to Paul, "I'm sorry that I couldn't tell you what I was doing. Though, as I've discovered, I wasn't the only one with secrets, was I? I've been told all about your work with Michael & Co. You should have told me at the beginning, but we'll pass over that; none of it matters now."

"I'm sorry too," Paul answered, "I've been trying to remember why I didn't tell you. I think I was worried that you'd think I was having a breakdown, and from a small beginning, the secrets built up out of control; it became harder and harder to say anything. On top of that, I was really worried about you and your work .... but as you say, let's put all that behind us."

Paul was experiencing a massive cloud of euphoric relief that Chris was on the side of the angels after all. She kissed him and then moved to sit beside him.

Malcolm took charge again, "I think it would be useful, Christine, if you would kick things off by telling Paul about your work for SIS."

"Yes, that would be a good idea. It all began while I was at university, shortly before we met. I was approached by a group who claimed to operate internationally. They wanted me to work as a language tutor and, incidentally, to pass information between their various contacts across the world. Effectively, I was to be an information hub for them. I wasn't entirely convinced about the legality of what they were up to. So, although I went along with them, I also contacted MI6 and expressed my concerns. The outcome was that I began acting as a co-ordinator for terrorists while actually working for MI6, or SIS as we usually say now. I've been doing that ever since then."

"That's such a relief," Paul said, "Since I've been working with Malcolm, I've known you were up to something, but I didn't know what it was. I've been suspicious of other people as well – Jacquie and Zara, and even the gardeners – though I did discount them eventually. On top of all that, the police have had me worried."

"You were right about Jacquie, she's my main link with HQ. You're right about Zara too, she's been my martial arts trainer for years, but what's this about the police?"

"They haven't been asking enough questions," Paul replied, "and there was also the thin story about a detective deciding to follow me to Acton."

"I must admit that's good thinking. You should join SIS. The police were told to back off, hence the lack of questions, and you're right, it wasn't a detective who decided to follow you. SIS has had people looking out for us recently, and one of them was tasked with following you."

Malcolm interjected, "Actually, he wasn't the only one. I had one of my people following your chap."

Chris looked puzzled, "It's odd that my guy didn't spot him."

"Firstly, it was a her not a him and secondly, you'd better teach your chaps about following from the front. My girl knew roughly where Paul was going, so she was mostly in front of him, not behind. She saw Paul being taken and your chap phoning for help, so she left you all to it."

Paul was stunned by all this information, "If the three of us had simply gone together, the kidnap wouldn't have occurred in the first place."

"That's true," Chris answered, "but then we wouldn't have caught the gang either, and they are currently our best lead for resolving this mess. Anyway, where were we? Oh yes, talking about thin stories. Your explanation about a colleague in Acton was the weakest one yet."

Paul was about to say something in self-justification, but she carried on, "It's okay, you don't need to explain. Malcolm has told me everything about the infection and what you were doing. I understand all about that, and you'll be pleased to know that I don't think you're both mad. On the contrary, I believe every word, and have no problem with any of it. In fact, it explains a few things, and I think it's going to be very useful for the future. But enough of that, I've been side-tracked again."

"Yes, sorry Chris, you were going to tell me more about your work with SIS."

"That's right. My recent campaign has been to foil groups of Russians who were planning to simultaneously bomb several churches across the UK. That plan was foiled, and my operation has just been successfully completed. Most of the miscreants are under lock and key."

"So, they were the ones we encountered a few days ago," Paul responded.

"No, they weren't, and that's where it all becomes complicated. I gather that Malcolm told you that you weren't in danger from anything I was doing. Well, that was true, but the bugging, the attack on Piers, and our recent experience, all come from something else in the quite distant past. A few years' ago, I was involved in a project to catch an international group who were making their fortune through illegal trading in drugs and weapons. We used to call them 'FourCo.' Our operation was all highly secret. So much so, that although I knew what I had to do, I didn't know who else was part of the enterprise or what they were doing. At the end of it all, we were told that the operation was a total success. The whole group of criminals were said to have been arrested, and they were all behind bars. Sadly, I've learned in the last day or so that our strategy wasn't as effective as we had imagined. We didn't actually catch everyone. The top echelon of the gang was supposed to have been arrested, but we now know that there was a level above the ones we caught. They escaped and are highly peeved that their trade was destroyed. Now, there are reports that their old trade routes are open again, and also that they are intent on revenge. These are the people behind the recent attacks. Piers was included, because they found out, what I didn't know, that Piers was the dog handler primarily responsible for finding their drugs."

"Yes, we heard about this from Piers," Paul added. "I knew they were after him. That's why he moved away. I didn't know anyone else was on their radar. Does this mean that there's a very angry Mr Big still out there trying to kill us?"

"Yes, it does, and that's why we're all here together now," Chris answered.

A mobile phone sounded in Malcolm's pocket. He pulled it out and glanced at the screen. He looked concerned as he said, "Excuse me a moment, I need to answer this." With that he left the room.

Paul was in a state of agitation about the danger they faced. "What are we going to do?" he wanted to know.

"We're going to pool our resources and catch them," Chris replied calmly.

When Malcolm re-entered the room, his manner had been transformed. He looked very solemn. "I have some very bad news," he announced quietly, "Piers is dead. The official version is that he was killed in a shooting accident. I don't believe that for a second and nor do Chris's bosses."

Paul was devastated. He'd come to think of Piers as a wonderful friend, who was indestructible. He broke the silence, "That's awful! Did he have family?"

"No," Malcolm answered, "there was just him. His death is a dreadful tragedy, and we will all want to mourn his loss, but for the moment we have a greater duty to the living. We must catch Mr Big, as Paul so colourfully calls him." He paused. "Before we carry on, perhaps I could leave you for a few moments to collect your thoughts."

Chris and Paul both agreed, and Malcolm left them alone in the room to remember their friend, until he returned with a determined look on his face.

"We must devote all our resources to catching this Mr Big and putting him, or her, behind bars."

"Is there a plan for that?" Paul asked.

"Only in outline. In a rare moment of unanimity, SIS has agreed that Chris and her team will work with us. It's up to the three of us to formulate a plan. I suggest that our starting point should be Paul's gang of kidnappers. They are available for questioning, and it would be useful to find out who was paying them."

Chris spoke thoughtfully, "Before we go too far, Malcolm, I do have another piece of bad news."

"What's that? Don't tell me someone else has been killed."

"No, it's not that. Information has been leaking from my team. In the popular parlance, we have a mole, and I have no clue who it is."

Malcolm was unperturbed, "That's unfortunate, but not altogether surprising. I was going to raise that possibility anyway and, especially in the light of your news, I hope that we can agree to keep all key information and planning within the three of us. Now, why don't we all go home and think about a possible course of action? We'll convene again tomorrow."

"Are we going to be safe in the meantime?" Paul asked.

"I think so. We have an opportunity to ramp up your security again. It's public knowledge that Paul was kidnapped. As far as the press are concerned, that was a ransom attempt, so no eyebrows will be raised too far if I arrange for an armed guard at your house, and that's what I'll do. I'm going to call for a vehicle to take you home now, and I'm afraid that, until we catch Mr Big, you'll have the inconvenience of bodyguards whenever you're out of the house."

Chapter 36 – Fresh understanding

Although Paul was devastated at the news of Piers' death, he was also mightily relieved to have all his secrets swept away. He wasn't sure whether he was relieved or not about the armed guard in an unmarked van outside the house, but that was as nothing compared with his joy at being able to discuss matters with Chris without fear of accidently saying the wrong thing. They had plenty to discuss.

Chris's martial arts skills needed more explanation. "Where did all the Ninja stuff really come from?" Paul wanted to know.

She grinned, "You know most of that already. I practise with Zara. I was given an intensive initial course of training early on, and now Zara keeps me up to scratch. It's quite amusing really. We use a room in the Leisure Centre, with gym mats on the floor, but we have to cover the viewing glass in the door. The way we throw each other about, we really don't want anyone watching. The staff there were okay about it once we explained that we would do high level stuff and were worried that a casual observer might hurt themselves by trying to copy us. Actually, I'm supposed to warn any would-be assailants that I'm a lethal weapon."

"I don't recall hearing that in the alley," Paul remarked.

Chris smiled. "No, when someone's coming at me with a great knife, and he has accomplices creeping up behind me, I'm inclined to forget. I wouldn't want to ruin their surprise."

"I wouldn't mind some lessons with Zara myself, if that's possible. No somersaults or throwing myself about – just some basics."

"Yes, we can arrange that once the present business is behind us."

"I must admit that I'm worried about the danger. You and Zara seem to take this stuff without undue concern. I can't be like that. They've already killed Piers, so they are capable of anything. Don't get me wrong, I do want to help catch these people, and I'm really pleased that we can work together."

Chris's response was action, rather than words, and they remained in tight embrace for a long time. They were only stopped by the cold nose of Siete, who didn't know what was going on, but wanted to be included.

The couple chatted over lunch as Paul attempted to make everything clear in his mind. As he thought about their life together, he spoke about their time at university, "We were both students when we met. Were you already a secret agent?"

"I'm ashamed to say I was. It sounds horrible, but at first, I didn't say anything, because I thought you might be a good cover for me. That all changed when I got to know you. Then I didn't say anything, because I didn't want to lose you."

They hugged some more before Paul mentioned the safe house and the impressive car. That produced a further revelation from Chris, "I'm afraid that there was a slight deception there too: Polly and Sam were working for me and they knew not to ask awkward questions."

"Oh, I see, that explains a lot. What do you think are the chances of obtaining useful information from the gang?"

"I reckon the prospects for that are encouraging, and I'm hoping for good news on that front tomorrow. We have specialists for that kind of interrogation. I don't do it, but those who do are very good."

Paul felt his tender neck with his hand, "I can give them some suggestions involving lighted cigars," he offered.

"We don't do anything like that, Paul. That would be illegal," she said daintily, "even if it is well-deserved. It's probably just as well that it's not me questioning them. I might forget about that lethal weapon part again – when I'm forced to act in self-defence of course."

Paul smiled, "I wouldn't mind seeing that. I do have a serious question though. How does Mr Big bring his contraband into the country? Do you know the entry point?"

Chris looked thoughtful, "There's likely to be more than one entry point. If we just think about drugs; they have a high value to volume ratio, so a small pack fetches a high price.

We reckon that Mr Big is currently bringing a fair proportion of his goods into the UK through the port of Newhaven. Just think from the criminal's point of view. Suppose you have a shipment of drugs to transport through customs. You might well decide to break it down into smaller shipments and hide them in several vehicles. If it was all together in one van, and it was caught, you'd have lost everything. With smaller shipments you might well lose some, but you could expect most of it to be undetected."

"What would happen if that changed, and Mr Big lost all his shipments?"

"Border Force would be delighted and Mr Big would be furious. He would soon conclude that he had a spy in his camp, and anyone he suspected would come to a sticky end."

Paul spoke slowly as a plan began to formulate in his mind, "There might be a way to make that happen. I haven't worked out the details, and I would need to talk it through with Malcolm, but we might be able to cause mayhem in the ranks of Mr Big's gang. If we did, do you think he might give himself away?"

"Well, yes, he might. He, or let's be fair, she, is very good at planning and keeping themselves out of sight. It's possible that if hasty action is forced upon them, their planning could become skimpy, and mistakes would become much more likely. I am intrigued by the whole idea. Presumably, your special skills are involved somehow. I'll hold myself in patience until you've thought it through and we've seen Malcolm again. One thing though, don't you dare suggest anything hazardous. I don't want to lose you now."

Even more hugs followed and there was no more work done that day.

Chapter 37 – A cunning plan

After an early start next day, Chris began winding down her current tutoring schedule. That wasn't too difficult because most of her recent tutees had either been arrested or gone into hiding. Over the years, she had infiltrated several terrorist groups, but that work had reached the end of its useful life. The time had come to register with some legitimate tutoring agencies. Paul began to tackle his backlog of insurance work, knowing that serious progress on their secret activities wouldn't be possible until after the meeting with Malcolm.

A car arrived for them, and an armed police officer escorted them, with Siete, to the vehicle. There was a short drive to 'Fort Knox' where Malcolm was waiting. On reflection, Paul realised that his meetings with Malcolm were unlike any other business meetings he'd ever encountered. There was no paperwork. Every matter considered was held entirely in their heads, and all their decisions were verbal ones. That would be terrifying in any other context, but somehow it seemed completely natural as they discussed their plans over coffee.

As they had hoped, the kidnap gang had been ready to part with information after very little persuasion. They had soon told all they knew – essentially because they hardly knew anything. Their instructions had been provided by phone, and the caller had used a non-traceable device. Payment had been in cash delivered by a man (they thought) dressed from head to toe in motorbike leathers and a crash helmet with a dark visor. Half the payment was 'up-front,' and they had never qualified for the other half. In fact, they rather feared that someone might take aggressive measures to reacquire the up-front payment. With that fear in mind, they were in no hurry to be released.

However, there was a little more hope from the assailant that Piers had put into a coma. He had been regaining consciousness and, in his woozy state, had been muttering something about Crawley and a lockup. It might mean nothing. On the other hand, it might be a tenuous lead.

Paul offered his thinking, "I wondered whether we might be able to use our ability to detect infection. If the drugs part of Mr Big's operation is using Newhaven as an entry point, could we identify the vehicles carrying the drugs?"

Chris looked doubtful, "Don't we already have dogs that can sniff out drugs?"

"We do," Paul answered, "but they have to be close to the drugs to find them. I'm much more sensitive to the infection, and it wouldn't only be drugs. I could rapidly identify people and vehicles with any guilty secret from many metres away."

Malcolm also seemed doubtful, "There are a few problems with that. A major one is that you'd probably detect far too much. No doubt you could detect drugs smugglers, but at the same time you might also identify a whole host of other minor offenders, and even those who had spent a weekend abroad with someone else's spouse. That would totally muddy the waters."

"That's what I thought at first, but then I realised that I can tell the difference between secondary infections and human infections – it's rotting apples or fresh citrus. If I concentrate on rotting apples, I'll be detecting mostly contraband. It may not be restricted to the drugs we are looking for; nevertheless, it will be mostly goods that Border Force would be interested in. I could guide them as to which vehicles are worthy of a search. Who knows, I might even detect someone transporting guns for Mr Big. Whatever happens, no-one who's caught will think I'm anything to do with their bad luck."

Malcolm was still to be convinced, "That sounds attractive, though it also seems like full-time employment. I don't mind that, but your insurance clients might have a different view."

"Yes, I know. I've thought about that too, and I do have a rather cheeky idea: is there any possibility of Steve and Ellie helping out, with Doce? With three of us we could work shifts, and I could set up a base at Newhaven to work on my other business from there."

"Who are Steve and Ellie?" Chris wanted to know.

"They are Spotters, like me," Paul informed her, "I'll tell you all about them later. You'd like them."

Malcolm was clearly thinking as he spoke, "Alright. You bring Chris up to speed. As for obtaining the help, I'll enquire about it. Your idea does seem like a possible line of approach, even if I'm not sure how effective it would be at finding Mr Big."

Chris was more enthusiastic, "It could produce some leads. Those who are caught could be questioned, but also, if Mr Big's operation is disrupted, it might cause dissent among his workers, and he might make mistakes. Not only that, a tweak to Paul's plan could make it more effective. If Paul were to detect contraband in a few vehicles, we could leave one or two to be followed, and we might find the next link in the organisation that way."

"Okay," said Malcolm with an air of finality, "let's do it. I'll have the boys in blue investigate the idea of lockups in Crawley without alerting the local criminal classes about our interest. The Newhaven idea does sound like fun. Whether it works or not, we could do a great deal of good by taking drugs off the streets. We could also curry an enormous amount of favour with Border Force, together with HM Revenue and Customs. So far as they are concerned, it would be best if they are left with the impression that any success is entirely due to highly trained dogs. In the course of our activities, we could quietly leave one or two suspect vehicles to be followed by Christine and some of her agents. Remember there could be a mole in among them, so we'll only tell them what they need to know. I'll get on to Sania to enquire about the possibility of Stephen and Gabrielle helping us. Are you both happy with that?" Paul and Chris agreed enthusiastically.

In the car home Chris asked about Steve and Ellie.

"Once I learnt to detect human infection," Paul explained, "I discovered that I was infected myself; not to the level of a major criminal, but infected none the less. It turned out that everyone I met was infected to some extent, though that level was low enough for me to tune it out for everyday purposes. Malcolm told me that my own infection could be removed using a special plunge pool on his country estate, and my overnight conference was to do that. While I was there, I met Steve and Ellie. They're a married couple, who were there with their dog, Doce. Like me, they were there for the plunge pool. They have their own version of 'Malcolm' – her name is Sania. All of them are really nice people, and I'm sure you'd love working with them if Malcolm can fix it."

"When you say 'everyone's infected,' Paul, does that include me?"

"At a low level, yes. I can only detect it if I try very hard."

"What about you? Will you become reinfected?"

"No, the plunge pool clears the infection and gives immunity."

Chris ended the conversation with a pensive, "Oh, I see."

Once at home, they both worked on their ordinary employment. They would have a few days to make progress with that, while Malcolm worked his magic with the authorities.

Chapter 38 – The Sunshine Coast

It was a week later when Paul, Chris & Siete had packed their bags and were being driven off, under guard, to an unknown destination in the Newhaven area. Apart from the guard, it was very much like setting off for a holiday by the sea. Appropriately, the sky was clear blue as they headed towards the Sunshine Coast of East Sussex. Their journey ended a mile or two outside Newhaven with a drive along a country lane between flintstone walls, which marked the edge of the rolling fields beyond. There they entered the world of a rural village, where time dawdled. They finally stopped in the forecourt of a large detached house, also with flintstone walls, that appeared to have defied the passage of time altogether.

There was Malcolm, waiting at the door with his usual broad smile of welcome. The man was a magician. How had he come up with this place for them to stay? The modern interior of the house was in dramatic contrast to its ancient external appearance. The ground floor included two enormous lounge areas, where the thick carpets and comfortable sofas would have graced any smart hotel. This clearly was not a hotel, and that made Paul wonder about Malcolm's domestic plans. He gave every impression that he would be staying with them, but did that mean that a cooking rota would be needed? For all Malcolm's impressive skill set, Paul couldn't imagine him at work in a kitchen. In the kitchen, the truth was revealed: Malcolm had hired a cook. Sheila was a robust middle-aged woman already efficiently at work preparing a meal. Though she was busy, her round face creased into a warm and friendly greeting when Malcolm introduced her. Even Siete's presence was cheerfully accepted, though with hindsight it was probably expected.

The garden was a dog's paradise, fully enclosed, with a large lawn that gave way to a copse. Siete was set free to explore.

Malcolm showed Chris and Paul upstairs to an ensuite bedroom with a king-size bed and a sitting area where Paul would be able to work. Malcolm explained that Ellie and Steve were due to arrive soon, with Sania and their dog, Doce. Paul asked about the arrangements for their armed guard, and Malcolm replied that the guards wouldn't be needed inside the house. They would be keeping watch outside and would be on duty for trips away from the house.

By the time Chris and Paul had settled into their room, a second car was arriving. After the introductions, Sania disappeared with Malcolm, leaving Ellie and Steve in the lounge with Chris and Paul. They all sat together round a table, where Sheila had provided morning coffee. Paul explained, with great delight, that Chris now knew all about Michael & Co. and would be working with them. Ellie wanted to know more, "When we last met, Paul said something about you having serious martial arts skills, Chris. Is that true?"

Chris made light of it, "I do have lessons, and I like to think that I could defend myself if I needed to."

"So, is it true that you disarmed a mugger with a knife and broke his arm?"

Paul intervened, "Chris is being modest. The truth is that she is supposed to declare herself as a lethal weapon, and I'm pretty sure she did break that guy's arm."

Steve was puzzled, "Is that anything to do with the armed guard outside?"

"Yes," Paul answered, "I'm sorry about that. I'm afraid that you may have walked into a hazardous situation. Chris is the target of a crime lord, who's after revenge for her part in damaging his business."

"Don't worry about that," Ellie responded, "the situation isn't a total surprise, and we're here to help. The idea of wrecking smuggling operations at Newhaven is a splendid one; we're really looking forward to it."

As they were speaking, Malcolm and Sania came into the room to help themselves to coffee. "I'm afraid there's some bad news on the ferry front," Malcolm announced cheerily, "The first ferry tomorrow arrives at 0500 hours in the morning, so breakfast will be available from 0345 hours."

There were four glum faces as Sania and Malcolm took seats to discuss arrangements. "There is a ferry at a more friendly time this afternoon," Malcolm informed them, "and I think it would be a good idea for us to view its arrival. We can introduce ourselves at the port while we're at it. The ship arrives at 1500 hours, so I reckon we should arrive 45 minutes before that. It will only take 5 or 10 minutes to reach the port from here. Consequently, and this is the key point, lunch will be at the civilised time of 12.30."

"What's the plan at the port?" Steve wanted to know.

As usual, Malcom seemed to be the fount of all knowledge, "During the week there are three arrivals each day. After the early one and the afternoon one, there's an evening arrival at 2100. At the weekend, there is a fourth ferry, docking at 0930. Unfortunately, that means that the early morning arrival on Saturdays is even earlier, at 0400. I'm hoping that we can spread the pain of the early ferries with a shift system."

"How will we work things at the port?" Chris asked.

"Subject to what we find this afternoon, I reckon that we can work in twos, with each couple having a dog. We'll need a Spotter with a dog to be in a secure place where all the disembarking vehicles will be passing slowly. The Spotter will have a radio link to the second person, who'll be with Border Force at their control point. The Spotter can advise on which vehicles need to be checked. I suggest that Stephen spots for Sania, Gabrielle spots for me, and Paul spots for Christine. That gives three pairs for three ferries on most days. We can rotate round who takes the early morning slot."

"When it comes to the searching of vehicles," Steve said, "surely the easiest thing would be for one of us to be involved. We could locate contraband very quickly."

"Yes, you could," replied Sania as she spoke with her usual precision, "but Malcolm and I have discussed that. We really do not want everyone to know that you have superhero powers, which means that Border Force will have to do the actual discovery, and everyone will be left to assume that it is our dogs that have the super powers."

"Mr Big has chosen his port well," Malcolm added, "at Dover, for example, there's a lorry scanner that helps the searches tremendously. It's rare for such a device to be in use at Newhaven, so Border Force has to depend on humans, occasionally with the aid of sniffer dogs."

Paul had other doubts, "Are they happy with the prospect of us arriving, Malcolm?"

"They've been told to co-operate fully. That's bound to cause initial resentment, but if our plan works and their successful search rate rockets upwards from its current low percentage, I reckon they'll soon be clamouring for us to stay. That's not all good news, because the statistics will be in the public domain, and they might take some explaining. The plan for that is to talk vaguely of SIS intelligence about smuggling operations. That's to say, I'm going to blame it on Christine."

"Why thank you, Malcolm," said Chris primly.

Now that Chris understood the training that Siete had been given, Paul was able to share the dog's exercise and training with her to a far greater extent than before. Chris played and trained with Siete in the garden with Ellie and Doce to keep her company. As the two women chatted, Chris asked about the dogs' names, "I've always thought Siete was an unusual name for a dog. I expect you know it's Spanish for seven and then your dog's name, Doce, is Spanish for twelve. Does that mean there are other dogs out there with Spanish numbers for names?"

"I don't know, but if there are I'd look for a Tres and a Cuatro – three and four. I reckon we might be dealing with numbers connected with the Bible. Then again, maybe I'm barking up the wrong tree; perhaps they just began with Uno and worked upwards."

By lunchtime, the two dogs in question were happy in the garden, Paul had finished working in the bedroom setting up the technology he needed for his work, and Steve had returned from exploring the neighbourhood. Sheila set a high standard for all the meals they would share together, and the provision of good food reinforced the two couples' desire for exercise during their stay. They studied the local map to identify some suitable runs for the four of them, with their dogs. It was left to Malcolm to inform the armed guards about the new duty that would be needed as a result.

For the afternoon, Ellie and Chris announced that they wouldn't need the car, as they would run to Newhaven. Again, a guard would have to come with them, but Chris, for one, had no intention of losing her level of fitness for the convenience of a guard, who should be keeping fit anyway. The distance to the port couldn't be more than three miles, and the two women reckoned they could make that well within 20 minutes. They were happy to run back again afterwards.

Malcolm and Sania gracefully declined all invitations for them to join in with the physical activity. They travelled to the port, with Steve and Paul, in one of the cars – with the two dogs. It was agreed between them that if the driver was armed, then no further escort was required.

Ellie and Chris had set off, with their guard, 15 minutes or so before the car. They were found waiting at the port security office, wearing track suits that Paul didn't remember them leaving with, and looking as though they'd just come from a stroll in the park. Their guard was seated wearily nearby. Paul never did work out how that state of affairs had come about, but anyway, the whole group was waved through to reserved parking beside the office, where they were to be met.

As they parked, a uniformed officer came out to meet them, "I'm Philip and I've been asked to look after you." He surveyed the motley group before him with interest before adding, "I can't imagine how many arms you've twisted to be here at all, but I'm ready to help you as much as I can. Now perhaps you'd like to tell me what this is all about."

Malcolm stepped forward, "It's in the nature of an experiment to add to your intelligence for making decisions about which vehicles are worth searching. I know that you have some high-grade information that leads to a good success rate in your searches. At the same time, there's a great deal of much lower grade data that produces a poor success rate. Our experiment is aimed at trying to improve that low grade information. Whether or not we'll be successful remains to be seen, but we'll give it our best shot."

Paul noted how Malcolm had underplayed their hand by not mentioning who had authorised their presence – he rather suspected a Cabinet level decision - and then by expressing doubt about their abilities. He listened as Malcolm suggested that one of the group would like to be with a dog, in a safe location near to slow moving traffic leaving each ship, while another one of them would be with whichever Border Force officer was choosing the vehicles to be searched.

Philip armed them all with high-vis jackets and took them to meet the 3 o'clock ferry. They observed the docking from a discrete distance. When traffic began to rumble from the ferry, they soon identified a spot where it would be possible to detect infected vehicles as they passed by, so they asked Philip about the feasibility of arranging an observation post that would be protected from traffic hazards. It was agreed that protective barriers would be arranged at the relevant point.

All that remained was to hope that Mr Big's shipments were indeed using this port and that they were sufficiently frequent for at least one of them to be caught during the few weeks ahead.

Chapter 39 – Working with Border Force

Chris and Paul were on the first early shift, but they were not stopping for breakfast at 3.45 in the morning. Instead, they took cereal bars for the car ride and vowed to breakfast after the shift. Siete would have to do the same. There was no cereal bar for her, though Paul had retained some treats from the previous evening. Malcolm had provided them with a communication system, and the couple wore earpieces with wires curling into their clothing. Paul was soon imagining himself, in a dark suit and sunglasses, on duty as security for someone like the US president. Back in reality, he quickly told himself to get a grip and not to do anything that would attract attention.

At the port, Philip was nowhere to be seen, but another officer, Sian, showed Paul and Siete to the spotting position that had been set up and took Chris back to where vehicles would be picked out for searches. As Paul stood behind a set of concrete blocks, he thought about the task ahead of him. It would be best if he was conservative in his suggestions of vehicles to be investigated. There could be some cars, for example, that had recently been used for dubious purposes and the secondary infection from that might still be evident. He only wanted to identify those that were currently up to no good. They would be ones that reeked of infection, and he would restrict himself to those, if he could.

He watched as the ship nosed into the dock and was secured. His mind wandered, as it frequently did, to memories of Piers and his own enduring sorrow over what had happened. Piers had been a good man and a great friend. Paul hoped that their work in Newhaven would begin to make a fitting memorial to him.

Eventually Paul's mind was drawn back to the present as the bow of the ship was raised, and the shore crew performed a mysterious set of preparations before, finally, the first vehicles trundled from the ferry. Paul wondered how many of them would show signs of infection. He wanted to assume that most of the population would be upright, law-abiding citizens, though his experience during Siete's walks each day didn't do much to encourage that kind of hope.

The first cars began to pass by, and Paul concentrated on making himself as sensitive as possible, taking care to sense only the rotting apples phenomenon. At first, he almost expected every oncoming vehicle to wreak with the indication of dubious activity, but only one or two displayed even a hint of infection. He ignored those. Of course, it was unreasonable to think that there would be smuggling gangs at work on every ferry that docked. It could be days or weeks before anything significant was found. Worse than that, he'd never tried to detect the infection in this way; the whole project might not work. Perhaps he had raised false hopes of success.

As these thoughts were passing through his mind, he was assaulted by a waft of fermenting apples, and Siete whined. Where was that coming from? The smell was becoming stronger as he saw a red estate car in the line of traffic. When it passed him, the smell reached a peak. He could see that the car was loaded with equipment for a camping expedition, and a young couple was in the front seats. He almost forgot to relay the information. Hurriedly he made a mental note of the registration plate and told Chris that the car should be searched.

That was his sole success of the morning, though, unless the search revealed contraband, it might not be a success at all. It was always possible that the car was involved in some bad activity, but that it was nothing to do with smuggling. It was also possible that there was contraband so well hidden that it wouldn't be found. In either case, he wouldn't have endeared their project to the Border Force officers on duty. No doubt word would then spread rapidly that they were just a hindrance that everyone could do without.

Once the traffic had cleared, Paul hurried back to the vehicle check point to find out what had happened. There was the estate car with Chris and Sian, together with other officers engaged in searching the vehicle. The car had been loaded up to the roof with everything needed for a camping trip, but it had taken only a short time to discover a cardboard box underneath the sleeping bags. The 10 kilogrammes of hand rolling tobacco in the box would have more than financed the couple's holiday.

Sian and her colleagues were barely concealing their delight beneath the stern faces they presented to the pair of smuggling tourists. Paul joined Chris and they quietly left the search team to process the offenders.

By the time they had been driven back to the house, Paul and Chris found everyone else at breakfast. They were met with a chorus of, "What happened?" Paul replied that they would feed Siete and then tell all. There was an excited buzz at the table, encouraged by the belief that there was something to tell.

When Chris and Paul were seated for their breakfast, Paul began to explain, "I was worried about identifying every vehicle that showed the slightest hint of infection. I thought that most of them would be wild goose chases caused by infection from previous activities. So, I decided only to call attention to any vehicles where the infection was very strong."

Malcolm nodded with approval, "That was a good call, and I think we should aim for that as a matter of policy."

Paul continued, "In point of fact I'd almost given up hope of finding any vehicles to be searched, when a red car came by which absolutely stank of rotting apples. I called that one in to Chris."

Chris took up the tale, "Philip wasn't there this morning. I had someone called Sian with me. She had the red car pulled over. There was a couple inside who'd been on a camping holiday. The vehicle was fully loaded with their equipment, but it didn't take much to discover that there was a large carton of tobacco underneath their gear, and I think Border Force were rather pleased with the find. We made ourselves scarce and left them to it."

Everyone at the table was beaming at the success. It wasn't a huge haul of contraband, but it was significant and they were now full of optimism about what they might achieve.

Chapter 40 – French Polish

Days at the house soon settled into a routine. The two couples would take their dogs for a 10-kilometre run before lunch on most days. By now, Paul's increased level of fitness meant that he could keep up, provided that the run didn't turn into a race. It wasn't quite clear whether their armed guards had realised that this kind of exercise might be part of their duties, but though they were encumbered with a weapon, they took it in good part, hoping that their activity wouldn't raise too many eyebrows amongst the residents in the village and the local countryside. On weekdays, before the run, there would be an informal report back over breakfast. During the busy schedule at weekends, the 9.30 ferry prevented everyone from being together at breakfast, so the report was delayed until the evening meal.

There had been a noticeable thawing of the relationship with the Newhaven Border Force officers. Although there had been no major discovery of illegal goods, there were sufficient relatively minor finds to generate enthusiasm for Malcolm's 'experiment.' The policy of only identifying vehicles where there was a very strong indication of infection proved its worth. Every car or lorry that was flagged up was found to contain contraband – until day seven. That morning Ellie and Malcolm reported back at breakfast.

"One of the first vehicles to leave the ferry," Ellie told them, "was an estate car carrying three young men. The car was heavily infected, so I called it in for a search."

Malcolm took up the account, "The car was pulled over. The three men claimed that they were returning from a tour of Southern France and the North of Italy. Their whole manner portrayed every indication of guilt, but that wasn't supported by the search. By the time the ferry had unloaded, and Gabrielle joined us, nothing had been found."

Ellie was eager to explain what happened next, "I was gobsmacked that nothing had been found. There had to be something - I could smell their vehicle and luggage from an enormous distance. I felt like sniffing at their goods myself to locate the problem, but I couldn't very well do that without giving away our special skills. Then it hit me. There'd be no problem if Doce detected their contraband, so I let him search. He went straight to a couple of packs of canned drinks; eight cans of Sprite and another eight of Cola. Except that they weren't." Ellie looked round at all the expectant faces, "You know that you can buy dummy food cans to hide money at home. Well, these guys had got hold of sixteen dummy drinks cans. Each one was stuffed with heroin so, altogether, they had a couple of kilogrammes of the drug hidden."

A day later, Steve reported back that a lorry driver on the evening ferry had concealed a particularly evil-looking knife in his cab. He'd hidden it in the fridge in his cab, underneath his food and drink. This was all good, but none of their finds so far could be anything to do with Mr Big's shipments. While the Border Force officers were becoming elated with successes, Malcolm's team were becoming dispirited. It was true that they were doing some good, but their purpose here was to find a lead that would help them to track down Mr Big. Although they hadn't set out with a fixed time scale to achieve their mission, they were developing a common feeling that if nothing was found within a month, they'd need to come up with a new plan. They were already at the end of their second week.

Malcolm attempted to bolster everyone's spirits at the evening meal, "If Mr Big is running regular shipments through Newhaven, it's unlikely that they amount to more than one or two a month. For all we know he may be running very large shipments less often than that. You've all proved that our approach can be successful – outstandingly so. In the scheme of things, we should carry on with the good work. It's true that we can't stay much beyond four weeks, or our cover of an experiment will wear thin. As it is, we're going to leave undesirable ripples of the Border Force group here clamouring for more of whatever mysterious scheme we are working."

Ellie and Malcolm were on the rota for the evening ferry two days later. A stream of innocent vehicles had already disembarked, when an unusual one appeared on the ramp. It coincided with a great waft of infection. The vehicle itself was a purple van of the type used by home removal companies, though it was on the small side for that purpose. The golden logos on the van advertised 'French Polish,' a company specialising in quality furniture from France. Ellie called it in to Malcolm, but when Malcolm suggested that it should be searched, he was told that the van was a regular. It had been searched before, and nothing had been found. The only thing that had been discovered was that it belonged to a genuine company based in Crawley that did indeed specialise in upmarket French furniture. They always declared the load and paid the duty required. Everything seemed to be above board. Nevertheless, Malcolm had pressed that it should be searched again. In the light of experience over the previous two weeks, his case was persuasive, and the van was pulled over.

By the time Ellie and Doce appeared on the scene a search had begun in earnest. Ellie suggested that the dog should take over for a few minutes. During that time the Alsatian led them to a couple of well-padded armchairs. Although all the furniture items were heavy, this pair did seem unusually so. The extra weight was due to 10 kilogrammes of heroin that had been packed into each one. Ellie and Malcolm left the port with its officers in a state of high excitement. This load would make the newspapers. Fortunately, the driver of the van had been prevented from making phone calls, and Malcolm had persuaded Border Force to keep the find to themselves for 24 hours.

Back at the house, despite the lateness of the hour, there was a flurry of activity. Malcolm informed everyone about the van. He told them that the van driver was claiming total responsibility for the drugs and was insisting that they were nothing to do with his employers at French Polish. His assertion was that he'd picked up the drugs in a French layby or 'aire.' He'd been instructed to deliver them in a quiet road just off the A23 – he would know the spot when he saw it. Malcolm didn't remotely believe that story and announced that they should all leave for home immediately. He wanted a raid on the French Polish premises in Crawley early the next morning.

Their two cars were speeding north before midnight.

Chapter 41 – Death comes calling

French Polish was based on an industrial estate in the outskirts of Crawley. Malcolm and Chris had arranged for the premises to be watched during the small hours and for a police raid on the premises at 9 a.m. in the morning. Sania had found overnight accommodation for Steve, Ellie and Doce. Paul and Chris had returned home, but the whole team from Newhaven was gathered again next day to observe the raid.

The proprietor of French Polish turned out to be a woman of Greek origin, named Sapphira, who must have been approaching retirement age. Her long, dark hair hung in natural ringlets over large, gold earrings. She had sharp features and wore a stern expression, suggestive of an employer who would brook no nonsense from her employees. When she was told about the drugs found in her van, she was horrified and promised full co-operation over any prosecution of the driver. Her main concern was for the return of her van with its load of furniture. She was keen to show how all the items in the van had been declared for import, and that she had paid the duty required on them. As Sapphira showed the police round the stock of furniture in her warehouse, she was vociferous in her assertions that the business was a model of honesty and decency; she even donated some of her stock to local charity shops in the town when she had items that didn't sell. In short, her business was a pillar of the community, and her reputation for fair dealing was second to none.

Despite all Sapphira's claims, she exuded a strong scent of citrus to Ellie, Steve, and Paul. They were fully convinced that her claims of probity concealed an active criminal mind. However, the warehouse showed no sign of any illegal substances. The only real mystery about the business was over how it made money. It was hard to believe that the Crawley area provided a buoyant market for expensive French furniture, yet the hard fact was that the search team was faced with a warehouse full of high value furniture from France. According to Border Force, the van brought regular loads across the channel. If the goods were not being sold, where did they go? That small mystery was rendered more mysterious when the Newhaven Border Force was asked about the outward journeys of the French Polish van. The perplexing reply was that the van also exported furniture from England to France. It was loaded in both directions when it crossed the Channel, so where did the out-going furniture come from?

The raid found nothing. The warehouse only contained furniture and a pile of empty cardboard boxes that had contained accessories for furniture, such as castors and drawer handles. In disappointment, Malcolm's team gathered for a conference at 'Fort Knox.'

Malcolm took the chair. "Any thoughts or observations?" he asked.

After a thoughtful silence, Paul spoke, "We all know that Sapphira is guilty of something. I strongly suspect, as I imagine we all do, that she knew all about the drugs. It would be a miracle if she could make money selling lots of French furniture in Crawley, but Crawley is an ideal base for smuggling operations. Gatwick airport is close by, there's good access to Newhaven, and the M23 is nearby for transport to the rest of the UK. The question is, if Sapphira is dealing in drugs, where does she keep them?"

Malcolm himself had a possible answer to that, "If you remember, there was mention of both a lockup and of Crawley from the chap Piers put into a coma. I asked the police to investigate, and I now have a list of lockup stores in the area. There'd be a lot of them to look at, but that's really our only lead."

"We could narrow the list down very easily," Ellie said, "Three of us are Spotters. It would be very easy to tour the list of possible premises. We'd know immediately which of them is associated with bad goings-on."

"Okay, if everyone's happy, we'll do that," Malcolm replied, "Of course, we're assuming that Sapphira is working for Mr Big, and if that assumption proves to be wrong, we'll be back to square one. For myself, I'm hopeful that we're on the right track. If we can identify Sapphira's store of contraband, we could set up a stake-out in the hope of following goods from there to someone more closely associated with Mr Big."

The group pored over a large map of the Crawley area and plotted out the possible lockups to be checked. Several of the premises were blocks of self-storage units. The group all felt that Mr Big would prefer an individual unit, where he could come and go without passing through any form of security. If all else failed, the group would have to investigate the blocks of storage units, but they wouldn't be the first priority. The whole process of filtering out large commercial storage companies and plotting the others on the map was slow, and it took a couple of hours to work out three routes that would enable them to visit all the likely contenders.

For the search, they used the same pairings as those used in Newhaven. That placed Paul and Chris together with Siete. Reluctantly, Malcolm agreed that for this outing, an armed guard would make them too conspicuous, so Chris offered to find another young couple of her agents to accompany them instead. Malcolm pointed out that she had a mole among her associates, so it would be better if he provided a suitable couple from his contacts. That was agreed. They would look like two couples out for a walk with their dog. Their main security, would be the self-defence training among the group and the protective nature of their German Shepherd. In addition to that there was the extra security that arose from the fact that the forces of evil wouldn't know their plans – they hoped! All the same, they had strict instructions to back out rapidly from any situation that seemed even slightly hazardous.

The three walking tours began next morning when three cars each delivered a group to the starting point of its route. Paul and Chris were left with Tim and Julia as their additional security. No background information was provided on either Tim or Julia, other than an assurance of their competence in tight situations. They were of similar age to Chris and Paul.

Although they clearly knew each other, their greeting sounded as though they hadn't worked together for quite a while.

The four of them set off with Siete on a walk that took them near sets of domestic garages. Those of interest were mostly in strips near blocks of flats or rows of housing. There were often quiet access roads for the garages, and the unobtrusive locations had been an open invitation for them to become the haunt of local gangs of youths. The gas capsules and other detritus littering the areas were frequently infected, and that hampered Paul's search for infected garages. From Paul's imagined criminal perspective, the problem of using these garages as storage was the danger of other users arriving and observing the contents when the smugglers were accessing their goods. Perhaps they would solve that difficulty by keeping their goods in boxes that were labelled as something boring. Nevertheless, he thought that this kind of isolated garage was their best bet.

As they were walking, Paul remembered the cardboard boxes at the warehouse. Why had French Polish needed so many boxes of drawer handles? Their furniture would already have handles fitted, and it would run counter to their business model to replace the French ones. Suppose those boxes weren't intended for drawer handles at all. They would make perfect containers to store drugs in a lockup store or garage. The French Polish van could deliver drugs in those boxes without triggering suspicion in any observer. Mr Big could then collect them in an unmarked vehicle, again without causing disquiet in anyone who might see his agents.

In one residential street, the stores on the list to be checked consisted of two rows of about twenty garages facing each other in a dead-end drive way. An unshaven young man in a leather jacket sauntered into the drive ahead of them. As they themselves turned into the drive, Paul began to sense fermenting apples. He could also see the young man leaning against a garage at the far end. He was looking at them as he spoke on his phone. The smell of citrus hung about him. This didn't look good.

There was the sound of a motorbike engine approaching. No, it was several motorbikes. Chris was already on her phone when the bikes drew up across the open end of the drive. There had to be six or seven bikes, and each bike carried a leather-jacketed pillion passenger as well as its rider. Paul and his group were heavily outnumbered by twelve or so men in black leathers, boots, and crash helmets. The approaching men carried an assortment of offensive weapons, with an emphasis on knives and batons, which were being wielded in a most threatening manner. Siete's growl and bared teeth made the men hesitate in their advance.

Chris whispered to the others, "If we get out of this in one piece, it would be good to detain the one behind us for questioning." The others nodded in hopeless acknowledgement of her words. She added, "Don't back up, and look confident."

Tim addressed the mob, who were slowly approaching again, "What's the problem?"

One crash-helmeted figure raised his visor, "You are, and especially the bitch with the dog. Give her to us and the rest of you can go, otherwise we'll smash you to a pulp and take her anyway."

Even though he didn't fancy their chances, lacked any training, and was trembling with fright, Paul was still not going to let Chris be taken without a fight. Two of the gang stepped forward to take Chris by the arm. That was a mistake. In the blink of an eye one of them leapt back in alarm as Siete sprang at him. The other found that his own arm had been grabbed. He crashed to the ground to find Chris standing over him, kicking his knife out of reach. He had barely registered what had happened when Chris stamped on his crotch and he doubled up in agony. There was a stunned silence in which Paul called Siete back out of harm's way. It was clear that an all-out attack was imminent. This couldn't end well. The bikers took a firmer grip of their weapons and were about to charge. It was in that moment they all heard the approaching sound of multiple police sirens.

The bikers rapidly reversed their movements and backed up to their bikes, leaving their fallen comrade rolling on the ground. Chris turned to the young man behind them who had called the gang. She pointed to the man on the ground as she spoke, "You're coming with us if you don't want to have that happen to you. Is that clear?" He nodded in sullen silence, and Chris followed up with, "Any move that I don't like the look of, and you know what will happen. Now, phone!" She held out a hand, and he handed it over.

Tim and Julia took the prisoner by the arms, and the group were heading out of the driveway as the police vehicles drew up. Chris went to speak to a couple of the officers and pointed out the man on the ground. She returned to the group, "Come on, let's go." The police ignored them as they left the scene of the action, which was becoming flooded with uniformed officers. A short distance along the road, Malcolm's original transport car stopped to pick them up and they drove off with their captive.

Chapter 42 – Preparing for action

The car took them a few miles out of town to a mock Tudor village hall. Malcolm and Sania were there to show them into a carpeted meeting room, where the rest of the team were waiting. Their captive was made to sit under a battery of searching eyes, including those of the two dogs. If Malcolm's intention was to unsettle him by the use of an environment that was outside the rules and regulations of a normal interview, he was succeeding admirably. The prisoner was nervously surveying the two German Shepherds that were both sitting just in front of him, giving him their full attention. "You can't do this," he blurted. He was ignored as the group found seats for themselves and began to watch Chris at work.

Chris was examining the phone she had acquired. She moved behind their detainee and thrust the phone in front of him with one hand, while her other hand rested firmly on the back of his neck. "Unlock it," she commanded. He hesitated briefly, she tightened her grip on him and he complied. She reviewed his call and text history, found the last call made, redialled the number, and switched on the speaker.

After a few rings, a rough voice answered, "Yea?" Chris paused for a few seconds, ended the call, and passed the phone to Malcolm, who left the room with it.

She addressed their prisoner, who was nervously running a hand through his greasy black hair, "Now your friends will know that we have you. They'll have no idea what you're telling us, but they'll probably imagine the worst. After a decent interval, we're going to let you go. I wonder what you'll do then. I guess you could walk home from here, though if you like, we could give you a lift to where we found you."

"You haven't even asked me anything. What do you want?"

"We already have everything we need from you," Chris answered, "I don't think there's anything else you can tell us, so we have no further use for you."

The captive was desperately trying to reassess his position, "But I could give you information."

"I very much doubt that you could tell us anything that we don't already know. Don't bother with the details of your biker friends. We know who they are and where to find them. I suppose you could tell us more about who pays them, but I don't imagine that you know that."

"I don't know who you are either, so if I tell you something you don't know, will you hand me over to the proper police?"

"Sure," Chris drawled, "you could try, though I really don't think you know anything useful."

Her victim became more animated, "You're right, I don't know who pays, but what if I could point you to an address?"

"If you can convince us of something useful there, we'll happily get the police to come and collect you."

He looked round apprehensively, "Is that a deal?"

"I need to check that with the boss," Chris answered. She left the room for a second or two and then returned with, "Yes, fine." Everyone else nodded in agreement.

"Okay then. You need to look at Rowhurst Manor. It's an estate in West Sussex."

The whole party prepared to leave the building. They ushered their prisoner out, with instructions to wait for the local police. He might ignore their instruction, but that didn't matter to them, and any deviation from it would probably end badly for him in any case.

Malcolm arranged a car for Tim and Julia, and then suggested that the rest of them should head for the house Paul thought of as Fort Knox. There would be facilities for Steve and Ellie to stay there with Sania. Malcolm gave the hall keys to a woman waiting outside the premises, and the group returned to their cars.

At Fort Knox, a meal awaited them. This set of premises was new to Steve and Ellie. In fact, Paul and Chris had only ever seen the ground floor. In the circumstances, none of them was paying much attention to the building. There had already been sufficient activity to fill a whole day, and the thought of food filled their minds. Much to the surprise of everyone, the meal was lunch. Surely, it was too late in the day for that meal; so much had happened. But their watches proved that it was indeed only lunchtime.

Malcolm confirmed that they had all the details for the leader of the biker gang. He'd been tracked down from information on the captive's phone. That was what Chris had been checking on before releasing the prisoner. Malcolm suggested that the two couples should take the afternoon off to wind down after the excitement of the morning. He also floated the idea that it might be convenient for Chris and Paul to stay on the premises for a few days. There was plenty of accommodation on the first floor. If they did want to leave the grounds, the armed guard was back on duty. In the meantime, he and Sania would work out a plan to investigate Rowhurst Manor.

Everyone in the group was very happy to stay together. They all went to explore the bedrooms, while the two dogs roamed in the garden. The rooms were not as plush as those on the country estate, but there was a choice of four well-furnished ensuite double bedrooms. There was unanimity over the need for a shower and change of clothing, and they agreed to meet in the lounge later in the afternoon.

Having showered, Paul and Chris laid on the comfortable double bed in each other's arms. Paul reflected on the morning's events, "You were amazing at the garages, Chris. I truly thought our time was up and that we were all going to die a horrible death. How did you stay so calm?"

"It didn't come easily, but I've learnt to control my fears. Even the most desperate of situations is made worse by panic. If I can keep the ability to think clearly, that gives me an edge which might prove to be the difference between life and death. This morning, we were saved by two things: firstly, Tim caused a small delay by calmly challenging the gang; secondly the two men who tried to take me by the arm helped us - their fate caused a further slight hesitation on the part of our attackers. Put the two things together and you have the few seconds that enabled the police sirens to be heard before we were hacked to pieces."

"I assume it was you who called the police in the first place."

"Effectively, yes. As soon as I saw what was likely to develop, I called the cavalry to respond with urgency, which they did."

"I'm still trying to work out exactly what happened with our captive."

"Most of the useful information was on his phone. I left Malcolm to contact the relevant authorities to ask for names and addresses. In the meantime, I wasn't holding out hope of there being any other useful information to be obtained. I didn't want to threaten our hostage overtly, but I thought he might eventually realise that his friends would expect him to be in the hands of the local police. They wouldn't know that it was us who had him, despite what I'd said. His fate would be unpromising if they thought he'd been talking to us. He worked out that he'd be better off in the hands of the police and voluntarily offered a deal to tell us the one useful thing he knew. So that was all good."

"Well, I know it has only been half a day so far, and I haven't actually done very much, but I feel exhausted. Let's just rest here for a while." They did. Paul snuggled up to Chris and they slept.

Chapter 43 – Rowhurst Manor

Paul strongly suspected that Steve and Ellie had also taken a nap during the afternoon. They all met in the lounge shortly before it was time for dinner. Paul had come to expect that, when he was with Malcolm, there would be no stinting on the quality of meals. The idea of an army marching on its stomach was clearly one that he fully endorsed, and Paul, for one, would not be complaining, though it did leave him wondering how Malcolm and Sania were managing to burn off the calories.

Over the meal, Malcolm indicated that it would take a day or so for Sania and himself to come up with sufficient information to enable intelligent discussion on the way forward. Therefore, his team and their dogs were free to amuse themselves for the next day at least.

After dinner, Paul set up his work station in the bedroom so that he'd be able to attend to his business during the following morning. Chris suggested that they might plan an outing for the afternoon. Perhaps they'd all like to visit the Leisure Centre for a workout and a swim. She could possibly arrange for Zara to meet them there, which could enable Paul to begin learning some basic moves in self-defence. Her thinking met with approval all round. Chris did point out that, although Zara was a secret service agent, she knew nothing about Michael & Co. Because of that, and the problem of a secret service mole, the present mission couldn't be discussed with her.

Paul made good progress with his work during the morning, while Chris exercised Siete in the grounds. After lunch the two couples left their dogs and set off by car to the Leisure Centre. The decision to use a car was made so that their armed guard wouldn't be apparent to every casual observer, and for the same reason, the guard would remain in the vehicle outside the centre. Despite the presence of a guard reminding Paul of all the recent traumas, he was in a very good mood. Here he was on an outing with his lovely wife and their friends, without him having to carry a burden of secrets. His sense of joyous freedom gave him a lightness of spirit that was impervious to all external threat.

Zara was waiting for them in the café area. Chris made the introductions, and they decided that Paul would go with Zara to the private room she used while the other three would use the gym. Later, they would meet back together for a swim, followed by refreshments in the café.

His time with Zara wasn't quite how Paul had expected it to be. She spent a good deal of time discussing how to avoid getting into a fight and more time on the value of maintaining distance between himself and a possible aggressor. In the event of a close-up conflict, she had no civilised rules for combat. Her aim was to use any means available to put an opponent out of action in the shortest possible time. Paul couldn't afford to be squeamish, nor should he be trying to copy any of the fancy moves that Chris might be capable of.

When they met for swimming, Paul swam a few lengths, but the other four must have clocked up at least a mile each before they were ready for the café. Paul thought the stilted conversation over tea and coffee was hilarious, principally because of all the things that couldn't be said. There could be no discussion of the work with Michael & Co. because Zara didn't know about that. Zara and Chris's employment was off-limits because Zara wouldn't expect Steve and Ellie to know about that. Steve and Ellie couldn't talk about how they'd met Paul and Chris because that was part of what Zara wasn't supposed to know, nor could they say much about their work as solicitors because that was mostly confidential. Paul and Chris could tell the others about the play they'd seen in the old London County Hall, but they couldn't talk much about the plot because the audience was sworn to secrecy. Neither could they tell about the attack in the alley afterwards because Zara would assume that Steve and Ellie weren't supposed to know the details of that. Paul could talk about insurance, but that was hardly riveting stuff. In short, there were quite a few silences. Now that he wasn't keeping secrets from Chris, none of this was a burden to Paul, and he could simply laugh to himself at the way they were all tip-toeing round their various secrets.

Back at the house, Malcolm and Sania called a meeting for the following morning when they reckoned that they would have reconnaissance details for Rowhurst Manor. After another superb dinner, the group enjoyed an evening of freedom together. Following breakfast next day, they assembled with eager anticipation in the lounge, where Malcolm had set up a projection system connected to a laptop computer.

Sania, dressed in her customary sari, informed them that the owner of Rowhurst Manor was known as Sir Karl Stuart. Her researches had found no evidence that he really had a knighthood. She presumed that he could get away with it because, apart from themselves, how many people would ever check such things? Bearing in mind that he was suspected of being Mr Big, Malcolm and herself hadn't wanted to show obvious interest in the Manor. They had to assume that Karl would know about the episode at the garages, and he might suspect that they'd identified which of the garages was Sapphira's store. The presence of the dog would produce the risk, from his point of view, that the Alsatian had sniffed out where drugs were stored. Sania was hoping that 'Sir' Karl wouldn't know that his name had been connected with the drugs. To maintain his level of ignorance, the authorities had given permission for reconnaissance of Rowhurst Manor to be carried out by a drone flying at high altitude, and Malcolm had compiled the resulting video.

Malcolm took the reins and commentated on the video as it was projected, "The first thing we discovered was that the estate has a high level of security. There are guards, almost certainly armed, and the whole place is bristling with cameras. The house itself is large, as you can see. We don't have a *recent* floor plan, but we do have the one on the screen, which comes from 50 years ago, when the manor was occasionally open to the public. You'll realise that there are four storeys, though one of those is a basement containing a kitchen and working areas for servants. The top storey contains bedrooms, also for servants. The ground floor has a grand hall, complete with a gallery for musicians and, at the time of the plan in front of us, there was a billiard room, library, dining room, and lounges. The first floor contains a set of bedrooms, each with associated sitting rooms and bathrooms. There's also a separate bathroom for general use. At some point, a two-storey East Wing was added to the original manor. That used to contain an art gallery and a music room, plus some bedrooms on the floor above. Finally, there's also an indoor swimming pool that is accessed from the East Wing."

"Apart from the manor house itself," Malcolm continued, "there are many other buildings on the estate. There's a gate-keeper's cottage by the main entrance to the grounds. You can see that it has been turned into a guard house. There are other houses in the grounds, which would originally have been used for estate workers and, judging by the parked cars, they're in current use. Karl is unmarried, but he's surrounded by employees who live on the estate. He also has several female associates who live in style with him. We suspect that they effectively form a small harem."

"The prospect of searching Rowhurst Manor is a daunting one. There's a stables block, which still does contain horses as well as cars. Part of the grounds is used as a walled-garden, complete with heated greenhouses. Plus, there's an underground bunker that was built during the middle of the last century; initially as an air-raid shelter for the Second World War. We think it's been extended since. You can only see the entrance; we know nothing about the inside."

"Presumably we'd like to search the place," Chris commented, "but it looks as though that would take a small army."

"Yes, and yes," Malcolm replied, "We must assume that Karl himself has a small army. If we want to avoid a gun fight, we'll need to go in with overwhelming force. The plan is to leave that in the hands of the police. We'll rely on them to clear the whole estate, hopefully to secure Karl for us, and then leave us free to question him and to search the premises. We expect armed officers to take control of Rowhurst Manor in the early hours of tomorrow morning and to have the property cleared for us by the afternoon."

After a pause to collect his thoughts, Malcolm moved on to a new topic, "When the police came to your rescue at Crawley, they thought they were simply dealing with a gang attack. I've now told them about the garage we'd like to search. There's a warrant to search it, so we'll set off to do that after breakfast, and the local police will meet us there. Sapphira has disappeared, so we haven't been able to ask her about it. Naturally, her employees are denying all knowledge of anything and everything. Once we've done with the garage, we'll head to Rowhurst. There's so much to search on the estate, that I anticipate we'll need to live in the manor for a few days while we search the house and grounds, so be ready tomorrow morning to change our address for a while. Sheila will be bringing a friend to the manor to help in catering for us."

Chapter 44 – Takedown and disappearance

Malcolm's team stood back while a locksmith made short work of the lock on the garage. The accompanying group of police officers watched with interest as the up-and-over door was raised for them. Inside the lockup, the walls were lined with steel shelves, where several cardboard boxes were stored. Most of them were labelled 'Furniture accessories,' like the empty ones that had been seen at the French Polish warehouse, but these boxes weren't empty. The contents were obviously drugs – perhaps as much as 50 kilogrammes altogether. There was one box that was different. Malcolm opened it and then turned to the others, "It's a pistol – Glock 17."

There was a brief discussion between Malcolm, Sania and the two detectives in charge of the police operation. Sania returned to the team, "We are going to leave the police to secure the contents of the garage while we make our way to Rowhurst. In case you are wondering, today's haul probably has a street value of around three million pounds. That is bound to end up being reported by the news media, but our part in this will not be mentioned. The credit will go to a combined operation between the Police and Border Force. The cardboard boxes leave no doubt that the drugs came from Sapphira, so she will be arrested when she is found."

As their two cars cruised towards West Sussex, Paul realised how Sapphira must have been conducting her illegal business. He presented his conclusions to his travelling companions, Chris and Malcolm, "I've worked out how Sapphira was using her furniture business, Malcolm."

"Do share," said Malcolm, "let's see if your thinking agrees with mine."

"Okay. Firstly, the furniture. I think she was sending the same furniture backwards and forwards to France. She was using the stock in her warehouse to vary the loads, but I reckon she hardly ever bought or sold any of it; she was just ferrying it between her warehouse in Crawley and another one in France. It all looked legitimate, because she was producing the appropriate paperwork and paying any import duty on every trip. The cost of that was small fry compared with the value of the smuggled goods hidden in the furniture each time. If drugs came into the UK on one trip, then the trip back to France would contain hidden cash. As we've already worked out, she didn't keep anything illegal in her warehouse. All that went to the garage, where it could stay until 'Sir' Karl arranged for it to be collected."

"Bravo!" cried Malcolm with a clap. "That's precisely the conclusion I came to. All we need to do now is to catch Karl and find something to incriminate him. But before that, lunch."

They were near Horsham when the cars turned off from the 'A' road and began to wind their way along quiet, rural lanes. The reason became clear when they approached a country inn. "I think you'll find the food here is acceptable," Malcolm announced. The proprietor greeted him with an enthusiastic handshake and showed the group to a private room, where tables were laid for them. Their dogs were left in the car park with water and the armed guard. That was going to be a surprise for any other customers!

The food was more than acceptable. As they ate, they quietly discussed their progress and their expectations. Chris was looking forward to having Karl locked up so that she could resume what she regarded as normal life; without the need for protection from a vindictive drugs baron.

They were in no rush, because Malcolm reckoned that the police were over optimistic in thinking that they could secure the whole Rowhurst estate by midday. He was correct. When his team arrived at the gates to Rowhurst Manor in the afternoon, the property and its grounds had just been secured. Paul and his friends arrived in time to see a line of captives being escorted through the security barrier into waiting vans. As they watched, Chris let out a gasp, "That's Jacquie!" she exclaimed. In a flash, she jumped out of the car. Fortunately, the police escorts reacted with commendable speed to prevent Chris from closing in on

Jacquie. The woman herself just looked at Chris with contempt and spat. Chris was left standing, and looking in amazement, as Jacquie was loaded into a police van. For Paul, light was dawning. That explains how they'd been bugged, with no sign of forced entry. He'd never known how that had happened, but of course Jacquie had easy access, without the need for a break-in.

Everyone in the group had seen a photograph of Karl when Malcolm had briefed them, but none of them could spot him among the line of prisoners. Paul was hoping that he was being kept for them in the Manor House, and he was full of optimism as a police officer approached their vehicle to address Malcolm, "The property and grounds are clear for you, sir. I take it that you aren't interested in any of the estate workers for the moment."

"We might like words with some of them later, depending on what we discover from Karl."

"There's enough to hold most of the workers, sir – illegal firearms etcetera, but I'm afraid you won't be having words with Karl anytime soon. There was no sign of him."

"That's a disappointment," Malcolm replied mildly, "In the meantime, we'll see if we can link him with crime, so that he can be held when he does surface."

"There'll be no problem with that, sir, we already have enough to hold him, not least for all the illegal weapons we've removed from his workers. In view of that, I'm going to leave officers guarding the perimeter of the grounds in case more of the gang have guns and attempt to repossess the manor."

"Thank you very much, Superintendent, we'll probably be here for a couple of days, but I'll let you know when we're done."

Chris came back to the car in a combination of distress and fury at Jacquie's apparent betrayal. She was seething as the security barrier was raised, and their vehicles swept along the drive. They crested a rise in the ground, and the manor house came into view. In front of the main entrance, the drive encircled a large lawn with an ornamental pond and fountain at its centre. With a crunch of gravel, their cars came to rest by the impressive wooden doors. Although the building itself suggested opulence and the casual authority of a wealthy owner at the end of the Victorian era, the multiplicity of cameras created a more sinister impression. For Paul, the subtle menace was compounded by the strong sweet sensation of ripe fruit. Somewhere on this estate there must be a primary source of infection.

As Malcolm instructed everyone to make themselves at home, Paul wasn't the only one who was uncomfortable. Steve and Ellie were also approaching Malcolm, "There's a primary infection here," Ellie told him. "It's pretty oppressive, so we won't be comfortable until we've done something about it."

Malcolm opened the boot of his vehicle and handed over a couple of spray cans. "Thanks!" they chorused. The three of them set off at a jog, calling over their shoulders, "We won't be long."

With no fear of opposition, they rapidly followed the scent trail to the door of the underground bunker. It was closed, but that didn't matter. The outside of the plain steel door was the source they were looking for, particularly around the lock. They sprayed the area and the cloying sweetness quickly died down to a level that they could ignore.

When they returned to the house, Malcolm was organising a search, "With three Spotters here, we should be able to uncover any guilty secrets very quickly."

"It's not quite that simple," Paul suggested, "the whole place smells of fermenting apples." Steve and Ellie were nodding in agreement as he added, "There's secondary infection everywhere, presumably because of 'Sir' Karl's whole lifestyle. We can live with it, but it will make it difficult to find contraband in amongst it."

"Okay, understood," Malcolm answered, "Do the best you can." He organised them into the familiar three groups: he would take the basement with Ellie; Sania and Steve would take the top floor; leaving Paul and Chris to search the first floor. They would all meet back in the reception hall to look at the ground floor together.

Paul and Chris took the main staircase to the bedrooms upstairs. For Paul, the background of rotting apples was all-pervasive. He could tune it out, but that wasn't the purpose for the moment. Karl had certainly made himself comfortable. His own bedroom suite was obvious from its size and the enormous bed. Also, it smelled more strongly than the others. One strange thing was the way that the bed had been slept in. The police raid would have been early in the morning, so it was understandable that there'd been no time to remake the bed. Strangely, the signs were that there had been two people in the bed during the previous night, so if neither of them had been Karl, who were they? And, if one of them was Karl, where was he?

Each of the six bedroom-suites was equipped with its own sitting room, and each was supplied with a bath and shower room. The sense of secondary infection was uniform, except for the increase in level that Paul had noticed in the master bedroom. There was nothing to indicate any particular point of interest. Cameras scattered the inside of the house as well as the outside. Although they couldn't spot any inside the bedrooms, they were certainly covering all the corridors and stairways.

When the group reconvened, none of them had found anything. Before investigating further, they unloaded their gear from the cars and trooped upstairs to choose bedrooms. Chris and Paul left their bags in Karl's room then re-joined the others to tour the ground floor. In the dining room, the large oval table had been laid for breakfast. Ellie was reporting that in the kitchen, food had been prepared for cooking before being left when the area was abandoned. At this point, they were interrupted by the clanging of a bell.

Malcolm responded to it, "Excuse me a moment."

He returned after a few minutes and announced, "That was Sheila and her friend, Martha. They've gone off to organise the kitchen. We won't starve because there's no shortage of food in the house."

They continued their tour without any expectation of finding smuggled goods on the ground floor. The main hall made a great impression on all of them. It was incongruously set up as a nightclub. There were heavy curtains across the windows, and the walls were festooned with disco lights. At one end was a long bar, while above the opposite end was a minstrel gallery filled with DJ equipment.

The library and the billiard room reminded Paul of the game, Cleudo. "You don't think there are secret passages, do you?" he asked.

"You can go round tapping the walls, if you like," Steve said with a smile.

The East Wing was more interesting – not because of the drum kit in the music room, nor because of the art work on the walls of the gallery. It was the faint smell of a swimming pool that drew their attention. They opened the access door to find a large wet room, beyond which was a 25-metre pool with a jacuzzi at the near end and a sauna unit in the far corner. This was a facility they would use – later.

Searching the other buildings on the estate was going to be no easy matter. One thing they were agreed on was that they should begin with the bunker. Steve pointed out that access would be a problem. He remembered the locked steel door they had encountered when the group had been spraying the infection there. Sania asked him what the lock looked like and he replied that it seemed like a Chubb-style of lock. Sania nodded, "Let us go and investigate. We might need some light." Mobile phones were waved in reply, and they set off for the bunker.

At the steel door, Sania produced lock-picking tools from somewhere about her person. After a minute or two of fiddling, the door swung open. Torches weren't needed because a light came on just inside the entrance, and when they flicked a switch on the wall, a tunnel ahead was also illuminated. A second switch lit another tunnel on their left.

The passageways had walls and ceilings made from prefabricated concrete sections and wooden shelving lining the walls. Each tunnel ran for about 40 metres before opening out into a large space, so they divided their forces between the two passageways. Malcolm led Paul and Chris straight ahead. Some of the shelves along the wall held cardboard boxes of exactly the same type they'd found in Sapphira's warehouse and again in the Crawley garage. This was evidence linking Karl to the smuggling operation, and the content of the boxes made a further link. The tunnel contained many millions of pounds worth of drugs. At the far end of the corridor was a room, where there were tables in the middle and a collection of machinery against one wall. Malcolm recognised the equipment, "This is where drugs are cut – 'diluted,' in ordinary terms – with icing sugar from the cartons on the shelves. All the equipment is here to press drugs into pills or to pack them in sachets. Karl's going to end up with a long prison sentence, once we catch him."

As they turned to leave, the group from the other corridor were arriving. Ellie was almost skipping with excitement, "Guess what we've found!" She didn't wait for any suggestions, "The other corridor is lined with weapons. There's everything from pistols to grenade launchers. Come and see."

They followed her to find enough stacks of weapons to start a small war. "I'll have a guard posted outside the bunker until this can be cleared," Malcolm decided, "Let's take ourselves back to the house."

By common, unspoken consent the main lounge area became their base of operations. Sheila had already worked wonders, and afternoon tea was waiting for them. After tea, Chris declared that it was time to use the pool, and she ran off to find her swimsuit. Steve and Ellie shot off after her while Paul hesitated. He soon decided not to be left out and went to retrieve his own swimming shorts. He passed Steve and Ellie on their way down the stairs, though Chris was long gone by the time he reached their room. He grabbed his shorts and set off for the pool.

Steve and Ellie were already in the pool when Paul arrived, but there was no sign of Chris. "Has anyone seen Chris?" He called, "I don't know where she's got to."

"Perhaps she used the servants' stairs down and found they came out somewhere different," Ellie answered, "I expect she'll be here in a minute."

Time passed, and Chris still didn't appear. Paul went to look for her, calling as he went. He knew it was a large property to search on his own, but the silence that greeted all his calls was beginning to alarm him. By the time his shouting and searching attracted Malcolm's attention, there was panic in Paul's voice as he spoke, "I can't find Chris. She went for her swimming gear half an hour ago, and that's the last I saw of her. I've been looking everywhere."

Malcolm asked where everyone else was then asked Paul to stay in the lounge while he went to the pool to gather the others. While Paul was waiting, Sania arrived in the lounge, and he told her that Chris was missing. Once they were all together, they went as a group to sweep the house from top to bottom. That yielded no results.

"It seems unlikely that she went for a walk," Malcolm stated, "but we can't discount the possibility. We should give her a little longer before we call in reinforcements."

Chris had not appeared by dinner time, and Malcolm, true to his word, called in reinforcements. Within the hour he had a substantial search party, with dogs, combing the house and grounds. He suggested that his own team should eat as best they could. There was now little they could do to help the search.

Paul had no appetite for food, and he just picked at it. The rest of the party weren't much better. The only appreciation for food that evening came from the two German Shepherds, though it was a matter for speculation as to whether they tasted it at all as they wolfed it down.

The search parties all came up blank and darkness fell. Every part of the estate had been examined without result. Chris had vanished. There was nothing any of them could do that night. Indeed, it was doubtful that they could do anything the following morning either. They would just have to wait and hope that there were developments. They all went to bed, with the exception of Paul, who couldn't face the bedroom. He remained in an armchair in the lounge.

Chapter 45 – In the bunker

Paul felt called to the underground bunker. Perhaps there was more to it than they'd already found. When he arrived, the steel door was ajar. Where was Malcolm's guard? It was unlike Malcolm to employ someone who wasn't conscientious in his duty. Never mind, the absence of a guard was all to the good; it gave Paul unfettered access to the bunker. He eased the door open and crept inside. It would be best to leave the lights off. If the guard returned, light inside the bunker might attract his attention. Illumination from Paul's mobile phone would have to do.

By the light of his phone Paul examined each section of the concrete walls behind the shelving as he made his way slowly along the passage ahead of him. He reached through the shelves to touch the walls. Ugh! They were running with slime. He looked down. There was a great deal of slime, and it was gathering in puddles round his feet. He began to move more quickly towards the room at the end of the tunnel, but after a few paces there was an enormous crash behind him. He swung round in time to see the shelves collapsing and falling like dominoes across the passageway. They were falling across the corridor from both sides, and as each one fell the next one in the line followed its neighbour. By the time the succession of crashes had ceased, his way out was totally blocked, and a white cloud of drugs dust was rising from the debris.

There was only one way he could go. He moved further along the corridor, treading as lightly as he could in case he triggered some further collapse. He was nearing the room at the end of the corridor when he heard machinery starting up ahead of him. The whirring of electric motors in front of him was becoming louder, and the creeping menace of the drugs cloud behind him was coming closer. He couldn't allow the intoxicating cloud to envelope him, yet he was terrified of what might be waiting for him in the room ahead. He was rooted to the spot, rigid with fright.

Chris had conquered her fears, so he must do the same. Paul forced himself to move, and he walked slowly forward, pulling his shoes out of the sticky slime with every faltering step. He entered the room at the end. There was nobody in sight, but pills were flying across the room from the pressing machine. The noise had become deafening. Pills were ricocheting from the walls and shooting off in all directions across the room.

He gritted his teeth and ran through the hail of pills to hit the large red emergency button on the wall. He struck the stop button with all his might, but the machine didn't stop. Instead, a second machine started, and sachets of drugs began to form a pile in front of the packing machine. He hammered the red button again with his fist. Suddenly, the wall beside him swung open. 'Escape' was his only thought as he threw himself through the opening. In his haste, he dropped his phone as he jumped. Recovering his footing, he spun round to retrieve it. He was too late; the opening had closed, and he was plunged into pitch darkness. He felt the wall for any sign of a lever or door knob. There was nothing. All his pushing and prodding was to no avail, there was no way back.

Onwards into the darkness was his only option. He took one cautious step, but regretted it immediately as a firm hand grasped his shoulder, and he felt the coldness of a gun barrel pressing into the side of his neck. "Paul!" The single word was spoken and reverberated in the blackness all around him.

"Paul!" The blackness retreated. Malcolm had his hand on Paul's shoulder. The gun barrel was the pressure of his neck leaning against the wooden top of the chair he was sitting in. He was still in the lounge.

"Paul!" Malcolm repeated, "Wake up. We've had an idea."

Chapter 46 – Survival?

Paul rubbed his eyes and found that the whole team was assembled in the lounge, except for Chris of course. Malcolm turned to Sania, "Tell them, Sania."

"Malcolm and I were thinking about what we have seen here at the manor. One aspect of it struck us as very odd. We have seen video cameras all over the place. What we have not found is any control and observation room for them all."

Light was dawning in their faces as they listened, and Paul's lethargic despair was transforming into lively interest as he asked, "So where are they controlled from?"

"That is what we asked ourselves," Sania continued, "So, we took another look at the old plans of the manor and found that we have a room missing. According to the plan, there was a large toilet and bathroom at the top of the main stairs. Karl's current bedroom was on one side of it, and the second bedroom was on the other side. We have looked in both of those bedrooms and found no sign of this extra room. Nevertheless, there is a room-sized space between the two bedrooms. What we have not found is any way into it."

Paul was now fully alert, "What about from outside the house? Is there a window?"

"No," Sania continued, "we looked for that. There is only a wall between the two bedroom windows. In the centre of that wall section there is a coat of arms. We think it might have been placed there to disguise the fact that a window has been filled in. We need to go to Karl's bedroom to examine the wall more closely."

Paul couldn't wait to look. He was first to arrive in the bedroom and to begin tapping the walls. When Steve saw him, he couldn't resist a comment, "I did say that you should tap the walls, Paul."

Malcolm preferred to examine them with a magnifying glass, looking for any sign of a crack that might indicate a concealed door. After a while, he focused his attention on a framed mirror that filled the space between the stone chimney breast and a tall book case. The mirror frame was about as tall as a normal door, but it was impossible to see whether or not it was concealing anything.

Malcolm stepped back, "I can't even see how this mirror has been fixed to the wall, far less whether there's anything behind it. It's not very old, nothing like the age of the house, and that makes me suspicious. There could be a life at stake here, so that mirror must be taken off the wall. It looks as though the only way is to break it, but we don't want fragments of glass flying everywhere, so we're going to need some sheets to catch them – and we'll need some suitable tools."

"Wait a minute," Sania said, "Can we not drill a hole through the blank wall on the other side of the fire place and then push a camera through?"

"Good thinking," Malcolm answered, "we'll do both. If you and I call in the equipment for drilling, perhaps Stephen and Gabrielle can concentrate on the mirror."

They set off on their missions, leaving Paul to bang on the wall and call for Chris. He tried putting his ear to the wall, but could hear nothing. He ran round to the bedroom on the opposite side of the void and beat the wall there, with his fists, as he shouted for Chris. Still there was no response. In renewed desolation, he sat on the bed in Karl's room and waited for everyone to return.

Steve and Ellie were back first. They fixed a sheet of canvas over the mirror and laid a sheet of plastic on the floor in front of the frame. Steve used a crowbar they'd found to break the glass. The canvas prevented shards of glass from flying everywhere, and most of the glass pieces collected in a rough pile on their plastic sheet. They loosely wrapped the glass pieces in the sheet and pulled the canvas away from the wall. Having carefully pulled the remaining broken glass from the frame, Steve was able to force the empty frame apart with the aid of his crowbar. There before them were the edges of a concealed door.

Steve tried hitting the door with the crowbar. His only rewards were the dull clang of steel hitting steel, and a shock wave that travelled all the way up his arm. As for the door, he had barely marked its surface. Ellie produced a credit card with the idea of sliding it into the cracks to locate the lock, but the cracks were too narrow even for that. They were forced to wait until Malcolm and Sania returned.

Paul's mind was in turmoil. What were they going to find in the void before them? He'd been able to hear no movement inside. Was Chris in there at all, or was this a wild goose chase? If she was in there, was she hurt? Was she even alive? It didn't bear thinking about, even though he couldn't stop thinking about it. He imagined all kinds of scenarios. Each had a worse outcome than the previous one.

Eventually, Malcolm and Sania returned with two burly men, who were carting a mass of equipment. They soon set to work drilling at the wall. "This might take a while," they declared, "We're going through solid steel."

There was half an hour of intermittent drilling. Liquid was sprayed on to the drill bit to keep it cool. Even so, the drill bit had to be changed before very long. When they were about to change the drill bit for the second time, they broke through the steel into something soft. They fitted a longer drill bit and were soon through into the void. Everyone wanted to peer through the narrow aperture. There was light in the void and possibly fleeting shadows passing over the end of the hole.

A small camera on a stalk was connected to a laptop, and the stalk was fed through the hole into the void. Now, they could see into the hidden room! Paul collapsed on the bed in relief. There was Chris, casually sitting on a chair, eating an apple. She waved to the camera. The picture also showed that there was someone lying on the floor, but he or she was close to the wall, and they couldn't obtain a clear image.

Chris was obviously in good health, so all that remained was to open the door to let her out. That required steel cutting equipment. While they were waiting for that apparatus to be organised, most of the group left the bedroom for a meal. Paul had his food sent up to the room so that he could at least see Chris. After their meal, the others went off to search the grounds and out-buildings. They looked in on Paul occasionally to check on progress. When the steel cutters arrived with their equipment and their protective masks, Paul vacated the bedroom to leave them at work. It wasn't until late in the afternoon that the door was finally opened and Chris could rush out into Paul's arms.

As they were sitting together on the bed, the steel-cutting men were clearing their equipment, though the whole bedroom still looked like a building site. Chris repeatedly reassured Paul that she was totally unharmed. The saferoom had been well-equipped with food, and it had its own bathroom, so she'd been able to look after herself without difficulty. She took Paul into the room. The first thing he saw was the gory body of Karl, gun in hand, with the top of his head missing. He rapidly looked away to see that beside the body was a console filled with lights, buttons, and switches. The whole of the wall behind the console was covered with computer monitors. One of them showed the rest of Malcolm's team sitting in the lounge. Paul suggested joining them so that Chris could tell everyone what had happened to her. She happily agreed, saying that it would be good to tell the story once to the whole group.

As Chris entered the lounge, she was met by a barrage of "Are you alright? What happened to you?" and "Did Karl hurt you?"

She sat down and began to recount events, "As I expect you know, I went to our room to collect my swim suit. When I entered the room, there was Karl, standing at an open section of wall. The mirror had opened out like a door, and he was fiddling with the lock. As soon as he saw me, he ran back into his secret room, but I rushed in after him. The second I was through the door, it slammed shut, and Karl whirled round with a pistol in his hand. I'd obviously moved faster than he'd expected, so when he turned, he was surprised to find that I was within grappling distance. A tussle ensued. During the struggle the gun went off under his chin and blew his brains out. Unfortunately for me, he'd done something to the door system, and I was then locked in. I obviously couldn't ask Karl how to unlock it, and I couldn't find any obvious way to open it myself. I imagined that the code needed had died with Karl. The room was fully equipped as a saferoom, and there was plenty of food, so I just sat it out and waited for you to work out where I was. I knew that rescue was at hand once I saw you all in the lounge, looking at plans for the house. The rest you know."

Malcolm responded for all of them, "Your vanishing act did leave us all with a mystery, and we were all desperately worried, especially Paul. I hope we can celebrate your safe return with a candlelit dinner together this evening. Before then, I'll arrange for the secret room and the bedroom to be cleared. By the way, may I assume, Christine, that Karl's will be the only fingerprints on the gun?"

"Yes, you may," Chris agreed with a nod.

"In that case, Mr Big can pass quietly out of all your lives, and the police can round up the rest of his gang. There's little more that we need to do here at Rowhurst, so let's enjoy a last evening together and go home after breakfast tomorrow."

Chapter 47 – Back at Bedford

After fond farewells to Steve, Ellie and Sania, Paul and Chris travelled home with Siete and Malcolm - without an armed guard. It was only when they were at home that Chris sprang a surprise on Paul.

"I hope you don't mind," she began, "but I've arranged with Malcolm for us to have an overnight stay at the country estate near Milton Keynes. If you're happy with that, we can go on the day after tomorrow."

"You mean the estate with the plunge pool?"

"Yes, that's the one."

"That would be great. I'd love you to see the place."

"I want to do more than just see it."

"What do you mean?"

"I want to go in the plunge pool. You said that I was infected, and I want to be rid of it."

"That's wonderful, though you can't sense the infection, so I don't think you'll notice any change."

"No, I realise that, but *you* can sense the infection, and I believe you when you say that I have it. I've seen what it can do, and I want it gone."

"That's really great! Let's do it. You say that Malcolm can fix it for us."

"He's fixed it already, unless I put it off."

"Don't do that, I'm a hundred percent with you."

And so it was that, two days later, the couple with their dog found themselves travelling north in the car Malcolm had sent for them. His smiling face was there to greet them at the door, and morning coffee was ready for them in the lounge. They spent the rest of the morning, hand in hand, exploring the estate with Siete. At lunch time, Malcolm let it be known that the plunge pool had been warming since the previous evening, and it was now ready for use.

Siete was released into the enclosed garden. Malcolm showed Paul and Chris to the basement door and opened it for them. As they passed through, Malcolm spoke to Paul, "You know how all this works, Paul, so I'll leave you to it.

There's no rush at all, so join me in the lounge whenever you are ready." Paul was almost convinced that Malcolm winked at him as he closed the door, but that might have been a trick of the light.

Paul led Chris down the stone steps into the warm welcoming atmosphere of the pool. As on his previous visit, the water glowed softly with its underwater lights. While he was on the stairs, Paul realised that Chris wasn't carrying any swimming gear. He assumed that she had a costume under her clothes, and he pointed out the changing cubicles. When he turned, he discovered that he'd been mistaken; most of Chris's clothing was already at her feet. The rest soon followed and she leapt into the pool. She dived under the surface, before she floated up on her back and called, "The water's lovely, come on in."

Paul needed no second invitation. He left his clothes beside Chris's, held his nose, and jumped into the pool beside his wife. They floated, wrapped in each other's arms, and all was perfect in Paul's world. He had no doubt that adventures and trials lay ahead of them, but they would face them together. Now, there wasn't the slightest hint of shadow in his life. On the contrary, the clear blue sky of his existence was flooded with the glorious sunshine of his paradise restored.

Postscript

If you have enjoyed this book, please give it 4 or 5 stars on Amazon. Better still, write a sentence or two in review, saying what you liked. This is the only way that it will come to the attention of others.

Free resource available

This novel was written as a result of reflection on the nature of the many evils that seem to exist all around us. Many aspects of this work of fiction relate to very real features of the world. It was never intended to provide accurate philosophical or theological information, but part of its purpose was to trigger thought and discussion. If you have any passing interest in that, you are most welcome to look at or download a resource to help such thinking. The document is available here:

https://drive.google.com/file/d/17GUW9Ap85usX_Rlf0jhZRc
7inFmS7AYf/view?usp=sharing

It may be printed, copied and circulated freely, provided that you do not alter it.

Thanks

I am enormously grateful to my wife, Elizabeth, who has carefully read, corrected, and advised upon the very many drafts that have led up to the final production of this book. Thanks are also due to other members of our family who have provided constructive comments that have greatly assisted my writing.

April 2024

About the author

Albert's relationship with literature has always been a stormy one and until a sudden inspiration one night, he never had the slightest intention of writing a work of fiction himself. The sudden compulsion to write this book has been one of the greatest surprises of his life.

He has spent well over 50 years working with young people, both as a volunteer and as a professional educator. He had a career teaching physics and retired in 2006 from his position as Head of the Science Faculty at Whitgift School in Croydon.

Albert is married to Elizabeth. They have 3 grown up children and 6 grandchildren. As a couple, they continue to present science shows for schools and other interested groups. They are leaders and administrators of a thriving group for children and young people. In addition, they are trained and active as Lay Preachers.